# CHERRY HEAVEN

# CHERRY HEAVEN

## L. J. Adlington

**Greenwillow Books**

*An Imprint of* HarperCollins*Publishers*

Cherry Heaven
Copyright © 2008 by L. J. Adlington
All rights reserved. No part of this book may be used or reproduced in any manner whatsoever without written permission except in the case of brief quotations embodied in critical articles and reviews. Printed in the United States of America. For information address HarperCollins Children's Books, a division of HarperCollins Publishers, 1350 Avenue of the Americas, New York, NY 10019.
www.harperteen.com

The text of this book is set in Tekton and Adobe Garamond.

Library of Congress Cataloging-in-Publication Data

Adlington, L. J. (Lucy J.), 1970–
  Cherry Heaven / by L.J. Adlington.
      p. cm.
"Greenwillow Books"
Summary: Kat and Tanka J leave the war-torn city, move with their adoptive parents to the New Frontier, and are soon settled into a home called Cherry Heaven, but Luka, an escaped factory worker, confirms their suspicion that New Frontier is not the utopia it seems to be.
ISBN: 978-0-06-143180-7 (trade bdg.)
ISBN: 978-0-06-143181-4 (lib. bdg.)
[1. Revenge—Fiction. 2. Orphans—Fiction. 3. Science fiction.] I. Title.
PZ7.A26157Che 2008    [Fic] —dc22    2007024679

First Edition 10 9 8 7 6 5 4 3 2 1

 **Greenwillow Books**

For the red-headed Mr. Smith

With thanks to Beverley Birch and Kate Shaw,
Michelle, Kelly, Gary, Wendy and Rachel, Gillian, Elisa,
Noriko and Sheriff Hutton Ladies Football Club!

## Factory

the last birthday i ever had, years ago, was the
one where i got shot instead of presents.

silence fell after the gunman fired. cherries fell
too, fat and juicy in the snow. i heard boots
crunching closer as the man came to see how
well he'd done.

i shake my head.

those thoughts creep in a place i'm not ready
to remember yet, and let's face it—where i
come from there aren't any cherries, it never
snows, and remembering's Against The Rules.

i come from a bad place. they wanted to keep
me there but i had other plans. plans are
Against The Rules, of course; in fact,
everything's Against The Rules. the crazy thing
is (and am i the only one who's ever noticed?)
there are no Rules where i come from, not ones

they tell you about anyway. you only find out what the Rules are when you break them. i know what you're thinking! you're thinking, *that's not so bad if you're smart.* you're thinking, *why not watch and see what other workers get punished for,* then say, *whoa, best i don't do the same.* that's what you might think if you'd never worked in Factory before. get this: here in Factory, even though the Rules don't exist, they change all the time. somehow Director always has a Rule ready to be broken whenever he feels in a punishing mood.

Director likes Rules. he also likes nice food, fine wines, and working out with weights so he's a lean, mean shouting machine. Director thinks he's young and handsome. is he young? i've forgotten how to count things like that. is he handsome? hardsome more like. Supervisor fancies him almost as much as he fancies himself. she tries to smile at him and looks to see how many buttons are undone on his shirt. while Director's up on his platform, Supervisor walks Factory floor. Supervisor doesn't have crinkly white Hygie socks like us workers. she walks softly softly in her no-sound slippers and you can only tell she's there when she hisses on your neck, letting you know you're almost breaking a Rule just by being alive. when her breath hangs in the air you feel so tense you could crack like a bent bone. you wait there wondering, *should i stand still?*—cos maybe standing still's Against The Rules. then you think, *should i keep on working?* only maybe that's Against The Rules too.

Supervisor's good at punishing people: smack 'em, whack 'em, watch 'em cry. one time a girl was hit so hard her eye fell out. i don't know if they put it back in again and i don't know what Rule the girl broke. there just isn't room for someone to know everything, unless you're Director, of course, cos he knows how to brush his own teeth, gloss his own hair, and how to send a spot of spit down from his platform onto whatever lucky worker's walking below. oh yeah, Director knows he's A1 Ace Supremo. except when Bossman calls.

Bossman's the baddest man, and he comes here once a year. Director shivers when the Bossman's shadow's near. maybe he wishes he had a hood to hide his face like i do. he shakes Bossman's gold-shiny hand and waits, and we wait too. will Bossman be pleased . . . ? will he smile his special Bossman smile and pull that envelope from his pocket? yes! he does! we're all ready to flop with relief. Director tears the envelope and looks inside. it's arrived! an invitation to Bossman's birthday. unlike me he gets one every year.

Director loves parties, especially this birthday party. even before the big day he drinks so much wine his eyes almost pop out of his orange-tanned face, and when he makes it back to Factory after the fun, he'll have a hoarse voice and maybe a couple of hickeys on his neck. some years he brings back strings of silver/red streamers. one year he almost didn't show up at all, but that was too good to be true. he was back three days later complaining of a monster headache.

this year Director's more excited than ever about Bossman's birthday. he presses his belly against the platform rails and boasts he's got an invite to the biggest party on the planet. bet you wish you could go! ha ha ha you can't. you'd kill it dead anyway, you funless lumps of mud. d'you think it would hurt to maybe crack your faces to smile every once in a while? c'mon, let's have some music, you soulless little shitzers! sing!

he makes us sing the same tune over and over and no one complains, cos we all remember the time when Bottle Seal 55 forgot the words to Director's favorite song, oh yeah. let's just say she won't be singing anymore, or talking, or working, or breathing, even, so now i'm the new Bottle Seal 55.

no i'm not! i forgot!

they'll have to get a new 55 cos i'm not going to be what they tell me to be ever again. now i'm the girl with the Plan, the girl-who-can, the girl who's breaking the biggest Rule of all. get this— i'm leaving. i've always known i'd go, as sure as high tide follows low. you see, there's something i've got to do.

*girl, you ain't got to do nothing,* is what Packer 67 always told me. *an' if you have,* she said, *it's this: look small and think small. work your shift, eat your food before some starving shitzer eats it for you, sleep your sleep, then get up and do it all over again.*

i do look small.

i bend my shoulders and pull my Hygie hood over my face. i don't talk much, pretending i've got nothing to say. at the end of every shift i peel off the Hygie gloves and rub my hands with Stingo. oh, Stingo! the only smell you'll ever smell in Factory . . . thick germ-killer cream that pops your blisters and crusts your skin. don't ever put Stingo in your eyes cos it bites like the nippers of a thousand becano bugs. Director's always complaining about the price of it, and boy do we get through a lot. *do you realize how much a multi-box of Stingo costs?* he bawls at us, only he doesn't call it Stingo. he calls it hyperantibacterialviraleliminatorsolutionA. try saying that when you've just been punched in the teeth. i can't.

i look at my Stingo-smeared hands and wonder what it would be like to have proper fingers, not these white sticks that are blue-black with cold at the ends. Director has lovely hands. once a week he orders Packer 109 up to his platform. he sprays liquid Stingo in the air and puts a towel over his face while she kneels at his feet. he likes that. she doesn't.

*what's he making you do to him?* we whisper, under the eversteady hum of the chill machine. *do you have to, you know, touch him?*

Packer 109 scratches her head. the bristles poke out through ridges of red-raw Stingo sores. *no,* she says. *i don't do that; i just do his nails. see—he's got his own fancy nail file with his own fancy letters on it.* she passes it around so we can admire the gold letters: A. L. *i get his nails done real nice with this,* says Packer 109 in a voice that's long since bled dry of bitterness. *i just trim his nails and condition his cuticles.*

again i look at my fingers. what are cuticles?

does she mean these strips of dead skin that
flap around the blister lumps? i'd bite them off
if they didn't taste of Stingo. Label-glue 11 says
they put Stingo in the food, but that's doop
talk: they don't really put that shitzer stuff
in the grub, whatever the goss-roster says. our
Rule about food, the Rule Director doesn't need
to tell us about, the Rule that never changes
whatever the day, whatever the menu, our Rule
is: eat your food before someone else does. but
like i said, i'm a girl who breaks Rules. i don't eat
all my food.

huh, strange, you might say.

no, not strange—clever. wait and see.

i don't eat all my food and i don't give it to
Label-glue 11 either. i know she's as hollow inside
as the rest of us, only i need my food for the
Plan, oh yes, my Plan about leaving. what a
beautiful word LEAVING is. i don't care what
anyone says, the world is full of beautiful things
if you only know how to look for them. look long,
look right, and you'll find beautiful. you won't find
my food, though, cos i hid it.

Label-glue 11's always looking. she'd lick crumbs off the floor if anyone was mad enough to drop them, but it's not like a few extra pieces of bread are going to save her. nothing will, especially not the white Hygie mask she wears to stop the glue glutting her head. it's safe, she boasts, pointing to the label at the back of the mask. see, it says extra-super-strong protection.

sure you'll be safe, i agree, except we all know Director wouldn't dream of visiting the Glue Department even with a mask on. and anyway, i can read better than Label-glue 11. it doesn't seem right to tell her the label only says: Made in Meander. Size Small.

so, no point in giving Label-glue 11 my bread. she's done for. her brain's fried. i remember what fried means. i remember fat eggs cracking in a pan, yellow in the middle, white around the yellow and crispy brown on the outside. i can almost smell the "fried" things too. (can you have smell memories? i think i would if i wasn't Stingo'd up to the eyeballs.) Label-glue 11 isn't that sort of

fried. she's brain-fried high . . . fly up to the sky
. . . or up to the ceiling at any rate. in Factory
you can't get to the sky cos the roof gets in
the way. i tell you what—the roof IS the sky,
here in Factory.

NO! you see how i did it again? i forgot i've got
the REAL sky now, the one they don't tell you
about. the one you have to stretch your neck
and unroll your shoulders to see.

i'm OUTSIDE.

oh yes, sweet pain of pins-and-needles, i don't
look small anymore and i never, not really, not
deep in my roots, i never thought small. now i've
got my Plan to prove it. i thought of the Plan
when i heard it was time for Bossman's biggest-
ever birthday party. there i was, just minding my
own business, working as usual, with Bottle Seal
54 on one side and Bottle Seal 56 on the other,
and it suddenly came to me: *i want a birthday
party too.* i can't exactly remember what a
birthday party is, but i know i had one once,
quite a few of them, in fact, plus i know i was
about to have one the day the gunshots

cracked over the treetops and made snow shiver. why not have another one?

lots of reasons why not, anyone sensible would say. none of us workers ever have birthdays, not once not never. you just can't. apart from the Rules, birthdays need things like friends and presents, which are hugely not-get-able in Factory. so my brain got busy building a Plan while my hands were sealing up bottles. believe me, i could screw on those lids in my sleep, so don't go thinking it was an accident that by the end of the shift there was one bottle top missing. i had it hidden in my Hygie suit, with the rest of my treasures. by then i'd figured out that if there aren't birthdays in Factory, then I'd have to get away.

no way! no one escapes! that's what we all thought. workers come in but they never go out. the doors have machines that only let the right people leave and the windows are too high to reach. one time, a girl from the Glue Department got so crazy she tried to escape and even Director looked shocked by the mess he made of

her as punishment. but she only tried to
escape. i'm not into trying. from now on i'm into
DOING. at least, i think i am. i've never had to
do much before, apart from the same stuff
everyone does, you know—the work, eat, sleep
stuff. how hard can this doing thing be? Director
does stuff every day. people outside do too.
Bossman certainly does stuff; in fact, he does
whatever he wants. no one knows everything
that Bossman does, cos he keeps it ssh-secret,
as quiet as snow.

even the moons do stuff. they make tides,
pulling the sea closer and pushing it away. when
they pull and push together it makes the high
swells, the happentide and oppentide, ebb and
flow, come and go.

now i'm outside i gaze up at the moons. they
look funny without a skylight in the way; all
wrong now they're not smeared in grime or
edged with mildew, or blotted with a red triangle
that says NO EXIT. just before the rain comes
and the gray squashes me down, just before
then, the moons glow ghostielike in the sky. i

touch them with my Stingo-stung fingers.

*ride the tide, Luka, say the moons to me now.
time to go.*

i know.

i'm like a tide: i've come from a bad place and now i'm going away from it.

ssh! if you're really quiet you'll hear me creeping in the shadows.

# LANDFALL I

The New Frontier was drowned in rain and shadows.

One day on the edge of deep winter a ship was pulled toward shore on the swell of a sturdy two-moon happentide. It was the vintage ocean liner *Marie-Cloud* and it was making landfall a day early. Out on deck sailors struggled with wet ropes, trying to slow the vessel as it surged toward Santanna port. Snug on the Top Class promenade deck, two sisters were waiting for their first view of the Frontier. Tanka turned away from her reflection in the rain-stabbed window.

"You got me out of the pool for *this*? I can't see any land!"

Kat sighed. "I heard the announcement: Santanna's on the horizon."

"Are you sure it's not one of the captain's hilarious jokes, like when she told us we'd enjoy the voyage?"

Kat smiled. "Over there, look."

"It's a cloud."

"No, I can see buildings on the dock."

"It's a building-shaped cloud. C'mon, Kat, I want to go pack."

"Your bag's already chocker with free towels and bubblies!"

Tanka grinned. "There's always Aunt Milli's cabin to raid—a girl can never have too many freebies. And if you want a much nicer view, come and watch Zee Homarlo's latest movie with me again. Boy, does that guy have a bod worth ogling!"

"I'd rather salt my gills in seawater. Anyway, you said you'd watch for the shore with me."

"I came, I saw, I got bored."

"Maybe it'll look better when the sun comes out," Kat said valiantly.

"*If* the sun ever comes out."

"It's sunny in all the brochures."

"Yeah, and one of these days you'll tell me it's scientifically proven that clouds have silver linings. Can't you get it into your thick head that the blurb on the immigration pack was just one big *con* to get people to up sticks from the *civilized* side of the world where we have cities and sunshine and little luxuries like *culture*."

"They have cities here. . . ."

"Towns, Kat, they have *towns*. Probably rows of mud huts where you have to pump your own water and wash in buckets."

"It won't be like that. . . ."

"Wanna bet?"

"It's an energetic new colony full of bright ideas for the future. . . ."

"Yeah, sure. And according to Uncle Prester we're going to be met by crowds of happy smiley people who want to be our friends and share local produce with us. If that actually is the dock, then all I can see are soggy sailor-types, and they are one hundred percent *low* on thrill factor."

"You're expecting half-naked men tossing flower petals and sugar candy?"

"Now you're talking!"

"It's too cold for naked."

In the Top Class quarters of the *Marie-Cloud* the temperature was set to "deliciously warm," just like their homeland on the far continent. The New Frontier was a long way northwest from the sun-baked bliss of the five cities. It suffered from strange phenomena called snow and cold—two very good reasons for never going near the place, Tanka thought.

"Fresh new place, fresh new start," Uncle Prester said, and Kat agreed. The New Frontier was a land of peace and prosperity which had never known war . . . unlike the cities.

"Hey—bright light!"

The clouds never parted, but a sudden strong

light glared over the waves. It came from the tall tower of the Linveki Hydro factory, soaring above the squat port of Santanna. Brilliant at the top of the tower was the silver/red sign of the Atsumisi— a welcome sight after three long weeks at sea. Both sisters rubbed the silver/red IDs meshed onto the back of their hands. This was a reflex action every time they saw the proud emblem of the Atsumisi gene clan. They could barely remember a time when they hadn't had the distinctive wetware grafted onto their skin. It automatically set them above the other gene clans—the Mazzini and the grossly inferior Galrezi.

"Hey," said Tanka, seeing the factory. "Is that the place where they make Blue Mountain water?"

"I told you we'd see it when we arrived."

"Oh, Blue Mountain brand—hand me a bottle and all is forgiven!" Just saying the words made Tanka think of lazy days by the pool back home, swigging on glassfuls of purest Blue. "Huh. No prizes for guessing where they get all the water," she sneered as the silver/red sign was swallowed by rain again.

"It's not just bottled rain! It comes from a secret mountain source, actually."

"Doop! You can't believe everything you read on the label! I bet there's no secret source, plus those mountains aren't even blue." That much was true. The far-off mountains were definitely a dull, scabby gray.

"There must be other ones, proper blue ones like on the labels. Besides, they're still mountains."

There were no mountains back on their home continent, just wonderful stretches of blue sky and avenues of sandy-colored buildings shaded by yellow-flowered cimarron trees. Mountains were no use to Tanka, since she couldn't flirt with them or drink them. She left Kat to admire the scenery and padded across the thick carpet of the promenade deck to the drinks machine. One flash of her ID authorized credit. She ordered a couple of bottles of water, feeling the fizz right to the tips of her gills as she gulped it down. Drinking Blue Mountain was the next best thing to being underwater . . . not to mention the fact that Linveki Hydro was running a promotion offer, where one lucky bottle top advertised the chance to meet the hunky Zee Homarlo himself.

"Face it, sis, Blue Mountain's all one big con too. One big, delicious, thirst-quenching con, with the tantalizing prospect of maybe winning a hot date with movie man of the millennium." Tanka stopped, slapped in the face by a sudden, horrific thought. "They will get Homarlo flicks in Meander town, won't they? I mean, we're not moving to a *total* backwater, are we?"

"Sheesh, they probably just sit around a fire at night roasting nuts and telling stories to pass the time. *Of course* they have movies, mush-head! Same as anywhere. It's a different continent, not a whole new world."

Tanka muttered something about it feeling like

the *end* of the world. Nothing would reconcile her to the fact that they were leaving civilized city life, all because Aunt Millijue had a job offer she couldn't refuse and Uncle Prester was determined to go with her. Worse still, the only way to reach the New Frontier was by crossing the great Santanna Ocean, and it didn't take long for that novelty to wear off. Sailing through a tempest had done little to sweeten Tanka's mood about the change of continents. An electrical storm had chased the *Marie-Cloud* through dark days and nights, shattering the sky with a violence that had both girls trembling from childhood memories of bomb blasts and raid sirens. That had been when the seasickness was most vicious; when Tanka had begged for death (or at least a temporary non-disfiguring coma).

*Have a pill*, Kat had suggested, since this was Tanka's usual remedy for any complaint, from migraine to missing homework. Tanka had moaned that there was no pill on the planet big enough to stop her body turning inside out, and would Kat please cremate her, along with her entire Collector's Edition of Zee Homarlo movie disks?

Kat had been more than delighted at the idea of Zee Homarlo going up in smoke, but she'd pressed Tanka to swallow the nice handful of pills before she died, saying that the pink ones really were very good, and kind of sugary, too. Tanka had wanted to know when Kat had left off believing that pills were bunkum pseudoscience designed to fleece gullible neurotics. *That's not important right now*, Kat said then, passing her sister a bottle of Blue Mountain to wash the medicine down.

*How come you're not sick?* Tanka had groaned.

*Mind over matter*, was Kat's sensible reply.

She was far too organized to be sick. She had Tanka to look after, for one thing, not to mention Uncle Prester and Aunt Millijue, groaning in the cabin next door. P and M Jones weren't real relatives, just foster parents. They hadn't exactly planned on adopting two girls, but the war ten years before had left orphans in unlikely places, Tanka and Kat included. Millijue wasn't exactly motherly—she'd never even applied to have children of her own—while Prester was more interested in history files than real-life problems.

In fact, it was quiet, clever Kat who kept the whole Jones family organized. It was Kat who'd booked the ship tickets, arranged the upgrades, and sublet the city apartment. Kat's last day in the city had been spent double-checking bill payments with the power board and fobbing off legions of Tanka's left-behind boyfriends. There'd barely been time to say good-bye to the city—just a few slow minutes walking out into the lazy plaza heat, where the cimarron fruit fell fat on the ground to rot at the feet of General Insidian's giant statue.

Back in the bad old days there'd been fierce competition between the three different gene clans—the Atsumisi, Mazzini, and Galrezi. Rivalry hadn't been helped by a severe drought that had everyone gasping for more water. Sly propaganda set the gene clans against one another, with citizens soon starting to judge one another on the color of their hand IDs. The red-stamped Atsumisi jostled for the best resources and the most respect. Stunned, the blue-hued Mazzini and green Galrezi barely had time to object before all five cities were scrambling to arms in a bitter civil war. His hand clenched in a dominating fist, General Insidian had led factions of Atsumisi to a supreme victory over the Mazzini and Galrezi, dominating all five cities for ten long years, as well as forging links with the far-off New Frontier.

Kat and Tanka had grown up in City Five, which had suffered some of the worst war damage. The general had pledged to rebuild everything bigger and better than before, but now his statue was wreathed in black plastic flowers of mourning because he was dead. Kat liked to remind herself of this fact. Even though she was lucky to be branded Atsumisi, there was something not-quite-likable about the slack-jowled general. He was one thing about City Five she wouldn't miss.

At the same time she said good-bye to the demolition sites, the buildings pocked with ancient bullet holes, and the clogged-up bomb craters. Long shadows still stretched across the city landscape from the war ten years before, no matter how hard the building crews worked.

Tanka never worried her head about war, even though she'd lived through it. For Tanka, ten *days* ago was ancient, let alone ten years. She occasionally met lads in the old ruins for a bit of dusty cuddling, but apart from that she somehow managed to walk from mall to pool to school oblivious to everything that wasn't BOY or NEW.

Kat was oh-so-ready to feel the same way. She knew there'd be no shadows in the New Frontier, far from the old war zones. Clouds maybe—but not shadows!

# LANDFALL II

—WELCOME TO SANTANNA
AND A WORLD OF OPPORTUNITIES! —
—WELCOME TO THE O-HA
AND THE NEW FRONTIER!—

The dramatic silver/red sign faced all passengers as they stumbled down the gangplank from the *Marie-Cloud* and onto Santanna quayside. Santanna was the first port of call for anyone visiting the continent. From here a team of ferries took people up the wide Annaflo river to the inland towns of Anabarra and Meander, or beyond that to the fledgling outposts clustered on the edge of unexplored territory.

Brilliant above the welcome sign was a screen showing scenes of life on the New Frontier, where people smiled as they worked, wallowed in hot spa pools, or went hiking in the heartland.

Everywhere there were adverts for Blue Mountain water, as well as the silver insignia of the O-HA—the Overseas Humanitarian Agency. The O-HA was responsible for hugely generous donations of water and aid to the five cities during the war. Without the support of peacekeepers from the O-HA, the cities would have suffered much higher death tolls. The O-HA had no interest in gene-clan distinctions. They had kept faithful to the original ideals of the planet's colony: peace, peace, and above all, peace.

The Jones family had arrived at the New Frontier in time for celebrations to mark the O-HA's tenth anniversary. According to plastic posters all around the quayside, there was to be a big rally at Meander town as soon as the first snows of deep winter fell.

"Mmm, yummy—that's more like it! Shame

about the scar on his cheek." Tanka perked up at the picture on the O-HA posters—a boy with his eyes closed and long lashes grazing his cheeks as he tipped his head back to enjoy a bottle of Blue Mountain, all under the tagline "*O-HA: One World, One People.*"

Kat rolled her eyes. Okay, so the boy in the poster was completely gorgeous, and the scar made him look edgy, but weren't there more important things to think about? Like getting a place on the Annaflo ferry to Meander?

"Too bad he's probably brainwashed by the whole O-HA thing," Tanka complained as Kat pulled her away from the poster toward Customs.

"Well, they have got a lot to boast about."

"Yeah, but do they have to keep bragging like they singlehandedly brought about world peace and everything?"

"Well, they kind of did, Tanka—"

"And just remember who paid for our Top Class travel," interrupted Uncle Prester.

"Wish they'd cough up for return tickets," was Tanka's rebellious reply.

"Do you think it ever stops raining?" Aunt Millijue sighed, oblivious to any other conversation. "No wonder they make so much money out of water here."

She had a point. Back in City Five a few fat drops clogging the dust was a positive shower, while here in the New Frontier they were expected to shelter in long tunnels of wind-battered plastic, all stamped with the O-HA logo.

Kat marveled yet again at Aunt Millijue's complete lack of enthusiasm about life. Millijue had been headhunted by the legendary leader of the O-HA—Quinn Essnid himself—in order to revamp the O-HA archive system. Q Essnid had made sure that Prester was offered an excellent post at the new Meander University, as well as arranging a spacious new home for the family on a cherry farm not far from Meander. Millijue was grateful for all of this, but not excited. Errant shrapnel from the war had left her permanently deaf in one ear and plain tense everywhere else. Tanka exhausted her; Kat kept her ticking along nicely. She patted them both on the shoulder and said, "At least we didn't drown on the voyage."

A few steps farther into the port and they actually came face to face with Q Essnid—or his image, at least. A high-quality projection of him drew people over to a fund-raising machine where anyone could flash their ID to transfer money to a chosen charity. Back home in City Five these sorts of machines were generally to raise money for people still homeless after the war. Q Essnid's charity wasn't so grim. A voice recording began as the machine sensed people nearby.

"Welcome to Santanna! I hope you had a comfortable journey and find everything satisfactory on your arrival. You probably feel like stretching your legs, and we all know there's no better way to exercise than in water . . . which is why I'm asking people to support our charity program for hospital patients who need a bit of a lift after treatment. Just a few credits could mean first-rate therapy for people who will really benefit from it. Don't think of it as fund-raising—it's more like *fun*-raising! If you could spare . . ."

Kat shook her head to tune out the charming voice. That was the trouble with the O-HA: you couldn't resent them because they were just so *good* at doing good, and Q Essnid was deservedly popular on both continents. There was something about the man that inspired confidence, since he looked so calm and capable himself. Physically he wouldn't be a match for Tanka's favorite heart-throb, Zee Homarlo. Q Essnid was a just a short man in a suit. However, even laid-back Uncle Prester couldn't say Essnid's name without glowing like a human lightbulb.

"You have to understand what he's done for the

Frontier and the cities," he enthused, whenever any-one would listen. "If there'd been more people like him back on Earth, maybe it wouldn't've got in the mess it did, and we'd never have needed ships to new planets. Essnid's a credit to the colonies—the father of peace in our time."

Over at the charity machine, the image of Q Essnid finished his spiel. Kat watched as a fair number of passengers went up to pledge credit.

"Make me one of those machines, Kat," begged Tanka, seeing how much money people were parting with. "It could be your next brainiac project. I'd be ace at getting people to cough up for a good cause."

"Since when did you start supporting charities?"

"It'd be for *me*, shitzer-brain, so I never have to get a holiday job again. It'd be like having birthday presents every day of the year. . . ." Tanka lost her-self in an avaricious reverie until someone standing close by coughed and spoke.

It was a porter, dressed in a damp set of shrug-ons with a cap pulled well over his ears. "If you give me your baggage tokens I'll collect everything for you and have it sent on to your next destination," he said, nodding toward the large cartons already being hauled from the *Marie-Cloud*'s hold. "I can put your hand luggage on the trolley now," he added, wondering why the family didn't reply.

It was their first encounter with a real, live Frontier type.

Tanka leaned over to Kat and hissed, "Push your jaw up, doop. It's rude to stare at the natives."

"I'm not staring. I just thought. . . ."

Kat didn't know what she'd thought—that the photos on the brochures would bear any resemblance to real life? This man was nothing like the pictures she'd seen of strapping young lads harvesting fruit or neatly dressed scientific bods doing engineering work for Linveki Hydro. This man was clearly a few stars short of a constellation, and as he bent over for the nearest bag, Kat saw that his

ID glittered with the silver/green of a *Galrezi*, not the comforting Atsumisi red. She looked again. Yes, definitely green—the first green ID she'd seen up close since . . . since a time she didn't choose to remember. The porter was a real, live Galrezi. How was that possible? Hadn't the Galrezi all been . . . ?

The porter saw her looking and for a moment was puzzled, then his hand automatically flew up to scratch one ear—a classic defensive gesture.

"*You* give him the tokens," Tanka whispered. She was openly disgusted by the Galrezi mark.

Kat tried to smile at the porter as she handed him the baggage checks, but he was already distracted by the address on the nearest label. His eyes widened and he grinned.

"Say—you're heading for Cherry Heaven!"

"Not by choice," Tanka muttered.

The porter shook his head, eyes bright with delight. "The cherries from there were legendary!"

Tanka sighed. It was hard to be moving to a

place that sounded like an over-enthusiastic ice-cream flavor.

"You'll love it, Tanka, you know you will," said Uncle Prester, who was turning around and around in ever-narrowing circles as he searched for the sign to Customs. "Just wait till you see the house."

"Stop-I-might-die-from-excitement. Who the hell's idea was it anyway, this cherry place?"

Prester came to a standstill. "That's enough from you, Tanka J.! Q Essnid himself is letting us live there."

"For a small fortune . . ."

"For an amount we can afford, especially since Essnid says there are *two* pool rooms. . . . Yes, I thought you'd like that."

The Galrezi porter loped off, still cooing under his breath at the memory of cherries from Cherry Heaven.

Tanka held her nose and sneered at Kat, "I don't know why *we* have to pass immigration tests, when they obviously let any old scum on to this continent! You've got Galrezi germs now."

"There's no such thing!"

"Galrezi germs in your hair . . ."

"Tanka, don't!"

". . . crawling up your jacket . . ."

"I haven't!"

"Tanka! Be quiet!" Uncle Prester did his best to look authoritative. "The O-HA don't like racist talk about Mazzini or . . . or those unfortunate Galrezi people. Er, Kat, have you seen my visa?"

"I thought you put it somewhere safe?" came Aunt Millijue's terse voice.

Kat grinned. Uncle Prester's "safe places" were infamous in the family. "Panic not, Unc. You put it in your left jacket pocket. No—the other left."

"I knew that."


Tanka was allergic to queues. She couldn't understand how anyone else's needs came before hers, which was why Prester and Millijue were in line behind the girls. She was also incapable of keeping silent for more than a few seconds at a time.

"This ferry we're going on, it will have a roof, won't it?"

"I guess so," said Kat.

"And we are still going Top Class, aren't we?"

"I don't think there are different classes."

"And we don't have to go anywhere near the fricking *sea* again, do we? It creeps me out."

"Only up the Annaflo river, and that's freshwater."

"Just so I know." Tanka lowered her voice conspiratorially. "Aren't you a bit nervous?"

"What's there to be nervous about?" Kat put on her best cheery smile.

"Oh, just the fact that we're on a completely different continent that's swarming with Galrezi and the sky's so full of water you could swim in it."

"I haven't seen any more Gal—of them. And it's only rain."

"I think it's messed up my *e.f.* I'm not getting a signal."

Tanka loved her little silver *ear.fone* and had it tuned to all her favorite music channels until her credit ran out . . . which didn't take long, given the number of calls she made on it.

"Probably just a blip," said Kat. "I bet it needs adjusting after that electrical storm. Apparently they get a lot of blips over here."

"Great. So you're telling me I don't have online entertainment 26/7?"

"I'll fix it for you once I've unpacked my kit. . . ."

"What if I miss some calls first? Sheesh—what if I just curl up and die of *culture shock*, for god's sake? Did you think of that?"

"Relax, it's going to be fine."

"Hey—who's not relaxed? And it's okay to be a

bit nervous sometimes. You should try it. You might get mistaken for human more often." Tanka discreetly popped a couple of peps to take the edge off her own anxiety.

Kat repeated her mantra—*everything's under control*—until it was their turn to face interrogation from the Customs officer, who had a silver/blue Mazzini stamp on her hand. The woman's face was blank, as if she'd been rained on too many times in her life. Listening to the endless spat on the glass roof, Kat could well believe this was true. She did her best to keep calm.

*Deep breath, don't worry. It'll be fine, it'll be great. It'll be . . . it'll be a miracle if Tanka manages not to get kicked off the continent within the next five minutes. . . .*

Tanka was chewing gum with gusto and loudly complaining that nothing was a patch on glamorous city life. The flickering computer console flashed up her biometrics, and a *very* attractive photograph—the one and only Tanka Jones. Only Kat knew how carefully Tanka's beauty was constructed each morning, how well the hair was conditioned, how often the skin drank moisture cream.

Kat's photo wasn't quite so flattering, despite the lovely caramel-chocolate color of her hair. Still, the information on the screen did proclaim academic awards above and beyond the call of duty, which was more than could be said for Tanka.

Then time slowed down as the Customs officer asked the big question.

"*At this present time, are either of you, or persons known to you, currently under investigation from the War Crimes Commission?*"

"Absolutely not!" Kat craned her neck around to see the computer screen, as if staring at her file would make it even more honest-looking. "We were only little kids when the war started."

"And your parents?"

"They're . . ."

"Dead," said Tanka helpfully.

Kat bit back whatever else she might've added to that stark admission. Their parents *were* dead, that much was true—two out of the many thousands of victims of the war. As for why they'd died . . . she knew that perfectly well, but she couldn't bring herself to say the G-word out loud. The memory of being torn away from her parents was muddied with other emotions, like anger that they'd gone, guilt at being a safe Atsumisi, and disgust, too. There was no getting away from it. In the cities, Galrezi always meant shame—*shitzer* people. Scum.

Pink with embarrassment Kat began to stumble through an apology, as if she was somehow responsible for the violence back home. "I know you didn't have war here, and we didn't mean to, and we're not all like that. . . ."

The woman never heard a word. She had just

finished reading their visa information. Her eyes widened and she visibly straightened her spine.

"You've been vouched for by Quinn Essnid! My apologies for asking about . . . unpleasant things. It's a routine question, no offense meant."

"None taken," said Kat, relieved.

Tanka was more mutinous. "I'm sick of everyone jawing on about war crimes and sucking up to survivors as if we should all be a million times sorry for things that we didn't do anyway, like all those Galrezi getting—"

"Tanka! Shut it!"

"What? I was just saying—"

"Well, don't."

Kat had already noticed that the Customs officer wore a twist of green ribbon on her jacket. This was the newly fashionable sign of solidarity with war victims. It wasn't catching on fast in City Five, but here in the home of the O-HA, people were obviously a lot more open-minded about living in harmony with Galrezi gene-carriers.

Fortunately, the Customs officer ignored Tanka's sullen outburst. She was distracted instead by their onward destination. Her smile shone suddenly, like sun after rain.

"You're moving to Cherry Heaven? Cherry Heaven farm, near Meander? *Supreme!* My word, I remember crates of those cherries arriving at the stores, and they'd be sold out before you knew it. Legendary, they were, just legendary! Too bad they don't grow fruit like that anymore—they were to die for!"

After that the sisters were allowed onto the continent with minimal formalities and a unanimous thumbs-up for their cherries.

## Flavor

this not-being-in-Factory thing is to die for!
there are clouds and rain and everything! big
thumbs-up!

the sky's all over the place except under my
feet. the thing called day's turned into night.
day and night, night and day—i'd forgotten
what they were like. a long time ago, before
Factory, night was when i was asleep and day
was when i played. it's hard to believe there was
a time before Factory, where night and day
aren't on the roster. they're probably Against
The Rules, since Director's decided we don't
need to know what's happening outside to do
the work inside. we sleep when we've finished
eating and when we're not doing either, well,
what else would we do apart from work? day is
when Factory skylights show blue or gray.

night's when there aren't any colors. at least, that's what i thought. i didn't know about the big dazzles on Factory tower—the brilliant red and silver signs that stab the night like a fork stabbing meat. they're very pretty, the Atsumisi signs, like the little holograms that Stickers 1 to 20 put on the water bottles. they're as pretty as Sticker 15's eyes, or Packer 67's smile.

Packer 67 has pretty snow white teeth. i told this to Label-glue 11 and her big food-looking eyes were bigger than ever.

*Packer 67?* she laughed. *what, that old sow? she's at least a thousand years old. huh, she remind you of your mother?*

silence to that. Label-glue 11 shouldn't make fun of me, or make me think of my long-gone mama. *do i have anything pretty?* i asked Packer 67 when we waited in the line for the shower. *what's the point of pretty?* she said.

and no, i'm not blind. i could see that Packer 67's eyes were flat and her skin hung off her face and she didn't bend down so well anymore, but i didn't care if she was a thousand or ten thousand or a thousand thousand years old. stars are older than you can count, and they're still beautiful, aren't they? mountains are older than you can remember and they're still solid and where you want them, aren't they? i always thought Packer 67 was pretty because she was nice to me in a place where nice was a very hard thing to be. so i didn't care if Label-glue 11 laughed. what i did care about was when Packer 67 shook her head and said, *think smaller, 55: pretty don't make the shift end any quicker, and it don't make the food taste any less mush. why'd you want to have pretty?*

i don't know, except that my eye still looks for it and i can't help thinking bigger than i'm supposed to. and anyway sometimes you can see pretty in Factory. you can if you look.

i look. sometimes when the water runs from the vats to the pipes it shines pretty in the glass and we all touch our gills, remembering. one time Director stopped shouting as a pretty blackling bird flew through in from the outside. straightaway it knew it had come to the wrong place, so it flew up to look for the sky. (i remember blacklings in the trees, going *caw caw caw!*) we could hear the flying-in-Factory bird over the eversteady hum of the chill machine. Director's mouth was a wide hole of surprised Open. he bawled at someone to get that damn bird down! i secretly enjoyed seeing Director freaked because something had happened that he couldn't control, that he couldn't bully or boast about. the blackling flew all around Main Hall, uncatchable at first. us workers sneaked peeks at each other. we were wishing hard that the bird would escape even if we couldn't. but Director wasn't powerless for long. i didn't see exactly what happened; i only heard the gunshot. it was enough to make me freeze, hit by my own memories—*silence falling after gunshot. cherries falling too—fat and juicy in the snow.*

i was sent to scrub the bit where the bird fell with extra-strong industrial Stingo, which is horrible, horrible stuff. it eats flesh and even floor, if you leave it on long enough. so there i was, getting on with the job (gagging on the

smell of the stuff) when Director mooched over
to check out the corpse and see how well he'd
done. i tried to hold my breath, not wanting to
get any part of Director inside me, not even
atoms from his sugar-sweet voice.

*hey cutie,* he said.

*hey, drop dead,* i replied in my mind.

he gave me a white-toothed smile. *guess our
lil feathered friend didn't know i never miss, huh?*

what was i supposed to say to that? was it a
day when Director wanted compliments, or would
just opening my mouth mean i'd end up sprawled
in the puddle of raw Stingo on Factory floor?
lucky me. he walked off before i had a chance to
screw up completely, so he never noticed me take
some of that strong Stingo, did he? he didn't
see what i did with it next either, although i bet
he would've loved to slurp on the tears that
stung my eyes as i rubbed the hot paste on the
back of my hand. more than that, he'd've loved to
hear the scream of pure pain that i swallowed as
the skin on my hand dissolved. that wasn't
pretty, not nice at all. but clever.

*how come clever?* you're probably thinking.

wait and see.

as for Director, i'd seen his eyes, seen into his heart, and i learned something. fact is, that man *looks* tall, but he thinks *small*, so he can keep his clean skin, his fancy smile, and his neat nails! who cares if he's got Factory? so what if he's buddy-boy with Bossman? i wouldn't want to be like him if he was the last person on the planet, not a smit, not a smidgeon, not the littlest of little bits.

i want to be ME. i want to be Luka P.

so that's what i'm going to be . . . as long as Bossman doesn't find me first.

Bossman's got long fingers that have never felt strong Stingo and he acts like he holds the whole world in them. Bossman comes and goes where and when he pleases, just striding through the door by magic. i came . . . i don't remember how i came. it was too long and nasty ago. i came a different way with lots of others. and i go . . . i go where i please now . . . go down alleys, over walls, along sneaky paths to the river, nothing watching over me 'cept the sky.

i love the sky.

i'd love it even more if the stars showed but you can't have stars and rain at the same time. never mind—i love rain, too. yet another thing we never get in Factory. we see so much water in bottles and pipes, but it's *look, don't touch; lick lips, don't drink.* bottles of Blue Mountain are for other people, never for us-people. we only get water at shower hour, standing under the cold spray, heads sideways, getting it on your gills if you can.

Director thinks he's Big News cos he's got Factory and cuticles and everything. Bossman thinks he's Big News cos he has a suit and stuff. me, i'm richer. i've got rain! water in my socks, on my head, in my eyes, drink it down— did you ever drink rain? tastes different from what i thought—nothing like bubbled with fizz bottles of Blue. rain is for real, not greenberry-redberry-blueberry colored, just rain, like the sky's just sky. no preservatives, no additives. no lies on rain's label, saying "greenberry" when no greenberries have been within a million miles of it. people have labels too, did you know that? not glued on, but there all the same, every time they try to tell you what they're like. want my advice? ignore what people say and watch what they do. taste them a bit and figure out for yourself what their flavor is, what their true ingredients are. no, really, i'm not being silly: it's important.

Color Tech 26 asked me one day, *do you know what greenberry, redberry, and blueberry are?* her voice squeaked with nerves because she was afraid that it might be a day when asking questions was Against The Rules. i shook my head. i was Bottle Seal 55; i'd never worked in the Flavor Department.

*are they real fruit?* she asked. *real fruit like the pictures the Label-glue girls put on? i mean, are there really green balls and blue balls and red balls as well?*

berries, i told her. you're supposed to call them berries.

she told me the Techs just squirted the

colors into the vats with a giant syringe, the flavors, too. *i tried redberry flavor once,* she said. *i didn't mean to,* she added quickly. *i would never break the Rules like that, only i was cleaning the syringe seal and my Hygie glove tore and i thought i was shitzered for sure: some flavor stuck on my finger and i couldn't help it. i licked it off.*

i stared at her when she said this. when was the last time we'd had flavor in our food? Director's birthday, probably, when he ordered chocolate paste for all the workers. some of us even had time to taste a bit of it before he came storming onto the platform shouting, *hey girlie-girls, i've got the happiest birthday present in the world for you! guess what? big bulk orders from the cities have just come in! so get out of the canteen and back to work!*

oh those new orders! sometimes it meant no sleep, no food till we'd finished. it was one of the new orders that finished off Color Tech 26, just before i felt the pull of the two-moon tide, telling me to GO. Tech 26 was the same as Packer

67—she just flopped, dropped, and stopped, an unhygienic lump on Factory floor. that made Director mad. he leaned right over the platform railings and shouted, Supervisor! Supervisor, why has that worker stopped?

*Color Tech 26!* shouted Supervisor. *Tech 26, stop resting!*

only Color Tech 26 had stopped doing everything, including living, just like Packer 67 stopped some days before. both times the Medic came. the Medic said Packer 67 stopped from old age, at least, that's what i heard on the goss-roster. people said that's just what happens when you get old. it seems it can happen when you're not old as well, but what do i know? i don't have Medic learning. Color Tech 26 wasn't old, she was just a girl like me. *weak heart,* i overheard the Medic say as they pulled the white Hygie bag of body off Factory floor. i kept looking small so they didn't see me watching. *good-bye, Color Tech 26,* i said in my head. *at least you got to try the redberry flavor once before you died.*

*what did it taste like, redberry?* i asked her that time when we were talking.

*sweet,* she said, *sweet and sticky.*

*nice,* i said.

she wasn't so sure. horribly, she started to cry. no No NO! crying's against our rules (a stick of shitzer to whatever Director says on this matter). you can lie, you can steal, but you can never never cry.

*i'm not crying,* she said. *i just got some Stingo in my eyes . . . only . . . only i was sad as well cos i didn't know if that syrup was really how redberries tasted. did you ever have redberries before you came here?* she asked me. *do you remember what they were like?*

remembering makes you feel . . . funny, that's why we don't do it. this time, though, i didn't tell Color Tech 26 to zip her mouth up, cos sometimes we all need to get stuff straight in our heads, to work out whether we know something or if we just made it up. in fact, seeing how sad she was, i decided to give Tech 26 a present, something to make up for all the birthdays she never had. maybe it wasn't much of a present. it was just a lie to make her feel better. i told her, *oh yeah, i suddenly do remember redberries, and you know what, they look exactly like the picture on the bottles, all big and bouncy by the Blue Mountain.*

*what did redberries taste like?* came her thin voice. i lied to her again when she asked that.

*what did they taste like? for real? sort of sweet*, i said, *sort of sweet and sticky.*

she smiled: a little bit of pretty that disappeared not long after. i had to lie. i don't remember redberry. what i remember, what i dream about, what i splash through the puddles to find again . . . what i remember are the cherries. so i made my Plan. d'you want to know my Plan? it's a Plan with two parts and the first part is this: i'm going to get out of Factory and have a proper birthday with friends and presents and everything, especially *cherries*—so DON'T ANYONE GET IN MY WAY.

# NIGHTFALL I

"So where the hell are the cherries?"

Tanka dumped her backpack on the soggy path and waited with her arms wrapped around herself, hopping from one foot to another to keep warm. Ferry number 9 was long gone up the Annaflo river, on its way to Meander town. The orchard began a few meters from the pier and it seemed to go on for miles, right into the pale lilac of late afternoon.

They'd traveled inland and upriver for a night and a day. Since the New Frontier politicians were particularly strict about noninvasive technology and low fuel consumption, all transport went at maddeningly slow speeds, making sure that there was no wanton environmental damage. Ferry number 9, generously subsidized by the O-HA, traveled from Santanna to Meander, taking passengers and also serving as the main delivery boat for all the small outposts on the edge of the Annaflo. Each stop had brought a fresh tirade from Tanka.

"Can you see all those crates of Blue Mountain they're unloading?" she'd complained. "Any one of those could have the Zee Homarlo prize, and they're doling them out to hicks on the riverbank!"

She was in no sweet mood after attempting to tune into a local music channel on the *e.f.* only to discover that the songs and chats were periodically scrambled. Oddly, having Kat give detailed explanations about the disruptive influence of an indigenous metal called mont-halo ore hadn't soothed her mood in the slightest.

Prester and Millijue spent most of the journey staring out of the ferry windows, pretending they weren't regretting the change of continent in the slightest.

Then they'd arrived at the orchard.

"I mean, look at this place!" Tanka snorted. "The trees are all totally dead and I swear I'm going to strangle the next person who says, *Cherry Heaven? Ooh supreme!*—like we need to hear that from every single passenger on the ferry! If they rate the place so much, how come they don't stop here? And are you sure this *is* our stop? There's no sign of a house, no sign of anything . . . no fricking *sign*, for godssake! How do we even know we're here?"

Kat filtered out Tanka's rant as she slowly surveyed the terrain. "We're here, Tanka. This is it—the orchard at least."

The landscape was so different it almost seemed like an alien planet, not just a foreign continent. On the long journey from Santanna both girls had grown uneasy, seeing the strange shapes of mountains and forests rise up beyond the riverbanks. Back home people didn't travel much, unless it was a canal trip to one of the other cities. Most journeys were virtual—tours of the known universe from the comfort of your own apartment. Seeing pictures of the New Frontier was no preparation for walking into the real thing. The sounds, the colors, even the smells were different.

A freaky parade of grotesque shapes lined the path ahead, with branches stretched mute to meet them. Some trunks were covered in a living mire of moss and mold; on some the bark looked flayed, hanging down in sad strips that didn't even stir in the breeze. The red wood laid bare underneath shone like mirrored blood. Far rows of cherry trees were drenched in a gray sheen of rain—the same rain that had turned the path into a mulch of sodden soil and dead leaves. Each tree looked bruised by the purpling gloom.

"Original Earth tree DNA," Kat informed everyone. "Brought here by the first settlers. Can you imagine a bunch of people sitting around wondering what there'd be room for on the ships, and getting to choose cherries?"

"Dud choice," said Tanka. "They're all dead."

"Not dead, just dormant. They'll flower in spring and fruit in second summer. I bet the harvest brings in a lot of money, and the land alone must be worth a packet. All last year's cherries are probably freezer fodder—easy enough to defrost if you want to try some."

"Do I look like I need cherries right now? I need a big dinner and a long, long swim in warm water before my gills shrivel up and drop off, that's what. Why's the sky gone all weird?"

"Must be what they call twilight." Kat craned her neck to see if any stars or moons showed through the muffle of clouds. Not a hope. Even her lucky star was out of sight, or perhaps she wasn't looking at the right part of the sky—they were on the other side of the planet, after all. She refused to be daunted, having every confidence that they'd make it to the house before it got too dark. Only it was a *little* unnerving to lose a proper sense of distance and perspective. If this was twilight, it didn't suit her practical, clear-vision state of mind at all. Still, it was important to make the best of things. "At least it's stopped raining."

"The air's very damp," Aunt Millijue piped up stubbornly.

"I don't suppose even Quinn Essnid can do much about that. Look, shall we just walk? It shouldn't be far from here."

"Walk!" Tanka blurted the word out, as if she was waiting for some miraculous form of transport that would somehow whisk them through the orchard. "You're joking, right? Hey, don't look at me like that! I'm *not* being unreasonable, or spoiled, or . . . or whatever that look means."

"It's just a look," said Kat.

"Oh come on—we can't just walk through . . . *that*. Anything could happen."

"This *is* the edge of nowhere, remember? Nothing happens here; it's why you didn't want to come."

Uncle Prester did his best to be masterful. "Let's just get moving—going at a nice brisk pace will soon warm us up. What do you say, Tank?"

"Putting me on High in the kitchen oven couldn't warm me up right now. I'm frozen!"

Kat handed her sister a long, soft, pink thing. "Have a scarf. Apparently they're all the rage in Meander."

Tanka looked at it as if it was something she'd trodden in by accident. "I'd rather chew off my right arm."

"Fine. Stay cold."

"Cold?! *Cold* is the little goose-pimply shiver you get coming out of the pool. *Cold* is the chill from the fridge when you've mooched inside for another bottle of Blue Mountain. *Cold* is having to wrap a sarong around your bikini. This isn't cold . . . this is some *shitzer* Ice Age!"

"Look, it's just like the early colonists, intrepid in the face of adventure. Think of Zee Homarlo in *Son of the Stars (yes*, the extended version) when he has to survive on that barren planet for five years with only a half-naked girl to keep him company. *He* didn't complain about the cold."

If there was a trace of sarcasm in Kat's voice, Tanka never noticed. Kat shouldered her bag and started walking along the rough path and, since it was *sisters stick together*, Tanka hoisted her bag up too.

"Mush-brained early colonists," Kat could hear her muttering under her breath as she followed. "Should've all been lined up outside their landing craft and shot. Should've all been nuked in space when they left Earth. Should've all been strangled as embryos in the test tube. Ow!" She stumbled and dropped her bag. "Great. I might just break my leg before we even get there."

"Perhaps you'd be better off in proper shoes," said Aunt Millijue helpfully.

"Yeah—these are getting trashed."

"I meant ones you can walk in."

"I wouldn't *need* to walk if you weren't making me hike out to the middle of nowhere."

Kat pointed to the roadside, where the ground fell away into a ditch and a green-mired stream gurgled sadly. "You could always swim."

"You think I'd let those weeds near this hair? Not in a million light years! This waterbaby will only frill her gills with one-hundred-percent filtered A-one-quality $H_2O$, no messing. I'm heading straight for the nearest pool, and after that you'll have to surgically remove my swimming suit."

"Don't mention pools yet," said Kat. Even in the Top Class pool on the *Marie-Cloud* the $H_2O$ had been so recycled it settled slickly on the gills and had left her wondering just whose runoff water she was wallowing in. Kat felt the scarf rubbing on her gills as she walked. She hoped that Cherry Heaven had a rainproof house and decent bathrooms, as well as these acres of orchard.

The sisters went on ahead. Prester and Millijue were by no means fit or active people—the only exercise they ever got was cerebral. True, Prester had been known to lift boxes of heavy printouts if he had a particularly obscure historical reference to source, while Millijue's perpetual tension burned off most of her energy and left her hollow thin.

As the purple sky thickened into nightfall, two lines of orange light began to glow on either side of the path. Tanka cheered up at the evidence of smart technology, while Kat got nervous. It was one thing to be able to see where you were going, quite another to have your eyes so dazzled that the shadows in the orchard darkened to night absolute.

*Easy for us to see the path; easy for anyone in the orchard to see us.*

Kat stopped dead.

Tanka swallowed her giggles. "What? What is it?"

"Nothing."

"Like hell, nothing. What's the matter?"

"Trick of the light: I thought someone was watching us. . . ."

They stood so still each second seemed a century.

Then Tanka breathed out. "Kat, there's no such things as ghosts, right?"

Kat's whisper was shot through with a thread of bravado. "Are you crazy? Of course not."

"I know. Only, what are those ghostie-shapes moving in the trees?"

"Birds. Probably. Prester said blacklings like to nest in the orchard."

"Are blacklings big?"

"Maybe."

"And that jangly ghostie noise?"

"Bird-frights, to keep the blacklings away."

"Oh. And the trees?"

"Trees *can't* be ghosts, Tank!"

"So you don't think this whole place is totally haunted?"

"There's no scientific proof for . . . *shitzer on a stick*! What's that?" Kat grabbed Tanka's arm, making her squeal.

A white streak with a black tail shot across the road and just as quickly disappeared. It might have been a cat. Or a ghost.

"No such thing as ghosts," said Kat. "Scientific fact."

"Sod science," said Tanka. "Let's get to the house. Like *now*."

The shadow man hiding in the trees watched the girls run. He wasn't a ghost, though he did keep company with them.

# NIGHTFALL II

Stopping on a low rise to blow clouds of cold breath, Tanka and Kat surveyed their new home. One by one smart lights came on in the near valley, as if the farm knew they had arrived.

First they saw the fence that kept the orchard at bay, then the gleaming roof solars of the house itself. It was a stunning place, with brilliant white walls, wide windows, and yes, the unmistakable shape of at least one large pool room at the side of the house, edged with wooden decking. Tiny lamps danced along the veranda . . . which strayed over the edge of sudden darkness.

Tanka whistled. "Now that's something you don't see every day."

Kat was aghast. "There's a lake!" she blurted out, as if they couldn't all see it for themselves. "No one said anything about a lake! Uncle Prester, did they say anything to you about the lake?"

But Prester and Millijue were both making a beeline for the front door, moving faster than they'd done for years. "Damn thing had better be open," Millijue muttered. "The air's so wet I can feel my skin getting mildew."

Kat didn't move. "Who the hell put a *lake* next to our house!" Her words idled out over the water and didn't echo back.

"It's a big one," said Tanka. She snuggled up close to her sister, knowing full well Kat had a horror of anything she couldn't see the bottom of. Kat didn't like long tunnels, deep water, or murky maths problems.

The sheet of water was vast, swallowing the valley as far as a distant range of mountains to the north. The mountain tops were lost in cloud, and they weren't blue by any stretch of the imagination. On the eastern side of the lake, opposite, a cluster of lights glowed—obviously someone else's country house. Away to the south three bright silver O-HA signs hung in the night sky, impossibly high.

Kat suddenly laughed as she realized what they were. "Oh god, I must've left my brain on the ferry! What a doop! Who put the *lake* there?! It's a *reservoir*, Tank. Remember the big O-HA dam that was in the news a while back? They flooded a valley when it was done, and there was that awesome opening ceremony on the newschat."

"Oh, not the *O-HA* again," Tanka moaned. "I can't see what all the fuss is about. So they're Overseas? So they're Humanitarian and an Agency? Un-big excitement! They needn't think *I'm* going to lend my gorgeousness to their little rustic rallies."

Kat's mouth twisted up in a half-grin of admiration. "Linveki Hydro Company did all the engineering. It's got a superstructure of tuffcrete and local quarry stone for the fascia—totally state of the art and entirely eco-friendly. Amazing! They must be the dam towers, away there where the lights are."

"Pretty. Can we go in now? It looks like the locals are harmless, since the front door isn't locked. . . ."

"Sure, yeah. I'll be right with you."

While Tanka bounded off to join Prester and Millijue in search of coffee, Kat stayed a few moments longer in the yard. The reservoir water reached close to the house. *Too close.* It lapped around the end of the decking, turning it into more of a boat pier than a picnic spot. Just beyond the decking a line of white wind turbines went out into the water . . . and under the water . . . until the last one finally disappeared from view, marching in darkness toward whatever was left at the bottom of the lake.

She was suddenly shaken by unsteady memories of another waterfront and the home she'd known before the war, where she'd lived with a real mum and dad. It had been a snug house with fresh flowers at every window and a long plank walkway over sparkling blue water. Seagulls and sawri birds bobbed between the pleasure boats. City Five marina. That was before the war. Before the horrible day when Security came, seeking out green-stamped Galrezi. They'd all run together, Tanka in Mum's arms, Kat in her dad's, escaping through the waterfront cafés and into the beautiful city boulevards. Door after door, they knocked on them all, begging to be let in to hide, but who dared help when they saw the green glint of a Galrezi mark? Then there was the terrible moment when her mum and dad were torn away; Tanka crying, Mum waving. Leaving. Gone.

That was then. This was now. No war or weapons or running away. It was the New Frontier and a new start. The clouds would clear, the sun would shine, and the mountains would, somehow, be blue.

She turned away from the reservoir and went into Cherry Heaven.

It was a beautiful house—every room warm and inviting. While Prester and Millijue went on a futile hunt for rodents, rising damp, or faults of any kind, Tanka flung open all the doors in delight. Cherry Heaven was much bigger than the apartment in City Five. Maybe there wasn't a rooftop sun-terrace or a flower-filled atrium, but there was a big wallow-pool on the ground floor, facing the reservoir, as well as a smaller pool room on the next floor up, by the bedrooms.

Both sisters raced upstairs, followed by the smell of freshly brewing coffee.

"I think I've found the best room," said Tanka, falling through an open doorway just as the light sensors came on. "Wanna share for now? Bagsie the bed by the mirror!" She hated to be alone, which meant the room would soon be a disaster area of clothes, makeup, and abandoned schoolwork.

Already she was tearing her backpack open to find her pajamas, letting her clothes fall into a squidge of damp on the floor—completely ignoring the lovely design of the room and its furniture. She bundled into a robe and twisted a towel around her hair. "I can't believe Q Essnid stocked the entire kitchen for us—did you see how crammed those cupboards were? *Food*, Kat! Hurry up!"

Kat unpacked her own bag carefully, setting each item out in order. Whoever Q Essnid had paid to get the house ready had done a good job making the room look homey. Everything had been deep cleaned and the beds were made up with extra-twice soft covers. Having bottles of Blue Mountain by each bed was a nice touch. Tanka had already opened them, hoping against hope to win the competition to spend a day with Zee Homarlo. She'd drawn a blank with both bottle tops.

Kat snuggled into her 'jamas and turned to go downstairs. Then, because she was Kat and because she noticed things, she stopped in the doorway. It had recently been decorated, but underneath the fresh white paint there were the faintest of faint marks visible. It was enough to intrigue a girl whose idea of a hot date was murmuring "enhance" to a digital microscope screen. She grazed the marks with her fingertips: three horizontal lines pressed into the wood, each with an initial. They were just like the mark she and Tanka used to draw back at the city apartment, showing how high they'd grown. They'd kept that up into their teens. Now Kat was tall, taller even than the first two lines gouged into the door at Cherry Heaven.

One line had an *H* next to it, the other had an *M*. She nearly missed the bottom line. It was much lower, slightly wobbly, and it was tagged with an equally uneven *L*.

Girls or boys? No way of knowing, but nice to think there'd once been a family at Cherry Heaven.

"Hey! Prester says we can't start till you get your lanky legs down here!" Tanka appeared at the bottom of the stairs. "You weren't switching my stuff, were you? I already bagged that bed."

Kat smiled at the mere idea of shifting Tanka's explosion of luggage from one bed to the other. "I didn't touch your stuff, and I'm coming."

After that, she forgot about anything other than food . . . and there was a good mountain of it laid out on the table in the front room. The heaters were cranked up to high and Aunt Millijue flung over a thermal blanket for Kat's lap.

"What a fantastic house! Will you just look at this feast!" Uncle Prester beamed. "There are three more crates of Blue Mountain, courtesy of the Hydro factory in Santanna, so drink up."

Kat was impressed. "Is this all stuff Q Essnid left for us?"

"Not personally. There's a note from his son, who delivered it specially for our arrival."

"Did you say the magic *son* word?" Tanka's boy-radar was always on Alert.

"A boy called Aran E," said Aunt Millijue innocently. "Your age, I think Q Essnid told me, or maybe a year older."

Tanka wiggled her toes in front of the heater and sighed. "Perhaps this place will cater to all my appetites after all! Can we eat now?"

They ate. Q Essnid's generosity was praised many times before the impromptu meal was over. Shutters were closed against the night and music programmed to fill the house. It was only after extensive gormandizing that Kat looked over the crumb-ridden plates and empty packaging, noticing that for all the luxury foods on offer, there was one thing oddly absent from a place called Cherry Heaven.

There weren't any cherries.

## Footprints

trouble is, i can't remember where cherries come from. In Factory there weren't any cherries, just those big vats of fruity flavor.

wish i could remember. something's sitting on my head saying, *hey Luka, don't be such a shitzer-brain, you know where cherries come from.* i don't like being talked at like that so i say, *Okay thing-on-my-head, if i know where cherries come from, how come i don't know where cherries come from?* in my mind i see rows and rows of trees with fat juicy cherry berries under the leaves. the branches are hung with metal ribbons singing jingle-jangle music the birds don't like. are these memories or made up? how can you tell the difference? it's hard when you're used to being in a place where *real* is whatever Director says it is.

except now *real* is the path i'm on, the bushes scratching my legs, the mud swallowing my feet. i've got mountains on the left and a river on my right. L for Left. L for Luka. L for LEFT Factory! R for Right. right and wrong, weak and strong. what is right? in Factory whatever Director said had to be right, but wasn't he wrong? Bossman was wrong but definitely strong. my legs are weak when they need to be strong. in Factory there's not much point in having legs, except to stand by the conveyor belt or to climb a ladder to sleep. now i've got to walk as far as i can away from that place, even if every step takes me farther into the world where Bossman breathes, and every footprint leaves a sign for Director to follow. faster, faster, running now, chased by the gleam of Director's white grin. his nails will be neat as his hands reach out to grab me. quick—look back—no one there. there's a not-real feel of his breath on my neck. bushes scratch, mud sucks, cold bites. i run past houses where windows are dark. won't be long now before people wake up. they'll get to wash in

warm water and eat yummy food, things as far
from Factory life as the ground is from stars.
how can both things be real at the same time?
and if the snug bugs looked out would they think
i was real or some kind of ghost all orangey-gray
in the day's last darkness?

they get up, i get up too. time to go hunting,
got some things to find.

*where'd you always find things from?* Packer
67 said that time i stole her some proper soap
as a birthday present. *if Supervisor sees that,
she'll kill you once a day for the rest of your life.
i bet it ain't even my birthday anyway.*

*who cares?* i said. presents are nice anytime,
and you need soap—you smell.

*me, smell? when i'm smeared up past my eyeballs
in Stingo!* she growled. then her face grew a fat
smile as she realized i'd done something only
Director was allowed to do: i'd made a joke. her
lungs puffed out wheezy laughs till she remembered where she was. *girl, you ain't right or real for
this hole. what in shitzerville keeps you going, 55?
why hasn't this place finished you off years ago?*

good question. i had a good answer, only i was afraid to tell her, in case she blabbed on the goss-roster. it was my secret. she liked the sound of a secret.

spill, 55—what secret? yeah, 'course i'll keep it . . . who'm i going to tell, huh?

you might, i said carefully. i don't want people to laugh.

just tell me and i won't laugh. Packer 67 did her serious face.

it's not a serious secret. it's a nice one, about people. nice people.

what about 'em?

well, just that there are some.

Packer 67 didn't laugh. she sort of coughed and shook her head and swore and shook her head again, but she didn't laugh.

haven't you learned anything in this dump?

oh, sure, i said cheerfully. i've learned many stages of water-bottling production, how to organize extra food rations, how to jump the queue for the shower, how to watch for Supervisor coming, and how to sleep when

Label-glue 11's snoring. the thing is, though, i met the nice people before i came here.

stuff your nice people, said Packer 67, only she didn't look quite so gloomy as before. she waited a moment then asked, what nice people?

lots of 'em. there's my friend Gim Damson who used to show me the stars, and Aran E and Harpo C, who used to play in the river with me, and the lady with the hot donuts, and the roast-nut man, and my sisters, of course. i've got two big sisters called Hikori and Mai. well, i did have.

Packer 67 shook her head at me.

you aren't supposed to remember stuff about sisters and things.

that was the end of that secret sharing. after, i'd catch her counting her bruises and muttering, you and your doop talk about nice people. believe it when i see it, that's what, believe it when i see it.

there were nice people, though, even if i can't quite see their faces. there were friends, and there was a place i lived with my mama and sisters, a place where all you can hear is silence falling after gunshots and all you can see are cherries falling, fat and juicy on the snow. *get real!* is what Packer 67 always told me when i went all misty trying to remember. *don't dream of the other days. they're gone.*

gone? maybe. can i get them back again?

can't worry about that now, got to keep going. mountains on the left, river on the right, and revenge . . . revenge is dead ahead, rising like the sun over shadows.

# WINDFALL I

A shadow watched from the orchard edge as the sun rose over the Blue Mountains and shone into the valley.

On one bed Tanka was snoring happily. Her cheeks were pink and one painted-nail foot had escaped from the duvet. Kat was already awake, dazzled by the strange magic of frost on the windows. She slipped out of bed and wiggled her toes in the thick carpet, ready for a long soak in the small pool. There hadn't been time for more than a perfunctory gill-wetting the night before, all four of them too dizzy with the Bliss of being underwater to appreciate their surroundings properly.

Cherry Heaven was warm and quiet in the new light. It was nothing like the old apartment in City Five, where they'd woken every morning to the sound of demolition crews on the plaza, or salvage squads still picking over the war ruins. Back in the city everything had seemed dusty, recycled, stale, nothing like the early-morning luster skimming the top of the cherry trees and flashing on the silvery chimes of the bird-frights.

The view from the picture window on the landing was sensational, although the Blue Mountains still weren't blue no matter how hard Kat squinted. South she saw the pale smudge of the dam at the narrow mouth of the valley. Once there had been a river rushing along the valley bottom to join the broad, brown Annaflo. Now the dam held it back, and she was pleased to think that under the three tall towers there were super-smooth machines that turned the water into good, clean power.

Just because she admired the technology, she still shivered at the dark gleam of the reservoir, where there should've been Cluff village and fertile fields. Was the village down there, collapsing gradually into the dark mud, with water snakes writhing through the windows? That would be one more reason not to dip even a toe in the reservoir. And who'd want to, when Cherry Heaven had two glorious warm-water pools? Like all colonists she lived for the Bliss of being submerged, when water bubbled across the streaks of gills at her throat and sent body and brain into a precious passion of other-self. Oxygen-enriched was best—that kept the mind alert longer. Normal water was fine, as long as you didn't mind the eventual drowsiness. Salt water was like poison. Deep water wasn't dangerous, just something Kat couldn't cope with.

Padding off to the pool room, she caught a flash of movement in the yard. If she'd been a paranoid sort of person, she would've said it was something slinking along the edge of the orchard. As she squinted into the long, low rays of the early sun, Kat found she was holding her breath. Which was silly. There definitely wasn't a man, a tall man, watching the house. She was imagining things. So why was her heart beating too quickly as she rummaged for a coat and boots? Why did she have to pause for a long moment outside Millijue's bedroom door, wondering whether to wake her? Just being overdramatic, obviously. Because when she stepped out into the sting of cold air, there was no answer at all to her timid, "Who's there?"

The cherry trees shivered but spilled no secrets. Around the yard the ground was too mushy with wet leaves to show footprints—or were those marks leading toward the orchard? Did she dare look closer? It wasn't so scary in sunlight, just shabby and rather sad, left untended for months, even years. Trees grew unchecked along the fence line, their roots snarled by brash tracts of undergrowth, nothing like the segregated olive and cimarron groves back home in the city. It was all strange, but not sinister. Suddenly she felt the horrible sensation of something sliding against her leg. She flinched . . .

then laughed at her own stupidity. It was a cat, just a little white cat with a black tail.

"Hey, puss! What're you doing? You made me jump!"

It shrank away from her voice, then skeetered over to some sheds on the far side of the yard.

"Don't worry—there's only me. Where'd you go? Hey—looks like you've found a nice spot for sun-bathing."

The cat was basking among the narrow branches of two trees tangling upward against a natural sun-trap along the shed wall. They'd been planted so close together they'd grown up as one, with roots covered by rotten leaves and branches bare of bird-frights.

"C'mon, kitty, I just want to say hello. Quick, cos I'm freezing. Here, puss-puss."

Just as her fingertips grazed the cat's white fur, it leaped away again, and Kat yelped as a branch swished across her right hand, leaving a thin trail of blood.

"Fine. Be like that."

She was about to suck the cut clean when she noticed something strange about the tree trunks. Long since split and splintered, the bark still showed signs that lines had been carved into them.

"Funny—the letter *H*, and that one's an *M*. So where's the *L*, like the lines on the door frame? Nowhere I can see. Stupid place to plant trees anyway, too close together; any idiot should know that. They ought to be cut. Could be tools in the shed . . ."

It wasn't strictly wrong to force open the warped doors. Who'd care if she cleared a path through the cobwebs and junk, if nothing else to find out what was making that soft electric noise? Who'd mind if she broke the thick seal of dust on three giant cryochests still freezing away at the back of the shed? Who'd even know if she opened the lids to see what was inside . . . ?

# WINDFALL II

An awful wail sounded from the big pool room. Aunt Millijue went rigid with nerves. She had a habit of holding her breath whenever something bad happened.

"That's Tanka!"

"No kidding." Kat didn't even bother to unwind from her comfy window seat. "Either she's locked herself in the pool room *again*, in which case I'll go hunt out my multi-tool, or she's just discovered a spot."

"Kat . . ."

"What? You don't think I should make fun of my sister? You know I love her to bits, only you've got to laugh when she spends the morning in tears because a bottle of nail varnish broke in her bag and now her eyebrow pencils are lacquered together."

"Oh dear. I'd better go and help, whatever the matter is."

"Don't bother. One rescue mission coming up."

It wasn't a dire emergency after all—Tanka thought she'd seen a white face looking through the window at her. Kat tried to reassure her. And failed.

"It *wasn't* a cat!" she argued. "It was a man! I saw him!"

"Tank, the windows are so steamed up in here, how could you see anything?"

"I can see you've been stuffing your face without waiting for me. When's breakfast? I'm starving."

"When Uncle Prester finds the pancake mix."

"Lead the way. . . ."

Tanka wrapped herself in layers of soft toweling and padded off to the sitting room, followed by a cloud of after-bath perfume. "Hey Milli—have you been in the big pool? It's extra-twice nice. This place is almost classy in daylight, real wood everywhere, and I kinda like the funny flying things carved on the ceiling."

Kat settled back on her seat. "They're papillons."

"Say again?"

"Papillons—like the butterflies we used to go see at the tropical house."

"Try not talking with your mouth full; you might actually make sense. What are you eating anyway? I don't remember Q Essnid bringing those."

"He didn't. Want some?" Kat held out a blue bowl filled to the brim with fruit. They were fat, shining cherries—some black, some red, some gleaming with straw-gold streaks.

"Ohmygod," said Tanka. "I can't believe you're actually eating *cherries*! After all the mush we've heard about, *ooh, Cherry Heaven, simper, simper, supreme!*" She leaned forward and looked in the bowl. "They don't look like cherries. What's wrong with the pink powder we had back home?"

"These are real for starters . . . straight off the

trees and into my mouth. Well, not exactly off the trees. I found a whole row of cryo-freezers in one of the outbuildings, all crammed full—I guess what you'd call a windfall, maybe left there when the last tenants quit. The wind turbines have kept 'em humming along nicely. I'm surprised Q Essnid didn't realize. Anyway, I nuked a few packets to defrost them, and they haven't killed me yet. In fact they're—"

"You just ate stuff you found in a freezer?" Aunt Millijue was shocked.

"It's fine. The packets are all dated. Ten years old is nothing to cryo. They're vintage, but very—"

"Well, who's the little culture integration star?" Tanka interrupted. "Next thing, you'll be signing up for the O-HA and saying you want to live here for ever and ever."

"I will not! Anyway, this *is* a famous cherry farm, so we might as well see what the fuss is about. And I've got to say . . ."

Seeing signs of an argument in the making, Millijue quietly escaped.

Tanka glared at her sister. "You're always messing about with things, aren't you? You can't just leave stuff alone. Maybe Q Essnid didn't want you to go opening his freezers."

"They're not his; they belong to the house. And since when do you care about what you're supposed to do?"

"I don't. You're the boring one. D'you think anyone would look twice at you if you weren't with me?"

"At least I *can* think."

"Like thinking's going to impress anyone at the new school. . . ." Bored with this argument already, Tanka looked around for another way to annoy her sister. "You keep eating those cherries, you'll end up looking like one."

"You keep messing about with that nail varnish, Prester and Millijue'll kill you and I'll spit cherry stones in your cremation urn."

"Oh come on—it's an improvement." Tanka made a flourish and stepped back to admire her handiwork . . . a neat bit of color on the pompous portrait of General Insidian that was hanging over the sofa. His eyes were now filled in with Neva-Chip Sun-Kist Sparkal. Scarily, it *was* an improvement.

Kat had to laugh . . . so hard she almost choked. Tanka very kindly thumped her—repeatedly—until Kat yelled for mercy instead. Sofa cushions were grabbed for a grand old fight that lasted until Kat got hiccups, Tanka got tired, and a very giggly truce was called.

"So those cherries . . ." Tanka began, eyeing the bowl warily. "Are they any good?"

"Good? Deliriously delicious, more like. If they're legendary, like everyone says, they deserve to be."

"Mmm. Pass one over. . . ."

Side by side on the sofa they ate cherries, then

pancakes with hot cimarron syrup. It was nice to know they wouldn't have to worry about school for a couple of days, although Kat was looking forward to the new curriculum and Tanka speculated on the local boy population. Peace lasted until their crates of possessions were delivered, all stamped with a pass mark from Customs and liberally plastered with O-HA stickers for good measure. Having decided to keep to the same bedroom because it was nice to share (nothing to do with feeling nervy about ghosts or white faces), it did look as if they could get through the unpacking without too many arguments. Kat agreed to keep all her geeky things on her side of the room, and Tanka said she'd try not to hog the whole of the closet space. Then, with a rustle of plastic wrap, the photos appeared—two old-fashioned prints salvaged from the little house by the marina all those years ago. One was of Tanka and Kat aged four, splashing around Waterworld park with polka-dot shorts and cheeky grins. The second photo showed their parents alone, holding hands in front of a forest of boat masts. It was just after gene testing became compulsory, so little twinks of light shone on the new silver/green stamps. Three weeks later they'd been running for their lives.

"No way are you putting those on the wall!" Suddenly furious, Tanka made a lunge for the photos but Kat jumped on the bed and held them high out of reach.

"They're mine. I can look at them if I like."

"What for? I'm sick of them!"

"It's our mum and dad!"

"Like I care! When are you going to grow up and forget about them?"

"When are *you* going to grow up and remember them?!"

"What's to remember?" Tanka yelled. "They're Galrezi, aren't they? Nothing to do with me; I'm

Atsumisi. No, before you go off on one of your lectures about being racist, it's not *my* fault what happened in the war. Did I go around arresting people? Did I build the chimneys? Did I light the fires? Did—? *Kat!* I'm sorry! I didn't mean to say that, I didn't mean it, honest, promise. Don't look like that, *don't look like that!*"

"Look like what?" Kat got down off the bed with unsteady legs, definitely not feeling like crying. "I'm fine."

Knowing she'd done something awful, Tanka searched around for some way of fixing things. She settled on a bottle of Blue Mountain. "Have some of this. I already checked the bottle top, though—nothing doing."

"Thanks." Kat took a long gulp. The cherry-flavor tasted flat after the real thing.

"I still don't want those pictures out," said Tanka.

"Fine."

"I mean it. You're too hung up on the past. Here—have a pill. Fancy one of these blue ones—they give you the warm fuzzies?"

"I don't need warm fuzzies!"

"You seriously do."

"I need a new sister."

"Just cos you can't handle the one you've got." Tanka took the pill herself, then settled with a movie magazine as if nothing bad had happened.

Kat put the photos back in the box and slid it under the bed. She didn't take them out again until Tanka was asleep and Cherry Heaven was dark. Moonlight made her parents' faces ghostlike and the tiny Galrezi stamps were dimmed to gray. She stroked the grainy paper. It was impossible to forget the past but remember her parents. Would it be better just to think about the here and now?

The man in the orchard watched in silence until Kat pulled the curtains closed and slipped into bed. He didn't seem to notice the cold.

## Fist

can't stand this cold any longer. never really
noticed it at Factory—that's all there ever
was—only now i'm watching people wearing
warm things, i want them too. they're waiting at
a ferry stop with tuff-cups of coffee and busy
faces. when the ferry comes they flash their
hands for a ticket. wish i could—legs are getting ground down from walking, only you got to
have a shiny hand square to go on board. very
opposite to Factory rules, where a shiny hand
square stops you going anywhere. workers can't
go out; others can't come in.

   that's why i burned my silver square off. and
yes, *of course* my hand hurts without it! your
hand would hurt if you rubbed it with pure Stingo,
industrial strength. yep, that's what i used. stole
it the day Director shot the blackling bird and i
had to scrub the floor clean. only raw Stingo

good enough for that. what a joke—almost like Director helped me escape. i wouldn't've got past the door machines without it. it stank, too, believe me. i was gag gag gagging as i smeared it on.

don't go thinking i had no idea how much it would hurt. i knew. i saw what happened the day Packer 14 decided she'd had Enough and she swallowed a whole bottle of the stuff. her lips blistered and burned like they were chewing themselves up. she dropped dead and the Medic came. poor Medic. all he ever does is pick up dead people.

so, if you're just burning skin stamps to escape, don't drink it, okay? wipe some on and wait for the pain. maybe it feels like it's killing you, but it ain't. 'course, if they hadn't started the whole hand-stamping thing in the first place, i wouldn't've had to steal Stingo or burn skin, would i? i never had a hand stamp till i was seven, my sisters were older. worst of all, we were sent to get ours done on my birthday—to the test center at school. go in with smooth hands, come out with a color. it made us late for my birthday, that and the snow. Hikori and Mai were trotting away, always long-leggier than me. *wait up!* i yelled. they never did.

so our hands were stamped. if you want to be top dog, you've got to have silver/red or silver/blue. you want to land in the shitzer, you get silver/green. like us. we're *shitzer-no-brain-waste-of-space-Galrezi-scum.* i know because Director said so. only, if i don't have green and silver on my hand, just this red-hot ridgeland of scars, does that mean i'm not a *shitzer-no-brain-waste-of-space-Galrezi-scum* anymore? and if i'm not a *shitzer-no-brain-waste-of-space-Galrezi-scum,* what am i?

i'm cold, that's what. tired of watching those people walk about in their world like it's the only one ever. bet they wouldn't give me their hats and gloves and scarves, not even if i asked all nice. that's what people are like, holding on tight to what they've got. you see it all the time at Factory, workers getting what they can when they can, a stick of shitzer to anyone else.

funny, though. about the warmest i ever felt there was this one time when this girl got really ill, her name was Freezer Store 24. since getting ill's Against The Rules in Factory she thought she was dead meat, only i said i'd work her shift since i'd just finished mine and i didn't want to sleep much anyway. (that was a lie. i was so tired i would've welcomed a ten-year zonk-out in the cryo-freeze.) in the end, she stayed in my bunk to try and get better. before i went to do her shift she gripped my hand in her fist and said *thank you*. i slapped on extra Stingo and went off to the Freezer Stores to be number 24. i should've been as cold as ice, and maybe i was on the outside, but inside i was toasty warm.

not like now. got to get clothes to be warm, inside and out. plus if i don't hide this crinkly white thing, Director'll just play hunt-the-Hygie-suit. here i am, at a garden by the ferry stop, stuck hiding so long my legs forget what to do when i unfold them, so i'm scrabbling on the ground like that spider in the corner of Factory Canteen—the one i accidentally scraped with

my chair, so it only had six legs, not eight. i felt
really bad when that happened, especially when
it tried to run away, taking two mangled legs
with it. then Label-glue 11 flattened it under her
Hygie sock, *to put it out of its misery,* she said.
horrible thought. if someone catches me, will
they put *me* out of my misery? i look around
quickly. no sign of Security yet—which doesn't
mean my neck's not stiff from looking this way,
that way, wondering which way they'll come for
me. i won't let them catch me.

it's not far from here to a washing line, with
clothes not too stiff from frost. just got to get
across the garden. Packer 67 used to have a
garden. when i first met her she somehow fixed
it so her bunk was on the row next to mine. off-
shift we'd lie awake for a while and she'd whisper
about all these things, growing things, telling me
their names and what sort of soil they like, how
much they need to drink. that was before
Supervisor heard her and told Director. then,
after the beating, Packer 67's brain was so

mashed she couldn't even remember what a lettuce looked like. Director had bruises too—on his fist. they matched the knuckle-shaped dents in 67's face. it took a long time for her smile to grow back, though Director was pretty perky for days. i guess there's no point in having all those mean muscles if you don't put 'em to good use every once in a while.

my knuckles get cut and dirty from digging deep in the hard ground. my mama always said it's wrong to steal, but it's wrong to be cold, too, isn't it, or hungry? and if i'm a good person can i really do wrong things? more importantly, can i eat, then nab some clothes without anyone seeing me? the first root i find is all whiskery like Supervisor's nose. i bite it hard. *crunch!* wow. what a taste! better than flava-paste and cracker bread.

on the other side of the fence people are wondering if the ferry's going to be late, or if it'll snow soon, saying the sunshine can't last. no one tells them off for talking. they don't have to hold themselves ready for trouble. i hear a ferry engine. good. everyone's looking that way. quick quick quick, grab the clothes, it's done. time to run and hide again—someone's coming. . . .

except i don't move.

i just stand there like a complete no-brain shitzer. can't rip my eyes away from the poster on the wall of the ferry stop. i'd never've noticed it if i hadn't straightened up to steal things. it's a boy drinking Blue Mountain with big O-HA letters over his head. not just any boy. i know that boy! he's bigger, older, grown a scar, but i can see it's Aran E! joint-best-friend with Harpo C! i shuffle up to get close—can't help touching the picture and dirt rubs off my fingers. quick, freeze, wait for Supervisor to knock me into the next universe for being filthy scum. no sign of her. i change the smear into a letter *F. F* for Friend. seeing his face is scary, cos looking at him reminds me of

*WHACK!*

*F* for freaking smack whack PAIN on my head! it's a thrown stone, here comes another. look,

duck, *smash!* it hits the wall. stones are a new
thing. mostly Director grabs whatever he can,
like bottles or chairs. now it's little stones, big
stones, any stones come flying at me.

is it him? where's his *hey cutie?* has he got
me? not yet. not while i've still got legs to run
on, scramble scrabble like that spider. hope i
won't be squashed flat, dead, put out of my
misery.

something's not right. i look back. drop jaw.
it's just children! two kids in the garden chuck-
ing things. just a boy with rocks and a girl with
roast nuts in a bag. she's taken her glove off to
lob stones, too. one thuds on my chest and
drops to the ground.

*hey, don't . . .*

the girl licks nut-flava off her fingers. she's
got fat pink fingers and rosy pink cheeks.
another stone thrown—misses—she throws
again—hits.

brain goes to sludge. F for Fear. F for something else . . . FIST!

i've got a stone for a heart and throw the

stone in my hand, as hard as i can, a damn good shot, a wham dam SLAM good shot right crack on the head. that makes her cry. she stands there, blood prickling out. *you should put Stingo on that.* i don't stop to give her any. i run this way, that way, dark way, damp way, all the way to the river.

shouldn't have thrown that stone . . .

tough. can't think about that now. my friend Gim Damson always said you do what you've got to do. Okay, he also said you shouldn't use violence. he also said it's important to stay alive, so—here i go, can't take it slow, fast-naked on the edge of the river, the angry Annaflo. it's not nice like the one in the valley where we used to play: me, Harpo C, and Aran E that was Cluff river, sweet and pretty with pebbly banks. this is not what i wanted for my first swim in ten years—no white towels, no soft smells, no flying papillons carved on the ceiling. too bad. i've got to get under before they find me. like stepping in a freezer my toes touch water—ankles next, swallowed by the muddy brown water coming up past calves and knees, over thighs, past tickly bits and belly, breasts, shoulders—then—you know what comes next—the best bit! the last breath of lung-air before *gills* go under—ohmygod now i remember what that feels like—closing my eyes and sliding straight under the water—the best most beautiful thing—dropping away from the bank and falling through the darkness to wet weeds on the river bottom.

Bliss.

# WATERFALL I

For a few moments, Kat sat on the edge of
Meander's biggest spa pool, almost giddy with the
warmth and the prospect of submersion. Then,
one after another, she dipped her feet, just her
feet, into the water. Her toenails were painted a
quiet shade of ivory that gleamed against her dark
skin. She bit her lip. This was going to be good!

Centuries before, there had been a time when
people didn't swim, not properly, not like the gen-
erations of colonists. Kat had seen archive images
of humans on Earth, clustered around the edge of
an ocean, splashing and jumping in waves of salt
water. It was the sort of thing Uncle Prester's university friends analyzed and lectured on: the scope
of evolution—looking back to a time when
humans weren't grown in tubes or gifted with gills.

Kat had seen ancient film clips showing swimmers in skimpy shorts, wiggling and gasping for breath after lengths of high-speed racing. She'd also seen long-since-dust babies in paddling pools, gurgling but not going under. It was all a bit sad.

How could anyone be happy just flopping around on the surface, when there was so much pleasure from sculling under the water, especially in the smooth luxury of Meander spa? Q Essnid had generously sent the girls e-passes so they wouldn't get bored before the start of the deep winter school term.

Tanka had almost exploded with anticipation, zinging through the streets of Meander like a loony firework, and only stopping to check out the local talent.

"Ooh, cute boy dead ahead! No, don't look now, Kat! What d'you reckon—seven out of ten?"

"How should I know? You're the one with a male-flesh fixation."

"Huh, no chance of seeing any *flesh* in this

climate. That could be muscle or it could be many layers of clothing. Six and a half?"

"He's too old for you."

"Mature."

"*Old*."

The young man passed them on the boardwalk, and as he swung his arm they'd spotted the silver/blue sign of a Mazzini mark on his hand.

Tanka failed to hide her disgust. "Yuk! Three out of ten, tops."

Kat merely grinned. "Oh, I thought he was an eight easily."

They'd stopped to snack at a place near the ferry stop. Tanka swore this was a dodgy proposition, since the man wore mittens and there was no way of knowing if he was Mazzini or Atsumisi or, worse, Galrezi. The sign on the side of his cart simply read, *J Reak—Best Hot Snax in Meander*.

"So long as they taste good," was all Kat said, watching as the vendor shoveled nuts into a plastic bag and sprinkled them with low-salt.

J Reak said, "They're roasted fresh today, just for you! And since it's you . . . how about I add an extra helping of these juli-nuts—you ever try juli-nuts? No? You'll love 'em—take it from me. Here you go, juli-nuts for free!"

They weren't as good as cherries—nothing could be—but they were delicious just the same. Kat pulled off her gloves and started crunching.

"Enjoy your trip into town!" the roast-nut man called after them.

"We can but try," said Tanka doubtfully.


Kat quite liked the look of the place. Meander was nowhere near as grand as the big cities back home, but there was plenty of evidence that money wasn't tight. The wooden boardwalks were all scrubbed clean, the shop fronts were crammed with goods (not a discount sale in sight), and there were exquisite arcades of colored glass protecting shoppers from rain or snow. Clearly, someone had gone to a lot of trouble to make it an attractive, dynamic Frontier town.

That someone was Quinn Essnid. He'd dedicated most of his life to promoting peace, nothing but peace. Whatever the cost, he said repeatedly, nothing would deter him from turning wilderness into prosperity. Back on the sun-baked continent of the five cities, people had at first mocked any attempt to make a miniature paradise in the harsh climate of the distant Frontier. They were more interested in comfort than new colonies. Then Q Essnid's hard work and investment started to pay off. Money as well as blizzards began to snow down on the Frontier towns. Employment was high—even when boatloads of workers came over from the cities—crime was low, and everything was clean. Without Q Essnid there'd be no hospital, no university, no industry or factories. His dream had been to build the great dam at

Meander, and he'd done it. Now the town had unlimited clean power and it was slowly creeping toward city size. Somehow he'd united Frontier people in peace while civil war tore the five cities apart. During the drought that had triggered the war, the O-HA was created, sending life-saving shipments of pure water. United behind Q Essnid, the Frontier was proud to say they'd never succumbed to the racism of the cities. Unsurprisingly, Q Essnid was elected Frontier governor every year without fail. His face smiled out from posters along the length of the town hall, advertising the O-HA's upcoming rally.

As if Tanka cared about stuff like that. She'd pulled Kat right past the politics and into the crowds.

No motors were allowed on the streets, apart from hydraulic trolleys used for delivering goods, which were easily managed by one person. Everyone got around by walking or using one of the eco-powered bicycles called speedeez. A pretty canal ran down the middle of the main street, arched over with bridges, each one a different design. One bridge led right into the columned entrance of the spa.

It was a dream of a building, the elegance matched with the same mathematical harmony Kat had noticed at Cherry Heaven. Nothing fussy, nothing brash, just beautiful clean lines and a lovely luminosity in the stonework. It was not at all what they'd expected to find in a grizzly foreign backwater. Even Tanka had been moved enough to murmur, "Not bad."

The biggest pool room was large enough to hold three good-sized waterball pitches. It was glassed over by one spider-silk-fine cupola that broke up the weak winter sun and sent it sparkling on the water below. At one end of the pool, near where Kat sat waiting, there was a waterfall created out of smooth blocks of volcanic rock. Not only did the sheen of water look lovely, it kept the pool constantly aerated. It also gave Kat a geological thrill, because she knew that the rock had been carefully chosen, since it was finely porous and could clean out impurities in the water better than any chemical or technical filter.

And that was how people liked things. Clean and pure.

Kat braced her hands on the smooth marble and . . . slid.

Oh—Bliss!

There was nothing quite like it—not sunshine, not cherries, nothing.

When she'd breathed the last air from her lungs, her brain flipped over and euphoria seeped in through the delicate slits at her throat. Her gills almost quivered from the pleasure of it. She let herself fall right to the bottom of the pool and grazed there for . . . no knowing how long; eyes closed, eyes open, fingers splayed, feeling the currents . . . then . . .

. . . *WHAM!*

Instinct made her curl around and put her hands out for whatever was hurtling toward her. It was a good catch. When she'd blinked a few times and come back to proper consciousness, she realized it was the leaden oval of a yellow waterball.

She surfaced, coming face-to-face with a boy. The waterfall flowed lazily behind him and waterlight reflected in his eyes. He was about the same age as Kat. He was also ridiculously attractive.

"Sorry about that," he began. "Our game got a bit wild, but, hey . . . nice save! In fact, one in a million. You play, don't you?"

"Defense—left back."

"Bet you don't let many shots past. Sorry to barge in. You were looking pretty Blissed down there."

Kat rubbed hair out of her eyes. It was hard to think straight and float right with the Bliss still swirling through her blood. She knew she should say something, anything, to keep the boy with her for a few moments longer. She found herself babbling about the tiles she'd been gazing at on the pool floor. Most of them were white, but every once in a while there were patterns of papillons, their wings unfurled and dazzling with colors.

The boy grinned. "You like the pictures down there? Not many people notice them."

"I guess I notice things."

She did. She noticed the way the boy's brown hair gleamed as the water ran down. She noticed the flecks of light in his eyes and the way his mouth curved when he smiled. His teeth were bright white—like the hairline scar running from brow to cheekbone on the right side. She noticed the muscles on his shoulders and his long fingers sweeping gracefully through the water.

"Papillons are the trademark of the spa architect," the boy said. "That was her name: Celia Papillon. Can you see them on the glass roof too?" Kat looked up, then flinched as the boy suddenly said, "*Cherries!*"

"Sorry?"

"No it's me—I'm such a mush-head! You're one of the new girls from Cherry Heaven, right? Tanka and Kataka Jones? I'm Aran Essnid."

"You're . . ." Kat stopped, embarrassed. *You're the fit boy on the O-HA posters* wasn't a high-quality conversational effort. She settled for, "You're Quinn Essnid's—"

"Son. Yeah. So you've heard of him?"

"I didn't mean it like that. It's just that you—"

"Hear about him everywhere you go?"

"—look like him."

That made the boy blink. "You're joking, right? You really think I'm like my dad?" For some reason this bothered him a lot.

"I don't know if you're like him—there's just something similar in your face. I've only seen him in pictures. It's not like you look old or anything. I mean, you look . . ." She stopped again. *Gorgeous.*

Aran E rubbed a hand across his face, as if he

could somehow change it there and then. His scar gleamed white. "Like father, like son," he said, more to himself than to Kat.

*Minus fifty million out of ten for good first impressions.*

She took a deep breath. "Actually, your dad's been really nice to us, fixing up Cherry Heaven and everything. He sent us passes to come here today. And . . ." *for what it's worth* ". . . I'm Kataka J. Kat."

"Good to meet you, Kat."

It was strange but nice to shake hands through the water. Then Aran E's eyes widened as he caught sight of a diver standing on the edge of the pool behind Kat.

Tanka stretched up once and executed a beautiful slice into the water. She always played better to an audience.

Kat let out her breath and sank to the bottom of the pool again. She knew when she was out of her league.

# WATERFALL II

Swimming wasn't enough. Once Tanka had collected a whole pool of admirers and swapped a multitude of *e.f.* numbers, it was agreed that they should all go hang at the local basement bar, called Chompers. Here the cream of Meander Junior College laid claim to comfy sofas and cheap drinks. Just a quick look around told Kat that these teens weren't short of money, and they weren't as uptight as the uber-fash kids on the scene back home. Designer labels were sewn on the *inside* of clothing and everyone apart from Tanka seemed to be dressed for warmth rather than style rating. Even so, Kat was still amazed at the way her sister somehow managed to propel herself into what was obviously the best clique in town. Watching Tanka sashay through Chompers zinging with confidence,

Kat could hardly be surprised that people clustered around her. She looked like everything Kat wasn't, like a living tableau of *have* and *have not*.

Which was a stupid way to think. They weren't enemies; they were sisters and their motto had always been *sisters stick together*.

Down in the basement room the walls were painted dull orange and crusted with photos of the regulars, who posed for the camera with varying levels of grinning idiocy. Aran E was in most of the pictures, arms slung around his friends and eyes smiling. Kat also noticed a couple of him in a group of pictures showing the virgin forests of the Frontier heartland. In one he was standing by a waterfall, surrounded by other healthy, outdoorsy types. He photographed well. Kat already had the impression he did everything well, but he was so friendly and easygoing it was hard to hate him for it.

*Who could hate a guy like him? Does he realize he's*

*sitting next to me? Does he realize how close his leg is?*

Kat moved away, even though things were pretty cramped on the sofa she'd chosen. Aran E didn't seem to notice. He was too busy being teased about the fact that his face was on all the new posters advertising the upcoming O-HA rally.

"Hey—it's sponsored by Blue Mountain," said a mouthy girl called Ellan N. "How many free crates of water did they cough up to get an Essnid on the promo, Aran? Enough to give you a good chance of winning that hot date with Zee Homarlo? Bet you're checking every bottle top, huh?"

Aran E colored, but from the way his eyes flicked over to Tanka at the bar, Kat could tell where his interests lay. "Tease if you want," he said. "I'm not ashamed of being an O-HA youth leader—you know I really believe in the stuff we do, and I don't object to the freebies!"

Ellan N laughed—no hard feelings—and when a tray of Blue Mountain appeared on the table, everyone was unscrewing the bottle tops to see if they were a lucky winner.

"Want some?"

Ellan N thrust a silver pill wrapper in Kat's face.

"What . . . ? Oh. No thanks."

Ellan N shrugged and pressed a couple of peps out of the foil for herself. Kat just wished there was a pill that would make her invisible until it was time to go home . . . or at least until Tanka got back from the bar to deflect attention. Then, with a friendly smile, Aran E twisted around in his seat to talk to her. Which was almost worse than being ignored.

"So how are you finding things so far? Pretty primitive, I guess? I was over visiting the cities with my dad last year. We can't exactly compete out here on the edge of civilization."

"Actually, I like it here." *Wrong answer?*

"Really?"

"Really." *Stop chewing your hair, Kat! Spit it out!*

*Good girl.* "I mean, I've only just arrived on the continent—the data's incomplete and all that, but so far so good. Cherry Heaven's seriously luxurious, the town's nice, and everyone's been friendly."

"I guess it could be worse."

Kat couldn't answer for cringing at herself. *The data's incomplete?! What sort of shitzer-brain says that?!*

Aran E smiled. "Sorry. I don't really think Meander's a dump. Between you and me, I love it here. You should've seen it ten, fifteen years ago, before the O-HA got things going. It was a total non-place, a real backwater in every sense." He mentioned a few of the projects being developed in the Frontier and was pleased—as well as surprised—when Kat knew what he was on about. For a few dizzy minutes she forgot her shyness to talk to him about a range of research interests.

"You know your stuff," he said, just as she was about to leave him in a vapor-trail of obscure information.

"Sorry. I go on a bit. I'm just interested."

He gave her a friendly shove. "Don't say sorry! My dad'll be psyched to hear what you're into. You remind me of a friend—Harpo C." He stopped short, suddenly looking serious. Kat had no idea what made him say what he did next. "It's funny how you've moved to Cherry Heaven. No one's lived there for ages."

"You can tell. The orchard's a mess, and pretty creepy at night." Kat tried to be lighthearted, to make up for her earlier embarrassment at being brainbox of the millennium. "Me and Tank got in a state the first evening, thinking there was someone hiding out in the woods." She noticed a frown cross his face and thought she must be boring him. "Sorry. That's crazy, isn't it?"

*Stop apologizing, girl!*

"Someone in the orchard?" Aran E choked on the words, then quickly turned away for a second or two, his hand lightly grazing the scar on his face.

"Someone in the orchard?" Ellan N butted in. Her voice was distorted by a surge of pep. "Ooh, it's Oklear Foster, come to get you!"

"Oklear who?" asked Kat.

"Shut it, Ellan," said Aran E.

"He comes creepsie creepsie in the night and *bang*!"

Kat actually jumped. "Who's—?"

"Nobody," snapped Aran E.

"A bad man," Ellan N giggled. "The bogeyman."

*Okay*, thought Kat. *Some kind of joke at my expense. I'm used to that.*

"Pack it in, guys. Oklear Foster's in prison and they've thrown away the key. Hey, anyone thirsty?" Aran broke into a grin and shook a bottle of Blue so that the fizz exploded everywhere as he waved it around, dousing everyone. They all shrieked and laughed. It was only later that Kat heard him say, "Funny. I haven't been in the orchard for . . . years."

She murmured, "Everyone tells us the cherries are legendary."

"Yeah? I mean, yeah, they were. I don't like cherries." He saw her pull away a bit, hurt. "Hey, sorry. Heaven *is* a pretty place. I think it's great you like it, I really do. We can see it from our house on the other side of the lake. You'll have to come out on the water sometime. In summer we have boat parties and go diving down to old Cluff village. When the reservoir freezes you can just walk straight to our place, or skate over, and wait till it snows—we can all go boarding down the Blue Mountain foothills. Does your sister snowboard? I bet she does. She looks sporty."

"Can I just ask—about these Blue Mountains . . . ?"

There was no time to find out why the mountains weren't blue. Tanka burst on to the scene, with a tray of coffee and hot donuts.

Kat couldn't help noticing Aran E wiping his

hands with antibac gel before he ate.

"Sad, isn't it? My dad's a complete hygiene nut. Our house is immaculate—guess it's rubbed off a bit."

"Hey!" yelled Tanka, reaching out and touching Aran E's face. "What's with the scar—how'd that happen?"

Aran E laughed quickly and said, "I get asked about it all the time."

But that was all the answer he gave.


Tanka pounced on Kat the second they left the bar to go back to Cherry Heaven. "Kataka Jones, pinch me so I know I'm not dreaming. Ow! Not *that* hard! Do you realize who that was? I mean, *Essnid*—Aran *Essnid*! What a catch! And did you happen to notice how *gorgeous* that boy is? Better in the flesh than on those posters! That girl on the waterball team with him, Ellan N, she said he's *available*—just ripe for the picking."

"Like a cherry?"

"Like a boy who doesn't know what's going to hit him! When I saw him in the pool with you, Kat, I just didn't know how to score him."

"Er, ten out of ten?"

"Don't be so drab! He's *way* off the scale. I mean, his dad's about the most important person on this half of the planet, and Aran's something big in the O-HA, *and* captain of the waterball team, and did I mention how gorgeous he is?"

"A couple of hundred times. Didn't you notice he's true-blue Mazzini?

"Yeah? And?" Tanka's eyes went hard. "No one gives a stick of shitzer for all that racist crap over here. The war's over, remember?"

"Hey—it doesn't bother me. I just thought you didn't like—"

"Look, he's totally the most popular boy at the JC, so already it's a match made in heaven. I told him I was the world's ace-est waterball striker and he said I could come along to tryouts at the JC pool once term starts. Oh, he said you could go too if you like. They need a new defender. Apparently Ellan N's a bit lame."

"Won't she be mad if I just take her place?"

"So what if she is? I bet you're light years better than her and that's all that counts. You *deserve* to be on the team. Hey, let's go in here for a moment. There's some stuff I need."

Tanka pulled Kat over to the strangest store she had ever seen. A peeling sign in the window claimed that it was part of the well-known "Mom 'n' Pop" chain of retailers, but it looked nothing like the white-light-clean foodie halls back in the city. It was called Challis Store, and once inside it was pretty clear it sold everything you could ever not mean to buy.

There were plastic stakka boxes hiding one wall, full of cereals, nuts, dried fruit, and fusty-looking tea leaves. Another wall was entirely given over to Blue Mountain water in a rainbow of flavors; yet another had a range of barbaric-looking fishing tackle, as well as flour sacks, reconditioned heaters, and as-seen-on-TV cleaning products. In one dark corner a stand of glossy O-HA leaflets was gathering dust behind some hefty home-use oxygen tanks. Tall pillars crammed the middle of the store. They were hung with every conceivable kind of cooking tool, cheapo toy, and tabletop lamp. *This* was exactly what Kat had expected in a rough-and-ready Frontier shop.

She stopped to examine a basket of used wetware basics. When she next looked up Tanka was nowhere to be seen. Unflustered, Kat moseyed over to a rack of pet collars, half thinking she might buy one for the little white cat at Cherry Heaven. While she was at it, she got a bag of malloey tea for Aunt Millijue. There was an impressive range of flavors, including cherry-malloey.

She chose that. Cherries were Kat's new love.

"I always like cherry-malloey best," said the woman at the front till, with a badge that read *J Challis, Here to Help!* and the silver/blue gleam of a Mazzini ID on her hand. She ran the scanner over Kat's red ID to debit her account. "Anything else?"

"No thanks. Oh, a bottle of water, please. Cherry flavor."

"Coming up."

"Blue Mountain brand . . ."

"Is there any other kind?"

Kat looked up, wondering if she'd just imagined the slight critical tone. Maybe. Maybe not.

J Challis kept her face cheerful. "Blue Mountain's on offer, you'll be pleased to know. Go on, open it now: I'm dying to find out if someone's won that VIP visit with Zee Homarlo. My daughter Clariss is just crazy about the guy. . . ."

Kat forgot to listen. She was staring at a page slowly grinding out of a memo-machine behind the till. Next to the Linveki Hydro logo there was a grainy photograph, showing a gaunt girl in a white suit. Under the picture—there wasn't a name—the text read:

—UNSTABLE HYDRO WORKER—
HAVE YOU SEEN THIS CRIMINAL?

J Challis stopped in mid-gush and turned to see what had caught Kat's attention. It looked as if she was going to ignore the memo, but then something about it made her peer closer. "Clariss!" she called, not taking her eyes off the image. "Clariss C— come and take over the till!"

Behind Kat a man with a sharp nose started to huff with impatience. "Excuse me, I'd like to pay for my things!" He waved his red hand stamp importantly.

J Challis never even noticed, then, when an elderly lady coughed, she snapped back to alert. "Oh,

I'm sorry. Clariss! Honestly, that girl's brains just leak out of her ears. *Clariss!* Look, why not take your things to Clariss C at the back of the store if you're in a hurry."

She tore the paper from the memo-machine and quickly screwed it into a ball—though Kat noticed her putting it in a pocket, not the recycling bin.

The man wiped a wet drop off the end of his nose. "I saw one of those posters up at the gym. Some psycho girl on the run."

The elderly woman nodded her fur-hatted head. "I heard it's a Galrezi. Such a shame, giving the others a bad name."

"She looks dangerous. . . . We don't want any trouble."

"Oh we don't have trouble here . . . it's the new Frontier, not the five cities!"

J Challis glanced up at that. For a moment it seemed she would stay silent, then she said casually, "Well, there was the Oklear Foster trouble. . . ."

"Oklear Foster!" the man exclaimed. "A bad business—very bad business. Years ago, too. Nothing to worry about now."

"I remember it well," said the old woman stubbornly. "All those poor people. Seems just like yesterday."

"*Ten* years ago, in fact," said the man stubbornly. "Now can I pay for my purchases?"

J Challis gave a little smile. "This young lady's first, aren't you, love?"

Full of questions, Kat forgot she was supposed to be buying things. For a moment her heart had flipped, hearing the talk about trouble and remembering the shadow she'd not exactly seen on the edge of the orchard. Was Oklear Foster waiting to get them? Crazy idea! Aran E said Oklear Foster was brain-drained in prison. A horrible punishment, that, having your memory and personality sluiced out of you by drugs that dissolved particular parts of the brain. "It's the only way to be sure," Q Essnid had said when asked to comment on this form of justice. "We can't just have criminals like Foster wandering around enjoying life, can we?"

No, Oklear Foster, whoever he was, wouldn't be going anywhere faster than a dozy, shambling walk . . . with a warden close behind. He certainly couldn't be camping out under cover of a run-down cherry farm. All that trouble happened ten years before. Nothing to do with the here and now, when everything was supposed to be wonderful. . . .

While the Atsumisi man blustered, J Challis bagged Kat's things. "You sure I can't tempt you to one of these homemade ginger donuts, hot as anything and heaven to boot? My son Harpo says ginger is good brain food."

"Well, I . . ."

"Go on—let me slip you some in for free; then you haven't lost anything, have you? Are you at the Junior College? Maybe you know my son, Harpo C? *Harpo!* There's a friend here!"

"I'm sorry, I just came to Meander, I don't know—"

"Well now! You must be one of the Jones girls, moved into Cherry Heaven? I used to sell cherries from there; they were legendary. Harpo! Harpo C! You come down here and say hi to our new arrival! He's doing his homework, as usual. Always up to some brainbox project or other. . . ."

"I'm sorry, I have to . . ."

". . . Get going. Bye!" Tanka appeared, grabbed Kat's arm, and dragged her out of the queue to the front of the store. Kat had a quick glimpse of Harpo C poking his face around a door at the top of the stairs behind the shop counter. It was a white face with a shock of bright red hair and a classic frown of annoyance. He had a set of lab goggles pushed up on his forehead and a big streak of cobalt blue across his cheek. One eyebrow looked suspiciously singed. Kat tried to smile. Harpo C just blinked.

Tanka was too loud as usual. "What a geek!"

Kat hissed. "Don't be rude!"

"Who's rude? You said geekiness was good, and you should know, being an expert in it and all that."

"You can't just—"

Tanka yanked. "Bye again!"

Once outside, she passed Kat her bag and quickly emptied something from under her jacket. "Hold this a mo."

"What'd you get?"

"Ssh!"

"Did you pay for—?"

"Look, shut up and have a sherbert."

"I don't want—"

"Sure you do. Hang on." Tanka slung her bag over her shoulder and rustled in another pocket. "There's a whole damn pharmacy at the back of that store—one of the guys in Chompers told me about it—dead cheap, too, if you like paying for things, and only this dopey redhead girl called Clariss trying to keep an eye on things. I got a stack of peps. You want?"

"Are you crazy?"

"No, just hyper-glad we moved here." Tanka washed down a couple of pills with a swig from Kat's Blue Mountain. "Looks like the New Frontier could be the land of opportunities after all! Oh shitzer—no Zee Homarlo on the bottle top, *yet again. . . .*"

As twilight crept in, lights began to go on all over the town. They were nothing like the big neon monsters that glared out over the city streets back home. These were delicate rainbow colors strung under the arcades in great bunches and hanging on low loops across the canal bridges. When the pep pills hit Tanka's system, her eyes looked just as bright and amazing.

## Flow

it's dark down here, dark and amazing. no clock
to keep me ticking to Factory time. maybe minutes pass, maybe days. i'm just sculling, lulling,
lazy in the water—first time in a long time. fat
chance of being lazy in Factory, where there's
only eat, sleep, and work! lying on your bunk at
the end of a shift doesn't count. it's just being
too tired to move.

i like lazy. what i don't like is the cold, the
mud, the weeds, and waiting for Director to find
me and fish me out. not that he'd jump in to
catch me *himself*—our dandy Director won't
want to chip his nails or stain his shirt. he'd be,
*hey you, someone else, dive in and drag the girl
out—now!*

Bossman's the same, no, worse. there's no
dirt on *his* hands. *immaculate*, that's what
Director calls him. i think immaculate means

you're so clean dirt never sticks, no matter how bad you've been. i'd like to get handfuls of mud and fling them flat in Bossman's *immaculate* face. maybe i will, one day, someday, soon . . . when i'm ready to breathe air again.

right now i like the darkness of the river-deep. yeah, i reckon they call this Taking It Easy.

when new girls come to Factory they say, *look at those old lags, going at it top speed, like sealing bottle caps or gluing labels is the most important job in the world.* new girls come to Factory and laugh. *relax a bit,* they say. *chill, Take It Easy.*

chill?

the only chill is the bite in the air.

relax?

when you're dead!

take it easy?

don't take *anything* in Factory. they'll find out. they'll get you. unless you're me. they haven't got *me* yet!

bet i've got Bossman shaking in his black boots, wondering where i'll go, what i'll say.

he'll ask, all nice, why Director didn't stop me escaping, then Director'll rub his hands on his gel-slimy hair and quickly blame someone else. yuk. even underwater i see Director, making my skin sting with his stabby eyes, licking the air with his sneer—hey cutie.

hey, *drop dead*. easy to answer back now, when my mouth's full of water and the current pulls the words away.

then, just when i'm loving being lazy, the river bugs, tugs, drags. i wrap myself in weeds at the bottom so i can hold on to this feeling of being a lazy, crazy, Blissed-out waterbaby. no good. ghost faces come here and gone so quickly i splay my hands in the water trying to touch them. Aran E and Harpo C grin and wave—can i come out to play in the valley? then Hikori and Mai, wisps just out of reach. then Mama, my mama, the faintest face of all . . .

i've been here too long. when i rub my eyes i see fireworks glow, then little patterns of mud-colored papillons. is it me getting weaker or is the current getting stronger? this is not good.

this is bad. what if the river goes all the way back to Factory to turn the turbines there? ugh. just thinking the word—the F-word—makes me sick despite the Bliss. in the dark i stretch, retch, reach for something to hold on to. *stop dragging me downstream! i won't go—won't flow.*

*got to flow*, the river says, pouring through my gills, through my mind, pouring past the mud all the way to where Factory waits. *all things flow and you've got to go with them. back there, where you belong, where it's safe and steady and the same.*

*shut up!*

*can't shut me up, can't shut me out.*

*i can do what i like!*

*yeah right. dream on. don't you know that nothing changes? Director still shouts, Bossman still bosses. that's just the way things are.*

*were*, i say. *the way things were.*

*it's where you should be.*

*don't have to be. nasty there.*

*what makes you think it's so nice anywhere else?*

the voice is right. Factory's nasty and outside's not so nice either. kids with stones. a man with a gun. gunshots—one, two, three . . . then four—then silence and cherries fall in the snow . . . *no! stop thinking that!* sprinkles of blood drops on the snow. *don't look!* Hikori and Mai stretched still on the ground. dead. not even knowing how cold they are.

shall i try it? stay down here and see what dead's like? the Bliss would blank me out, my brain would stop breathing, and i'd doze first, then dream, then die, dragged along by the river wherever it wants me to go.

if i was dead people wouldn't throw stones at me. if i was dead Director couldn't sneer at me, saying *work, damn you, you soulless little shitzer—coffee! get me coffee!* if i was dead Bossman couldn't make me slather myself in Stingo so his Factory was a Hygie-heaven. if i was dead maybe i'd see Hikori and Mai again. i stop swimming. brain droops.

blood sags. life trickles away, easy, lazy, soft. . . .

STOP!

up through the water, snap the surface, drag cold air into my lungs. making yourself dead's *stupid*. when you're dead you don't eat cherries, you can't smile, you're nothing and nobody. you're *dead*, no stars. yes, stupid dying-trying girl, stars! look at them all, prickling the newly night sky.

i shake the water away, feeling better already because it was Gim Damson who first showed me the stars. i met Gim Damson in a place before Factory, called Quarry. he was a boy from a big city over the ocean, older than me, very tall. they said he was a *shitzer-no-brain-waste-of-space-Galrezi-scum* but he never believed that. one time in Quarry, when we had sky all around us, he pointed up and said, *head high.*

*why?*

*cos then you can see the stars. they're always beautiful, whatever happens to us down here.*

i said, *they're bigger than me and they're
laughing.*

*bigger and laughing? is that what you think?
watch.* right away he did this amazing thing. he
put one grimy hand in the air, saying, *i used to
play this with my little sister. she was younger
than you and not so clever, i reckon. see what
happens if you get one finger, just one small finger? look—you can put out a star.*

he was right. you can!

i haul myself onto the riverbank and hold up
one finger. splat! a star disappears. just cos
the stars look huge, they don't have to be bigger and better. Gim D called it *Perspective.*
*Perspective* makes things appear different,
depending where you're looking from, so when
you're in *Factory, Director* looks as big as the
whole universe and when you're *Free, Director*
looks smaller than a dot on a spot of spit.
*Perspective* still works even when you're freezing
cold on a riverbank. after i've put one star out i
let it shine again.

*think about it,* Gim Damson said that time.

*the sky goes all the way around the world, so if you miss someone miles away you still know the stars'll be shining on them, too.*

*he missed someone—lots of someones. he missed his sisters, Carla D and Pelly D, and his mum and his dad and his friends in the city far away. he was worried about them, i could tell.*

*what are your sisters like? i asked, trying not to think about mine.*

*he said, oh, Carla D's really young, not much more than a baby. she's got this toy iguana she totally loves, way more than me. and Pelly, oh Pelly's a pain in the ass! everyone loves her, she's so sassy and fun and gorgeous, you know, the works. all my mates are totally mad about her—what a boy magnet. yeah, Pelly's a star and Carla's a cutie.*

*are they going to be all right? i asked him.*

*i hope so, he said. and you've always got to hope, Luka Papillon. whatever happens, the stars will shine on them.*

*whatever happens?*

*yep.*

*what if the people you miss are dead? will the stars still shine on them?*

he never answered that. he knew as well as i did that you can put people out like you put stars out, only you can't always get the people back again.

# ROCKFALL I

It started with a trickle, just a few pebbles sliding, but once she'd lost her balance Kat couldn't get it back again.

She was high on the side of Cluff Wood quarry, climbing higher to get a better view of the dam, which was startlingly close by. Although the dam was a state-of-the-art tuffcrete structure, it had been clad in stone hewn from the foothills to add an old-world feel to the architecture. The phenomenal curve dwarfed the landscape all around and apparently, when the hills were winter bare, it was hard to tell where the hills left off and the dam began. Shining out from each of the three towers was the red Linveki Hydro Co. logo, linked with the silver O-HA sign.

Kat was glad she couldn't see the reservoir

stretching out beyond the dam turrets. As far as she was concerned, it ruined the strange beauty of Cherry Heaven, no matter how much she told herself it was only the old river Cluff and the big spring snow melts, backed up behind the dam. Logically there was no reason to resent the still, dark water. It was now being used to power unseen machines at the base of the dam, creating enough eco-energy for the whole of the New Frontier—and then some.

She paused to steady herself on the uneven ground and took a deep breath of cold air before setting off again. It was exhilarating to be able to see for miles. There was the river Annaflo, heading northwest to the sea at Santanna port. Southwest were the virgin territories of the heartland, which were rich with possibilities for anyone interested in planet studies. The heartland was home to cutting-edge research facilities and it was also where the prison was—

the place where bad people had their brains drained to make them fit to live again. Beyond the top edge of the quarry the Blue Mountains were out of sight. They still weren't blue.

The New Frontier was now home and the Jones family were feeling settled, even after such a short time. As often as not they all walked through the orchard together to catch the same ferry into Meander. Once in town, Prester and Millijue went off to work while the girls hooked up with other school students. Early morning was a good time to marvel at the patterns of frost and brown winter leaves on the ground, to talk over the oddities of New Frontier people, and to plan new ways of enjoying the cherries from the cryo-freeze. Uncle Prester was loving his teaching and talked of directing a prestigious history project funded by the O-HA. Aunt Millijue was well on her way to revolutionizing data storage at the O-HA headquarters. She'd even managed to be sociable once or twice and was due to go and see the new Zee Homarlo movie with a few of her colleagues from work.

"Great progress!" said Tanka approvingly. She'd already dragged Kat to see the film twice, as well as going once again with the JC waterball squad. "Now if I could just win that hot date with Homarlo I'd die happy."

"Less talk about dying," Kat had grouched.

Occasionally there were arguments. That was just part of being a family. Tanka was absolutely one hundred percent dead certain she always remembered to lock the front door when she was last out; Uncle Prester sorrowfully insisted he'd come home from work to find it open—twice. When Aunt Millijue wanted to know who'd been snaffling the cimarron waffles and running off with packets of food, everyone protested their innocence. Tanka accused Kat of rootling through her stuff, while Kat swore she'd done no such thing.

There was also a friendly competition as to who

would be the first person to coax the little white cat into the house, even though it had never come closer than the front doorstep.

Both sisters had to admit that Meander Junior College was fun. Tanka loved being a minor celebrity, surrounded by a crowd of people who wanted to know about life in the big cities overseas. They never seemed to tire of boasts about the sunshine, the heat, and the fabulous luxury of the Waterworld resort. As for Kat, she had to admit that training for the new waterball team was fantastic, the JC teaching was excellent, and the other pupils were surprisingly nice. No one seemed to take any notice of the fact that she was officially the dull, geeky sister. People stopped to say hi in the corridors, and she'd even been told off for chatting in class—something Tanka had rushed over to congratulate her on after the lesson.

And then there was Aran E.

Kat halted in her climb. She could no longer

hear Tanka's voice rippling up from below, or see Aran E planting kisses in her sister's hair. Good. They were supposed to be on a Geology Club field trip, not a hickey-rich flirt fest. It was fine, absolutely fine, that Tanka and Aran were dating, but did they have to be so noisily *obvious* about it? All the way from the JC they'd been wrapped around each other, swapping kisses and laughs.

Kat was already out of favor with her sister for daring to suggest that she should stop telling silly Galrezi jokes. That argument had started as a little trickle, just like loose stones underfoot.

"It's only a bit of fun!" Tanka had wailed. "Lighten up—everyone did it back home."

"I didn't, and I'm embarrassed having to listen to you."

"So don't listen."

"You yell so loud they can probably hear you up at Santanna. And I wish you wouldn't keep banging on about the war."

"Oh, what's this—censorship from my own sister? Who do you think you are—General fricking Insidian? For your information, people want to know what it was like."

"They're just getting a cheap thrill hearing about gory things, and you're just milking sympathy with the whole war-orphan sob story."

"At least it stops people saying how mean the Atsumisi were during the war."

"But they were!"

Tanka changed tactics, hating the fact that Kat was probably right. Again. "Why don't you stop spying on me and do something useful, like fix my *e.f.*? You're supposed to be good at messing about with knackered crap, aren't you?" She'd tossed the *e.f.* over as they'd edged around a pool of murky water at the bottom of the quarry. Kat had made a brilliant catch, stopping it from disappearing into the gunk.

"It's not broken," she'd muttered, just as Aran E swung by for more smooching. Tanka was supremely arch once she had Meander's coolest boy draped over her arm.

"It's okay if you can't mend it, Kat. They're very complicated."

"I know that!"

"It doesn't mean you're stupid or anything."

At this point, Aran E had unwisely tried to make the peace. "You're right, though, Kat. It's probably not broken—we often get interference from a local ore called mont-halo. It's why things are generally so low-tech on the Frontier."

"Fine, take her side!" Tanka had hissed, whipping her arm away.

Aran E had his work cut out for him, smoothing her ruffled vanity. He managed it, though. The last Kat saw of them they were snug together, sharing secrets.

"Stuff you don't need to know about," Tanka had said airily.

Which was fine.

Kat was much happier exploring the quarry on her own anyway. She liked rocks. You knew where you were with a chunk of granite. Rocks didn't stare at you, expect you to talk, or flirt noisily with your sister. Better still, the geology professor, Kristie Rahbin, had a real passion for her subject and was fast becoming Kat's latest inspiration. K Rahbin was somewhere on the quarry floor, angrily explaining that the 3-D computer imager *wasn't* to be used to map out Tanka J's vital statistics, attractive though these might be to certain young men.

K Rahbin's Mazzini tattoo was drab compared to the shocking blue of her eyes. She wore her black hair smoothed back in a knot, and she had a magic touch with cosmetics that kept even Tanka on the right side of respectful . . . that, and the rumors that in her private moments she drank beer like gills drink water. It was K Rahbin's charisma that had herded fifteen students up the path from Meander JC to study rock formations in the disused quarry at Cluff Wood, on the dam's west side. Having a self-professed soft spot for the place, she'd arranged a visit there for the first Geology Club outing of the term. Kat was a genuine club member, as was Aran E. Tanka had joined as an excuse to bunk off double maths. Like most of the students she saw it as an excellent opportunity to carry on with the important business of teasing, gossiping, and making out. Kat simply planned on getting up close and personal with hard, cold stuff instead.

She hadn't meant to climb so far so quickly. Ordinarily, common sense would have told her it wasn't safe, but that afternoon she was too busy being indignant and frustrated, not really noticing she was in trouble until the trickle of stones underfoot slid farther and faster down the quarry wall. She quickly splayed her hands out, getting cut straightaway, but there was no way she could stop skidding over. It was a horrible sensation, losing balance—worse, losing control. While her body fell, her mind was clear, racing through possible options for emergency tactics.

*This is an avalanche. What are you supposed to do in an avalanche?*

There was no way she could stay upright. The second she went down, a river of small rocks cracked her skull and collided with every part of her body. Soon there was nothing solid to seize hold of. For one awful moment she thought she'd be rushed right to the bottom of the quarry and crushed under the debris. Then the noise stilled, the rocks settled, and dust fell softly on her face.

She was trapped.

Gradually she eased her upper body loose and freed her arms. She tried to prompt Tanka's *e.f.*, which she still had clenched in one fist. Nothing. *Of course.*

Her neck was jammed against a jag of rock, giving her a clear view of the cold blue sky. Silence settled on the scree and a flock of blacklings flew westward. No one had seen her accident, which was good . . . in a way. How undignified, to climb a quarry in search of geological enlightenment, then to end up flat on your ass in a rockfall!

She experimented moving her legs. One was fine. She could just about bend forward to clear it from the stones. Her right leg was definitely stuck, though. She gave it a wiggle. A couple of pebbles shifted, nothing more.

She swore. A lot.

Which was a shame, because just at that moment help arrived.

## Flesh

i was trapped, waiting for help that never came.

the memory whacks me in the gut. the high electric fence in front of me spikes the ground in a big jagged circle. coming back here wasn't part of my plan. i know this place. Quarry. Quarry One of four. no cherries or birthdays here, just hard ground, dead stone, and silence, guarded by a sign.

—CLUFF WOOD QUARRY—
NO ENTRY WITHOUT PERMISSION

that's almost funny, cos time was, it was no EXIT without permission. time was, if you went anywhere near the e-fence you'd be t-zzzzzz frizzled to your hair tips—fried like eggs in a pan. makes my skin prickle just thinking about it. i only saw it happen once, mind. after that one time, none of the Quarry workers tried to escape that way again. closing my eyes i see it all again . . . the great flat-bottomed barges on the river, taking stones to the cofferdam—the baby dam that held the water away while the big dam was built. workers on the shore tugging at cranes and lugging stones over rollers. ferries going past with the window shutters closed so the passengers couldn't peep out, even if they wanted to.

over there, the blast site. away there, on that flat stretch, the workers' miserable huts. near that sludgy pool, offices for the Capos and Supers. Capos were Captains, with silver badges on their coats and a bite worse than their bark. Supers supervised, telling everyone what Bossman wanted them to do. right from the first day in Quarry the Capos screamed and shouted at us—i'd never heard a noise like it!

ten years. ten cold years since i first came to this spot. it's bad beyond bad to see it again. they shoved me in a line—never even asked my name, just checked the green stamp on my hand. i wasn't made of tuff-stuff like i am now. i was made of snowmelt, ready to dribble into the ground like the other Weeds, Weaklings, Wimps, Worse-than-useless Workers. the Capo shouting was like sun on icicles: it made people grow small until they dripped away to nothing, then these nothing-people were taken someplace else.

   *what use are you for building the dam?!* the Capos screamed at them.

   all i kept thinking was, *why do we need such a big dam anyway? didn't we have enough water already?* we always played in pools and puddles and snowdrifts—never knew you could make money out of them. Gim did his best to explain about the O-HA—the people with big shiny meetings and little shiny badges. he said there was a war in the faraway cities, because Atsumisi bully-boys wanted all the water that other people had, so the O-HA said they'd send as much water as anyone wanted as long as there was no more fighting. Gim thought that was a great plan. he came all the way across the sea from his city to join the O-HA, thinking they were the good guys, out to stop the bad guys. when he got off the ship at Santanna the good guys said, hey, Galrezi boy, you can help us by building a dam. they said they'd play fair, be nice. all their words were like silver bark peeling off a rotten tree trunk. all their talk added up to work! you shitzer-no-brain-waste-of-space-Galrezi-scum!

F for Figure-it-out-if-you-can. i never could, not now, not then, not on my birthday when the good life ended and the bad one began with gun-shots, snow, then silence.

but Gim Damson was good, even in the bad. look long, look hard, and you're bound to find something beautiful. when i looked i saw Gim, beautiful on the inside but bruised everywhere else. he was older than me, way older. i was on the edge of seven, he was past seventeen. that first day, he was caught trying to escape (again) and they beat him so hard his legs didn't work right and his voice was hoarse. when he saw me shivering like a scaredy-cat kitten he could barely manage a growly whisper. i still heard him, even through the swearing and shouting.

*hey, puss! c'mon over here! you want a saucer of milk, little kitty?* as if he really had a saucer of milk! people were eating snow to stop the thirst. he just said that to play. *maybe you want a little mousling, hey?* he didn't have a mousling—he couldn't have! any critter with half a brain would already be miles away from Quarry . . . but you know what? i dared to creep closer to him, ready to bolt, wondering if he really could make a mousling appear. and he did! he took a corner of his gray shirt and with a bit of magic and a bit of tweaking from sore fingers, he really did make a cotton mousling that danced on his knee. after a while i forgot to be scared and went close enough for him to use that mousling to wipe cold blood off my face.

when he smiled i saw two broken teeth. *i'm Gim Damson, who are you?*

i got pulled away before there was time to answer. Blue Capo had found me. i called her Blue Capo because of her stabby blue eyes that were sharper than razor-cold ice. she bent over me like a cat crouching to kill.

*too tired to stand up straight? let me help—WHACK! aw, is poor little baby crying for her mammy? go on, cry for her, sweetheart, cry. Mama's not going to come and get you—Mama knows you're here and Mama doesn't care!*

she was lying! if my mama knew i was in Quarry she'd come running to rescue me. wouldn't she? where was she? where is she? somewhere i can't remember yet, that's where.

Blue Capo's lies went on and on.

*you're nobody now. nobody cares!*

how could she say that when i was Luka, the birthday girl?

besides, someone did care.

somebody with a gray mousling shirt who'd called me kitty cat and shared a secret smile. all the lies slid off my skin and soaked into the ground. i got to thinking that the soggy soil in the middle of Quarry was made from all the sludged-up shitzer Blue Capo tried to make me believe, going stinky-rotten in a pool.

it didn't me long to figure out the Supers and Capos couldn't build their fancy dam without us *shitzer-no-brain-Galrezi-scum*, that's why i learned to be useful. so what if i wasn't grown-up? so what if i couldn't cut or lug rocks? i could zip through the puddles of snow melt faster than you could say, *deliver this*. i was the best runner in Quarry. took Red Neck Capo his e-pads, told Head Capo the rock ton tally, even fetched Big Stick Capo when he was needed to stop slackers. what, you reckon i was helping them? no. it's called staying alive. in Quarry places, if you're not useful you're *nothing*. a pool of snow melt on the floor.

here's my advice when you're in a bad place: look out for trouble and stay away from it. watch to see which Capo's coming close, which one's just going past. learn to tell who's going to leave you alone, and who's got a dangerous swagger-stagger after boozing. they throw the empty beer bottles around a lot. if you're lucky, you've already scarpered and don't get one in your face. that hurts, though not as much as

getting blown to pieces. i know this because
there was one day in Quarry when they were
blasting sector 7—a special job some of us
were waiting to see because of secret reasons
of our own—only the two men setting the explo-
sives got blasted by mistake and the blobs of
meat landed all around, rolling still and shiny in
the grit. no amount of Stingo was going to
make those men all right again. Bossman probably didn't mind: they were only *shitzer-no-
brain-waste-of-space-Galrezi-scum* after all.
(ohmygod, if i could blow up Factory like they
used to blow up the woods to make Quarry, i'd
do it! a thousand *K-BANGS* as Factory flies in
the air! bits of ceiling and pipes and bunks and
vats of Stingo fall all around, and bits of
Director, too!) when the men in sector 7 got
killed, Capos shouted for people to come and
pick the bits up before someone skidded on
them and there was an accident. NO WAY was i
getting that job. i ran to hide under a hut and
that's when Blue Capo found me. she reached
and grabbed me, pulling on my leg like it was a

log of wood, when clearly it was flesh—white
flesh, with purple-flower-finger-bruises left over
from the last time we met.

she yelled, *come on out, you bitch-little-
shitzer, you can't hide!*

there i was, trapped and waiting for a rescue
mission that never came.

but i knew something she didn't. . . .

# ROCKFALL II

Harpo C didn't know he was a one-man rescue mission. He was happily clambering around a sturdy ledge on the quarry wall in search of something chunky to chip with his rock hammer. Unlike Kat, he'd kept well clear of unstable areas and was safely rapt in a private appreciation of stratification. Some pretty savage language coming up from the ground broke his reverie. He jumped. There was a girl, half buried and wholly irritated. "Er, hello?"

Kat twisted her neck to see who'd come to glory in her downfall. *Great. The ginger boy.* The clever geek who'd already beaten her to top of the environment science class and who'd claimed joint first in a prelim statistics exam. Kat had tried being friendly to him one time, when they met at the JC pool after her waterball training. Harpo Challis hadn't made the slightest effort to be friendly back again. He'd hardly been able to drag his eyes away from the silver/red Atsumisi stamp on her hand. It was a strange kind of snobbery, looking down on something that most other people respected. Knowing how smart Harpo C was, Kat couldn't understand what made him so anti-Atsumisi. It wasn't as if there'd ever been any trouble between gene clans in the New Frontier . . . had there?

"You're stuck," he said, approaching slowly so he didn't set the rocks falling again.

"Well spotted."

"The quarry walls can be pretty unstable."

"Really?" *I will not cry! I will not let one single tear squeeze out!*

"Are you okay? Your eyes are red."

"It's the dust. Look, could you just . . ."

Forgetting her usual shyness, Kat was about to

let rip about the idiocy of sitting watching someone be trapped, when she realized that Harpo had
actually been assessing the situation. When he did
move, it was carefully and with purpose.

"If I clear your leg, will you be able to ease it
free? Can you still feel it?"

"Ow! I mean, yes, I don't think anything's broken. I just sort of slid."

"Easily done if you don't stick to the safe bits.
People shouldn't really be in the quarry, I suppose.
That's why it's fenced off."

"Well, I promise I won't sue Q Essnid for letting
us in here to do school projects."

Harpo moved the stones away one by one, occasionally glancing over his shoulder to see if K
Rahbin had noticed the accident. No hope. As far
as he could tell, she was busy trying to stop Aran E
skimming stones into the scummy pool at the
quarry bottom. Harpo thought about shouting for
help, but hollering wasn't really in his repertoire.

Stilted conversation was about as noisy as Harpo usually got in public.

Kat was relieved. The last thing she wanted was people seeing her so helpless. Not that "people" would care. Tanka would sneer at her again, with that *so much for clever sisters* look, and Aran E would think she was pretty pathetic too. At least Harpo C hadn't made fun of her, and it was nice to have someone else take charge while she concentrated on not feeling hurt.

"I'm just going to check if you've got any fractures," he said. "Can you wiggle your toes?"

"Jeez, your hands are freezing!"

"Are they?" He looked down and realized he wasn't wearing gloves. He'd forgotten to put a scarf on, too, which explained why he'd been cold all afternoon—too preoccupied with more important things to notice. He rubbed his palms together and blew on them.

Kat was instantly ashamed of being so fussy.

"Hey, I'm kidding. They're fine."

Harpo C had a surprisingly gentle touch as he felt along her leg. "Do you mind if I just . . . ?" Kat nodded, knowing he'd have to cut her trousers to feel more clearly. She approved of the fact that Harpo C carried a decent penknife. "Seems okay to me, unless this swelling's from a simple sprain. We won't know till you're putting weight on it. Look—the bruises are coming up already!"

Harpo C suddenly realized he was holding a girl's bare brown leg. A blush started at the base of his neck until it covered his face, right to his earlobes, making his skin flame almost as red as his hair.

Kat winced. "Give me a hand up, will you?"

Harpo C blinked, reluctant to have any more contact. It had been impossible to ignore the arrival of the new city girls, particularly since every day his mum was asking if he'd met them and did he like them and how were they getting on at

Cherry Heaven? Tanka Jones was hard to miss, for obvious reasons, and harder still to block from hearing when she was off on one of her interminable, self-inspired monologues. He'd heard her boasting about *Atsumisi this* and *Atsumisi that* and privately he was disgusted. The cities must be lousy places if they could breed such obnoxious, narrow-minded opinions. When everyone raved about how gorgeous Tanka J was, Harpo just couldn't see what they meant.

As for Kataka Jones, he definitely related to the fact that she watched more than she spoke, and she was smart, too—really clever. She didn't bleat on about the war like her sister, though Harpo did wonder how long it would be before she was chanting *ra-ra-ra for the O-HA*, now that she was thick with Aran E and the waterball team. Harpo had nothing against Aran—or waterball, for that matter, since he was actually a pretty good player himself. His problem was with the hero worship most people in Meander had for the O-HA. Harpo was wary of swallowing the happy pap about everyone being equal, everyone being valued. If the whole gene-tagging thing was mush, then why were people still being tested and having their hands stamped? Aran Essnid always followed his father's philosophy, which was that people should be proud of what they achieved, regardless of the color of their hand stamp; Harpo preferred to argue that people shouldn't be labeled in the first place.

Not that Harpo and Aran ever argued. They were polite when they met, sometimes swimming a few laps together, sometimes catching each other's eye at a joke they'd once have shared . . . then looking away. All very different from the easy, everyday friendship they'd had years before, when Aran E would race Luka P to see who'd be the first to reach the red front door of Harpo's house in Cluff village. Aran lived on the valley east side in a shiny new villa; Luka lived to the west. The three of them played together all the time, when school didn't get in the way. Then, on one snowy day, all that was exploded forever.

Harpo had tried to fix things between him and Aran. "It wasn't our fault," he started once, when they were alone in the locker room after a match. "It was Oklear Foster."

"I don't want to talk about it," was Aran's reply.

Everything bad could be blamed on O Foster. Ten years before, the gene-clan trouble began. After more than a century of peace in the colonies, compulsory gene testing was introduced in the cities, and a subtle pattern of discrimination emerged, with no actual logic or common sense behind it. As soon as there were colors, there were labels. With the labels came prejudice. Nothing too noticeable at first, just the Atsumisi holding their heads a little higher, the Mazzini scurrying around the edge of the Atsumisi gangs, and the

Galrezi slowly being ground down into undesir-
ables. Prejudice swelled into race riots . . . and
worse.

No matter how hard the New Frontier struggled
to keep free of the trouble, the roots of hatred ran
deep. Propaganda crept into the most unlikely
places. Frontier people began to talk of war, whatever the cost to their community and economy.
Peace might have been trampled in the rush for
righteous excitement if it hadn't been for one man
who set himself the mission of massacring as many
Galrezi as he could get in his gun sights. The sniper
terrorized Frontier life for two long months. There
were deaths in Santanna, Anabarra, Meander . . .
all along outposts on the Annaflo river. When
Foster was eventually captured near Cluff—thanks
to an anonymous tip-off—fifteen people were
dead. They were all Galrezi. Since Foster was
Atsumisi it was touch and go whether the murders
would spark off violent gene-clan clashes like those

in the far-off five cities. Maybe even war.

"And he'd seemed like such a nice guy!" everyone said.

Then the miracle happened. Disaster was averted. Q Essnid smoothly slipped into the role of savior, begging the Frontier people to unite against violence, to use their hatred of O Foster's crimes as a foundation for a stronger *peaceful* society, where weapons were only used as a means to an end. "We'll show the cities how to stop the madness," he promised them. "Together, with my leadership, we'll build a humanitarian army that will defeat the waste of war and build a peace that no one can break."

And they did. The O-HA became the most successful organization in the Frontier. It looked like good had grown from the bad.

Unfortunately, Oklear Foster murdered more than Galrezi. He killed the old valley friendships, too. The dam was built, the village flooded, and

Harpo's family was forced to move to Meander. His mother, Jo Challis, opened a shop. His sister, Clariss, quit school early to help out. As for Federic Challis, their dad, he'd left for a secretive Security job in Santanna. That was fine. Harpo resorted to looking at the world through a digital microscope. He downloaded *New Colonist*—the planet's best and most technical e-mag about all things brainy. Every year his school projects got more sophisticated, until this year he was hard at work learning about a fabulous new 3-D audiovisual system called INTENS, due to be unveiled at the upcoming O-HA rally. If all went well he could even submit something for the Young Engineer of the Year award, pioneered by the senior award judge—the great Q Essnid himself.

Kat quite fancied a stab at Young Engineer, and she knew Harpo C would be her strongest rival, even though he hardly looked like tough competition. In fact, he looked entirely awkward and odd.

He'd grown tall too quickly and was too thin for his bones, with skin so white it dazzled and hair so red it could almost glow in the dark. She noticed that he'd bitten down his little fingernails, but kept the others neat. His right eye twitched when he was het up about anything and his voice had gone deeper than someone with such a slight build had any right to expect.

His right eye did indeed twitch the minute she said thanks for helping her.

"Um. Never mind. I mean, I'm glad I haven't made it worse. I picked up some medical stuff from my dad—he's in Security at Santanna."

Was Kat imagining things, or did Harpo's pale eyes darken when he said this?

"He taught me first-aid basics—what to do if you accidentally swallow poison or apocalypse happens or something. Fortunately, I reckon we can rule out on-the-spot amputation. You don't seem to be injured much, apart from a few nasty scratches, though maybe you ought to bind that ankle up and get some ice on it—just in case."

"It's fine," Kat lied.

"Instead of bandages, could you wrap these around as a bit of a buffer? You can strap them in place with my scarf, except . . . I forgot to wear my scarf. Maybe use some of your trouser fabric instead . . . ?"

Awkwardly Harpo tore a wad of papers from his clipboard, bulked them up, and passed them over. He immediately tried to grab them back when Kat unfolded the sheets to take a look.

"Hey—these drawings are really good, Harpo."

"You're not meant to . . . Jeez. It's a facsimile of the rock layers, to scale. I, er, find drawing is better than photography or e-pads for stratification analysis. You kind of . . ."

"Get a feel for the lie of the land?"

"Something like that."

Kat forgot she didn't want to be near anyone

and cautiously sat upright. Harpo C forgot he didn't want to bore anyone and stayed crouching down beside her, so close they almost touched.

"See this, this layer here?" He traced a finger along a line on the picture, showing light-colored clay about the width of his pocketknife. "I analyzed a section of it once. It's clay mixed with spherical particles of carbon, clustered like grapes. Interesting, huh?"

Just as oblivious to her potential injuries as Harpo now was, Kat studied the drawing. Meanwhile, Harpo C watched Kat's face.

*Maybe she's not like the others*, came a thought from a corner of his unusually tidy brain. *Maybe it doesn't matter that she's from the cities and she's got that silver/red square on her hand*. He'd been watching her in classes, hoping she wasn't the sort of girl who lived for playing in the pool or who worked to pay for the next batch of pep pills. She didn't have to guess the significance of the clay layer straightaway—if ever—she didn't have to know everything, she just had to be . . . on his wavelength, that was all.

Kat stared at the drawing, somehow sensing that she was being tested. She was cross with him.

*It's not fair of him to expect a decent analysis from a 2-D image. I don't have a decent sample . . . my microscope . . . I can't do any proper chemical tests. And I've got cramp in my calves, an ache in my ankle, and that dratted cut on my hand is prickling again. Look how the skin tightens and another scab tries to form. Amazing how the body heals itself, after big hurts and little.*

Aloud she said, "This layer, does it run right across the north face of the quarry?"

Harpo C allowed himself a bit more hope. He simultaneously noticed that Kat J had streaks of caramel running through her chocolate brown hair. All he actually said was, "Yep."

"At a consistent level?"

"Give or take a few major jolts where mining machinery has compromised the line, yeah. It's unbelievable how much damage blasting did, when they were building the dam. . . ."

"Any similar levels found at other sites?"

Oh, Harpo C was getting excited now. The girl was thinking—she was really thinking! He almost had a quick fingernail chew before he answered. "Sample digs at six sites in the heartland confirm layers of the same measurements and compositions. I, er, haven't seen them myself, but I saw the reports online. The same at sites near three of the five cities abroad. Maybe you knew that already. I heard you're from overseas?"

Kat straightened her shoulders. "This is just a guess, but according to the figures jotted here, the level's consistent with other evidence of meteorite impact about fifty-five million years ago, hitting the planet surface at about forty times the speed of sound . . ."

". . . and sinking a crater one hundred and eighty K wide in the heartland."

"You read Q Essnid's article in *New Colonist* too!"

"He's an expert on heartland geology. I'm wondering about joining one of his research trips next spring, if I can drag myself away from work on the INTENS project." Harpo C frowned. What had come over him? He didn't normally volunteer information randomly—certainly not to gorgeous girls who downloaded the same brainy e-mags he did.

Kat was on a roll. "So, I reckon we could be looking at a one-centimeter-wide mass grave of carbonized life. Pretty much everything that walked, talked, swam, or swarmed on the planet surface—all turned to toast by an impact explosion equivalent to about a hundred trillion tons of TNT."

"Exactly. *K-bang!* Cool for our colony, though:

no advanced life-forms to get in our way: most forests fried worldwide and most things in 'em." Harpo C fished in his pocket, took out a small gray lump, and passed it to her, unconscious of the fact that as he ruffled his hair again he smeared clay all over one side of his forehead. "This is a sample I took. Amazing, isn't it, that you stand in a place like this, this quarry, and you think it's all dead stuff, but everything's got a story to tell."

Kat thought about this for a moment. She also thought about the wind turbines disappearing into the reservoir and the *H*, *M*, *L* lines on the door to her bedroom at Cherry Heaven. Yes, definitely the very trees and stones had stories to tell. She rootled in her pocket and handed Harpo a small, round fossil she'd found just before falling. There were fossils of mini-beasts all over the quarry, now immortalized in the stone-clad dam too. She'd read that on-site geologists who'd supervised the mining had been forced to admit that there was nothing major enough to stop blasting stone for the dam. That was a big blow for ardent paleontologists, who'd been hoping the quarry would reveal the first evidence of large dinosaur-type remains on the colony planet. K Rahbin herself had been eager to make her name with a big find. Q Essnid had funded sample digs all around the site, but no one had made any awesome discoveries. All of which unfortunately meant that no one knew for sure if there had ever been significant life-forms on the planet before humans arrived with their do-it-yourself DNA animals and plants.

"Cool! A two-million-year-old becano bug, immortalized in quarry ore." Harpo didn't let on that he already had boxes full.

Kat gave a weak smile. "I suppose people always think the past is over and done with—gone away—but it isn't, is it?"

"No siree. And people say geology's boring! Meteorites, cataclysm, worldwide fires, death and destruction, all laid down in the land as evidence. What more could anyone want?"

*A bit of peace and a fresh new beginning*, thought Kat.

Seeing her frown, Harpo C figured he'd gone too far. Seeing Harpo's smile waver, Kat figured she'd best cheer him up. "Are you hungry?"

"Hungry?"

He watched her pull a foil packet from her dusty backpack. She wasn't going to offer him pills, was she? Didn't she know what they did to your . . . Oh. It was fruit. He licked his lips.

"Are those . . . ?"

"Cherries? Yes."

"From . . . ?"

"Cherry Heaven. Want one?"

Harpo C swallowed. "I haven't tried one of these for years."

Kat smiled to see his face flush with pleasure at the first bite.

"Ohmygod," he said. "These are . . ."

"Legendary?"

"Oh yes! Mind if I . . . ?"

"Help yourself."

He ate each cherry slowly, carefully, as if a real connoisseur of taste, not a teenage boy who'd missed lunch because he'd been immersed in a computer program.

"They're from cryo," Kat explained. "It doesn't look like anyone's harvested fruit recently. The whole farm's run-down. I can't understand. . . ."

"They just don't grow cherries there anymore," Harpo said quickly. "Q Essnid rents the place out now the owner's dead. The farm's closed down."

"I know. I just wondered. . . ."

"*Don't.*" His face changed, all pleasure gone.

He'd dreaded this moment ever since he heard that Q Essnid had found a family to live at Cherry Heaven—a family with two *sisters*, for god's sake! He wished they could just have left the whole fruit farm alone, let it fall down, let it rot, anything but stir up long-squashed memories.

"Do you want a drink?" he asked hurriedly, anxious not to alienate this new-found phenomenon called "interesting girl."

She took the bottle from him, commenting, "It's not Blue Mountain."

"I never touch the stuff."

"I didn't know there were any other brands."

"There aren't. This is tap water."

Kat looked alarmed. "Is it safe to drink?"

"Yeah—of course! Who told you it wasn't?"

"No one. I just assumed. . . ."

"Exactly. It's what the Linveki Hydro Company *want* you to think, so you'll buy their water."

This gave her something new to mull over. Mention of the Hydro factory made her remember the escaped worker whose face was now on posters all over town. From thoughts of escape her mind turned to prisons . . . and to one prisoner in particular.

"Who's Oklear Foster?"

"Who? Nobody! What're you asking me for?"

"No reason. I heard people talking about him and wondered if he was still in prison." *Or if he's the man I imagine in the orchard shadows.*

Harpo C blinked so hard he made himself dizzy. What did Oklear Foster have to do with anything? That was years ago. Almost exactly ten years ago. He didn't want to go thinking about all that again. Eating cherries had already brought back enough memories of that day in the snow. . . . Poor Hikori, Mai, and Luka . . . that awful silence falling after gunshots cracked in the valley.

"Foster's definitely in prison," he eventually managed. His voice was so croaky he had to cough a bit to sound sensible. "He, ah, committed some crimes years ago. Shot people."

"Are you sure he hasn't escaped?"

"Why would he? He's a walking vegetable now. Got brain-drained straight after his trial."

"And he shot people?"

"Some. Well, quite a few. He wasn't right in the head—kept saying he was innocent even though they caught him with a gun and everything. That's all old news—a blip. We're totally pro-peace now."

"Who'd he shoot?"

"Look, I, er, need to get some drawings done before we have to head back to school, so . . . thanks for the cherries and everything."

"Oh. Sure. I'll just . . ." Startled by Harpo's abrupt change in attitude, Kat scrambled to her feet. She bit her lip at the sudden pain, hoping he wouldn't notice.

He did.

"Grab my arm, I'll walk down with you. Careful—we don't want to start another rockfall."

The light faded as heavy clouds slunk across the sky.

Tanka came running up to fold her sister in an

exuberant hug. "Where've you been? Are you okay? I was extra-twice worried about you!"

"I just slipped. It's nothing."

"I thought you'd had an accident or something. . . ."

"Well, I did. You should see the cut on my—"

". . . and that you were dead and I'd always feel guilty because the last thing we ever did together was quarrel, and I'm really sorry I was narky. Are you still mad at me?"

Harpo C stared at Tanka like she was some strange specimen in a petri dish. "Er, I think she's more hurt than mad."

Aran E was close behind Tanka. He took one look at Kat and said, "You should get some antibac on those cuts."

"It's okay—we sloshed some water over them."

"He's right," said Professor Rahbin, edging around the nearby pool of water with an unusually strong curl of disgust on her lips. She made Kat sit down and crouched at her side to examine her leg. "It feels okay—no fractures. You did well to bind it up, Harpo. Look in my medi-kit, Tanka, and get the hyperantibac out. Pass me the Hygie gloves, too—I'm highly allergic to the stuff."

"It stinks," said Tanka helpfully. "No way would I ever use it."

"Really, I'm fine," said Kat. She looked around for Harpo C, but he'd edged away, thinking he was no longer needed. He still had Kat's fossilized becano bug warm in his hand.

Tanka wrapped her arm around Kat's shoulders while Aran E hovered nearby. "Let's get you home, sis. You can have the best comfy seat and I'll wait on you hand and foot. We can spend the entire evening watching Zee Homarlo reruns."

"No-o-o!"

"You know you want to, really—you're just delirious after your fall. Give me a hand with her, Aran. . . ."

Kat flinched to feel Aran E's arm supporting her around the waist. "I don't need help walking!"

"Shall I call some medics?" asked K Rahbin, a little aggravated at the disruption to her geology. "One of the students could run to the dam for help—they have personnel at the monitoring station there."

Kat had to laugh. She no longer craved being the center of attention, and had to work hard to persuade everyone she wasn't crippled for life. It was also embarrassing to have Tanka fawning on her so energetically.

She set off limping, not at all sorry to go. There was something oppressive about the towering quarry walls, or perhaps she was still nervous after all that talk of Oklear Foster's shooting spree. She sighed. It was no use trying to pretend that everything was calm and lovely on the New Frontier: like a trickle of rocks turning into an avalanche, little thoughts were setting off big worries in her mind.

When no one was looking, she tossed Harpo C's lump of compressed carbon into the pool of rank water on the quarry floor, thinking, *Why can't rocks just be rocks, and places just be nice? Why are there always secrets waiting to be dragged out into the open?*

## Friends

i was under the hut, waiting to be dragged out into the open while Blue Capo shouted, *come on out, you bitch-little-shitzer, you can't hide!*

that was an awful day. i can still remember how the ground was shaking as they blasted sector 7. it was Bossman's fault. he shouldn't've made us build the dam in such a hurry. Bossman's to blame for a lot of things—oh yes. just wait till i get close enough to smear that blame all over him. Blue Capo thought he was brilliant, of course.

she had me by the arm that time, practically pulling it off at the shoulder. i kept my fist closed cos i had a secret safe in my hand, something she'd want to know about. should i have told her? showed her? i meant to. i'd gone running to find her the day before the blasting, because the secret was so exciting. only things don't always work out the way they're supposed to. i found her all right—facedown in a pool of muddy water, stunk-drunk in the gunk, and it didn't take a Medic to realize she was well on her way to being totally shitzered. i mean, it's one thing to feel Bliss in the water, another to have your gills sludged with silt and slime. if someone didn't pull her out *quick* she'd be dead and done-for, dust-in-the-making, as dead as the bit of fossil i'd just found in sector 7. i looked around to see if anyone would help haul her out, but the other Capos were huddled around a heater in the tuff-build cabins, the workers were all off working, and there was only me. i could've left her there to die, really i could. after all she'd said to me, all she'd done! only i didn't, cos dead is bad. i tucked my newfound fossil away and lugged her out of the mud. i thumped her chest till she choked back to life again and took greedy gulps of lung-air. then she opened her eyes, saw me, and spat at me—one spot of spit that slid down my face.

that's why i didn't tell her what i'd found, what i had tight in my hand. that's why i said nothing when sector 7 was blown to smithereens and all her dreams went with it. she had no idea. when she pulled me out from under that hut i still had my secret safe.

well, the huts are all gone now. Blue Capo's gone, too—who knows where? who cares where? so many years since that day, and i'm on my way to better and brighter things now! all that's left of the gut-busting dam-building is this quiet, tidy Quarry and the ohmygod-have-you-ever-seen-anything-so-big DAM we made from the stone.

after a while i get tired of standing at Quarry fence, looking in at the shadows of long ago. i turn to go back to the path by the river, to the slope where the barges used to wait. that's when i see them. the people, real ones. since they're inside Quarry i figure they must be people with PERMISSION, like the sign says. they look as small as becano bugs from where i am, beetling around all the blank spaces where Quarry things used to be. they're just more people i don't know, who don't know me—probably don't want to know me. i watch them move past the glint of water, going to the far side of the fence and clanging the gate behind them as they leave. they're in friendly twos and threes, not a friend-free ONE like me. how come they get to be them, and i get to be me? Gim D told me people get what they deserve, one way or another. he can't have been lying—he didn't tell lies—only he can't have been right either, can he? do i deserve to be here? am i so awful those things had to happen to me? NO!!!!!! NO a squazillion times to infinity Plus One! IT WASN'T ME. it was never me. it was the *bullies*—the people who are all-stone-and-no-cherry—they're the ones who should get what they deserve. Bossman told them what to do and they did it, no questions, no problem.

i did nothing except be Luka . . . oh, and get the silver/green Galrezi thing on my hand. there wasn't much i could do about that. when we

went in to get our test results we were normal;
when we came out we were scum, so don't tell
me what people deserve, Gim Damson! oh. you
can't anyway, because you're not here, are you?
none of my friends are here; they're just shadows shuffling past my eyes, like i shuffled down
the path the day they took me away from
Quarry to work in Factory.

i'm out of here, going going gone, but suddenly
there's a sound. voices, *real* voices not just the
ones that rocket around my head. laughing, too,
yes, *real* laughing. i haven't heard that since . . .

since

since

Aran E!

that's *Aran E* laughing!

no it's not. can't be! but that *hair*, my god i'd
know that red hair anywhere! Harpo C! i'd like to
hurtle into him for hugs and laughing all around,
only i wait . . . just a second too long. they
go past, grown big with long legs like me, only
they're NOTHING ELSE like me. they're wearing
*warm* clothes and white smiles. Aran E's got his

arm around a girl, helping her walk, not helping me. Harpo C's got his hands in his pockets and his eyes on the ground, *not* looking for me.

*hey you! hey you with the hair!* the words can't get out past the fat lump in my throat. in a trance i trace the letters of his name on the palm of my hand. H-A-R-P-O-C. it's really him, right there! you see how i shouldn't've drowned myself in the river! you see how i was right to fight the flow! you see how it's worth escaping from Factory—worth the cold and the cramps and the hunger and the horrible pain of my hand. i'll call him, catch him, tell him—*it's me!*

but there's another voice asking, *what's the matter, Kataka J? are you sure i can't send someone for a medic?*

the girl called Kataka J's looking back, nearly noticing me. *it's nothing,* she says. *i just thought i saw . . . nothing.*

the other voice turns my blood to ice. *i'll call your aunt and uncle as soon as i get an e.f. signal again.*

*honestly, i'm fine!* says Kataka J.

*i should never have let you go up the quarry
side like that. . . .*

*she's fine!* comes a chorus in reply.

SHE might be fine but i'm not. i'm as stiff as
stones. shitzer a million times! shitzer to *infinity!* i know that voice. I KNOW THAT VOICE!
what's that woman doing in Quarry again?
what's she doing even being alive? oh, this is
NOT GOOD. this stinks worse than Stingo.

they all walk away except me. i'm still stuck on
the spot shaking when the first snowflake falls
out of a cloud and lands on my shoulder.

# SNOWFALL I

"Snow means no school!" Tanka was ecstatic to see a few white dots falling as they left the JC after their trip to Cluff Wood quarry. A few steps behind, with a very slight limp, Kat wasn't so impressed.

"Only on the first day, so they can do the festival thing. Deep-heat machines will clear paths so no one gets stranded."

"That's still a whole day off! Oh, I forgot, you'll get learning withdrawal symptoms, and you won't be able to see your funny little ginger boy. . . ."

"He's *not* my ginger boy! He's not little either—he's taller than Aran E."

"Er, excuse me, *no competition*, sweetie. Is Harpo C's dad holding a huge party to celebrate deep winter? Is Harpo C's house a completely supreme villa on the side of the valley? Is Harpo C *at all* interesting in any way? Honestly, you're my sister—you don't have to make do with dregs."

Kat felt angry at being forced to defend someone she didn't have the slightest interest in. Then she was stung by how easy it was to stick up for the boy. "Harpo's kind and clever and not obsessed with being what other people expect of him."

"Neither's Aran E! He's just . . . just got a lot to live up to. His dad *is* about the most important person on this side of the planet. And . . . nothing."

"What?"

"Nothing. Just looking at the snow. Pathetic, isn't it?" There were only a few fragile flakes drifting through the late afternoon. Cherry Heaven orchard seemed bleak and bare as they walked home. Any snow that reached the ground vanished. "Still, it means we get the Yuki Matsuri, with fireworks and bonfires and everything. I heard Challis sells the best rockets in the world." Forgetting to be bitchy, Tanka dropped back to her sister's side and they linked arms comfortably the rest of the way to Cherry Heaven. While Tanka called Aran to chat, Kat put an ice pack on her ankle, made hot malloey tea, and defrosted some cherries—they seemed like a cure for pretty much everything. She found Tanka sitting like stone on the sofa with her arms crossed.

"What's with the long face?"

"Prester and Millijue left a message. They're staying in town tonight for some bash at the university and they'll catch up with us at the festival tomorrow."

"And that's made you look furious because . . . ?"

"It's called having an *emotion*. You should try it sometime."

Kat felt a whole wad of emotions stick in her throat, but she was used to Tanka's careless comments, and it was *sisters stick together* after all.

"You're not mad at them. Have you had a bust-up with Aran?"

"No! Well—maybe. Just now. He called. All I did was make some crack about when am I ever going to meet his amazing dad, cos he's never around, and Aran just like blew up at me and said I didn't know anything, and I'd be lucky if I *did* meet him, blah blah blah. I don't get it, I mean, I know Aran E loves his dad but I don't think he particularly *likes* him, only he won't hear a word of criticism against him. It's weird. As if I care."

*Oh you care all right*, thought Kat. *You're sweeter on Aran E than all the previous boyfriends put together. He is really lovely, you can't fake that, so why do I get the feeling he's never entirely honest with anyone? He's always so popular, so perfect— what would we see if he dropped the act?*

"Have some cherries and call him back when you're calmer," was all she said out loud.

"Like I'm taking advice on dating from *you*, boyless brain of the century."

"Ouch!"

"Sorry. I mean, *really* sorry. Thing is, I asked if he'd come over—he's got the boat, after all, and how could he refuse me anything?—but he *always* makes some excuse for not setting foot in this place, and he did again just now, so I don't see why I should bother going to his stupid party at the villa. . . ."

"What party?"

Tanka blushed and tried to look airy. "The one I told you about. The totally exclusive get-together for the cream of the cream. It's tomorrow night."

"Nobody told me anything."

"It's just what we were whispering about at that stupid quarry place. Aran's fixed up invites for all four of us. Don't you think he's supremely infuriating? In fact, he's a complete extra-twice loser. And who needs him anyway, especially since I'm so going to win that hot-date prize with Zee Homarlo?"

"Right."

There was a long pause while Tanka thoughtfully nibbled her hair. "So, maybe I *should* call him now I'm calmer. Pass me some cherries, will you? I mean, his dad is actually very important and can't help being away a lot, especially now he's planning the big O-HA rally. Aran probably misses him, which is extra-twice sweet."

"Totally."

"And he probably doesn't like coming over here because it's not as nice as his super-supreme villa. . . ."

"Right."

Tanka soon lost her sunny outlook when even Kat's *e.f.* failed to pick up a signal. She threw it away in disgust and went to soak her frustrations in the big pool. Kat rescued the tiny silver device from the garbage. People in the New Frontier tended to rely on archaic paper messages, or computer net access, since other communications were so temperamental. There seemed to be no way around the disruption caused by thick layers of mont-halo ore—one reason that the original colonists had chosen to build the first cities on the other continent, where mont-halo was rare. That, and the fact it was stacks warmer there. The New Frontier managed fairly well, but it was hardly an efficient way to work. Somebody ought to think of a way around the problem. They could . . .

She snapped alert, her brain suddenly buzzing with a brilliant new idea. No, a crazy one. Brilliant! Crazy . . . Brilliant *and* crazy. Surely someone had thought of it before? Forgetting about sore feet and grumpy sisters, Kat fetched her computer down to the dining-room desk and pulled her best boxes of software off the shelves. She had some *serious* research to do. . . .

"Watch out, Harpo Challis—this idea is so potentially supreme it'll leave you light years behind. Or make you laugh so hard you explode."

• • •

Morning came with a strange white light, as if strong lamps shone in at every window. Kat had fallen asleep while she worked, so when the light woke her up she had a forehead creased with keyboard marks. She stretched and stumbled toward the window, then stopped herself and returned to the computer. The screen saver cleared to show *Message Sent*. So she had submitted her crazy idea after all. It would have arrived at the chatboard of *New Colonist* e-mag some time in the odd, dark hours of early morning.

*What have I done? Too many cups of cherry tea and not enough injections of common sense! I bet Security will roll up later today and arrest me for being such a loon—thinking I could crack the continent's communication problem after one mad brainstorm! Me and my stupid need to fix everything . . .*

Tanka came pounding downstairs in as many layers of clothing as she'd been able to load on top of her pajamas.

"Have you seen what's out there?"

"Out where? Oh, outside. No, I—"

"Slept on the computer? Weirdo. Come on!"

Together they went to the porch and opened the front door.

It had snowed.

"It's just cold rain," Kat said slowly.

"It's magic!" Tanka breathed.

"Well, it's actually a natural process where water crystals—"

"Spare me!" Tanka pushed one fluffy slipper outside and was delighted to hear the snow crunch and see the print she made.

Kat couldn't move, she was so amazed. Where had the world gone? Everything was changed! The sad trees were smothered, the barren yard softened, and the air filled with numberless slow-falling flakes. Despite all the science, maybe it was magic after all. Cherry Heaven had never looked so lovely—and so strange.

Holding safely on to each other, they stepped into the snow, deep enough to reach over their slippers and wet the bottom of Tanka's pajamas. Kat didn't know what sensations to expect. It was nothing like stepping in a puddle of water, more like walking on frozen sugar meringue. Looking back she saw their footprints from the house. Looking ahead there were more footprints, coming out of the orchard, close to the house, then off to invisibility.

*Who's been out in the snow already?*

Before Kat could say anything Tanka shrieked, skidded, and fell flat on her back in a crumple of snow. For a moment she was too stunned to complain, then she started to laugh. It was such a typical Tanka reaction, Kat laughed too.

"Snow's falling in my mouth!" Tanka shouted. "You can eat it! Pull me up; I want to skid again!"

"Hang on a mo, I just want to look—"

"You can go really fast! Zipeeeee!"

"Tanka!"

Too late. Tanka's pink dressing gown flapped behind her as she hurled herself into every snow-drift with complete jubilation. The unspoiled foot-prints Kat did manage to find were mostly filled in with snow, suggesting whoever had walked around the house had been and gone some time before, since snow was still falling.

Was it the nonexistent mystery man? Where had he gone? Into the trees? Surely there couldn't be anyone actually *living* in the orchard? Why would he do that? How could he survive? Worse, what was he waiting for?

She shivered, not exactly comforted by the fact that bogeyman Oklear Foster was absolutely brain-drained in prison. Feeling the cold bite, she couldn't believe that anyone would last long in this strange snowy landscape. She'd overheard people speculating about the runaway worker from the Hydro factory, saying the girl must have frozen to death already. It was horrible to think of someone once alive curled up solid, with snow falling on them. Security were out in force, some drafted from Santanna, all looking for the worker's body.

"Aha!" She stopped dead in the snow, while Tanka scooted past in another superlative skid. "That's it—*Security*! I bet they've just been trawling through the trees."

Before logic could point out that Security alerts had actually been posted *after* the girls first sensed someone in the orchard, a large splat of snow hit Kat full in the face.

"You can make it into balls and throw it!" Tanka needlessly explained. She quickly learned that Kat was a much better shot, and deflated even further when an enormous sneeze stopped her mid-mêlée, followed by a fit of coughing. When she straightened up, her face was whiter than the snow in her hair.

"My nose! What's happened to my nose! What's

all this green stuff running out? Ohmygod, it's the snow—I'm allergic to snow! You bring me a million miles round the globe and I get struck down with some evil Frontier infection! I *knew* it couldn't be natural, all this weird cold. I mean, if people were supposed to survive in this stuff they'd've evolved furry skins and blubber, right?"

"We can swing by the medic's on the way to the festival," Kat suggested calmly. She followed Tanka back into the house on a quest for pills. "Go easy on the peps, doop. The hospital might prescribe other medication."

"Bring it on! And hey, if I'm lucky the medic'll be some extra-twice gorgeous guy who'll need to give me a full physical."

"Oh, *please*." Kat tried to get Tanka to be serious for more than one second at a time. "I know you think you're fine, but you take stuff to perk up and stuff to cool down again. It can't be good."

"I'll be good when I'm old and gray."

"If you live that long."

"Gonna live forever! Oh *shitzer*! Pass me something to wipe my nose on, will you?"

They wore as many clothes as possible for the trek through the alien landscape to the ferry jam-packed with people heading into town for the festival, the famous Yuki Matsuri. Quite a few kids from the JC waved hello as the sisters pushed through the crowds to find a space by the port windows. Kat looked for Harpo C, but of course he didn't take the ferry into Meander; he already lived there. Not that she particularly wanted to see him. Not socially. Just for a moment, maybe, to tell him about the ideas on mont-halo ore she'd cooked up the night before. If nothing else, he could share the joke. He had a nice laugh and a lovely smile.

On second thoughts, it was best not to go anywhere near the boy.

Voices poked into her private thoughts: there'd been a sighting of the renegade worker from the Hydro. It seemed she'd been spotted—alive and not nice.

"Over at Anabarra," a stringy girl from Kat's art class was saying. "All the newschats are full of it. They say she just randomly attacked these two kids at the ferry stop, then ran off, and they didn't find her after that."

"Beat them to pulp, I heard," a tall older boy butted in. "Probably killed them."

"I heard they're dead."

"She wiped out their parents, too. Blood everywhere. She's a total psycho."

"The children weren't that badly hurt and no one was killed," said another ferry passenger, a woman in a bright yellow coat and hat. "Mind you, she sounds like a supremely nasty sort of girl, though I'm not saying that just because the newschats claim she's Galrezi."

As she spoke, the woman stroked the twist of green ribbon that was pinned to her coat lapel with a silver O-HA badge. People in the New Frontier often wore the ribbon to show their solidarity with Galrezi. They were especially popular now that the War Crimes Commission was starting to publish details of the terrible race crimes that had been committed in the cities during the war.

"No smoke without fire," the stringy girl muttered.

"Psycho," the tall boy agreed.

Conversation stopped as the ferry slowed close to the base of the great Meander dam. It was too wide and high to view properly from river level. Kat spotted the spillways sending frothy water pouring into a giant runoff pool that eventually fed into the Annaflo. She rubbed condensation off the window to try and see why they were stopping, but the woman in the yellow coat blocked her view, complaining, "What's going on? We never stop here!"

There was a gentle bump as the ferry came to rest at the dam quayside. Then a line of thick-shouldered workers went past, huddled into heavy-duty coats. The ferry would be even more crowded now they were squeezing on board.

"Builders from the cities," said the woman, her blue eyes narrowing. "I heard they'd drafted work gangs from abroad to set up for the O-HA rally. Quinn Essnid can pull favors like that. I suppose they get a day off for the festival, too."

Tanka looked up in alarm. "They're having the rally *outside*? At the dam?"

"Sure, honey. We all think it's going to be wonderful—Q Essnid's idea, of course."

"But . . . it'll be freezing!"

The woman laughed. "Not with deep-heat machines. And you think this is bad, wait until the real cold starts."

"*Real* cold?"

"Oh yes, ice on the reservoir and everything—

thick enough to walk on in a matter of days. I bet those boys from the cities had a bit of a shock when they felt our weather!"

"*I'm* from the cities," said Tanka loftily. "And I think the weather is rather boring, actually." Her performance was spoiled by a big, wet sneeze.

Surprisingly homesick, Kat watched the builders come aboard. Most of the workers looked ridiculously young to be doing hefty work—they were about her own age. She was too shy to ask any of them if they knew City Five, not even the quiet sun-brown lad who had turned away from the others to read something tantalizingly technical looking.

"Hey, Toni V!"

The boy pushed the papers deep inside his thick coat. Kat figured he was used to being interrupted in his studies. She heard him answer, "What's up?"

"You got any credit left for fireworks?"

"Sure do."

The builders were excited, thinking about all the

big explosions and the bonfires. The other ferry passengers smiled indulgently. They'd always suspected that New Frontier culture was superior to the fancy life that overseas cities were so proud of. After all, there were no war ruins on the Frontier, were there? No nasty mopping up of messy gene-clan conflicts . . . thanks to the power of the O-HA's peace.

As the ferry set off again, Kat craned her neck to take in as much of the dam as she could as they passed. The woman in yellow watched her reaction to the white wonderland.

"Won't it be nice for the rally? It's an omen, I'm sure of it. I love it when there's so much snow you can't hardly tell what's underneath—all pure white, nothing ugly showing. Magic, it is, just magic."

## Fossil

the snow's not pure white anymore, not since
the pavements have been sludged up from a
million footsteps.

if i didn't have a home to go to, i wouldn't mind
living here in Meander, even if there's no sign of a
single cherry at any of the stores i've seen. here
at Mountain View Apartments there's heating,
lighting, and plastic pot plants. not a mountain
in sight, of course, and security's not so hot. i
got in through the lobby okay, looking like just
another snow-dusty shape. after ten years of
cold it hurts being somewhere warm.

*knock knock knock*

the door's shut but i know she's home cos i've
got ears that can hear someone nasty a mile

off. question is, will she know it's me like i knew it was her? can't tell till the door opens. c'mon, Blue Capo, let me in—i've got a present for you!

Blue Capo thought she was clever—*whatever!*—that she knew things. she might've known about building and bullying, but she didn't know shitzer about being nice, did she, so what the hell use was she on this planet? she thought she was brainy, banging on about rocks and ridges and clay deposits. huh. that was only *half* her brain she was using, not even the best half, in my opinion, and yes, Blue Capo, i DO have an opinion. i know what opinions are. here's one for you: if you were suddenly squashed under a rock like a becano bug i wouldn't be sorry, unless someone shouted at *me* to clean the mess up.

oh yes, Blue Capo always said she was WHACK civilized, unlike us WHACK Galrezi-WHACK-scum. she said she was going to teach, be an expert, win prizes, go far. hah! she went as far as the junior college and the only way her name will ever be in lights is on the shiny sign telling me which apartment is hers.

she's hung a line of Matsuri lanterns above the door, like the ones we used to get when i was a kid, you know, the orange ones with stars on. they're supposed to make you smile and say, *happy snow festival!* actually, they make me sick. nothing happy about the last snow festival i had.

*knock knock knock*

it's always polite to knock before you go in, i know that. i know lots. Blue Capo told me a shitzer-load of stuff i never wanted to know, about rocks and crystals and mont-halo ore. she couldn't care mush about tuffcrete; she liked stones. especially she liked stones with dead things in them—fossils. always she was looking around Quarry, her bright blue eyes searching for just one big find, she said, one big skeleton in the rock. she was hoping to discover something huge, something they'd name after her.

*it's here,* she told me once, when drink had rubbed the roughness off her tongue. *my fame is here somewhere. i'll find it: the first on the planet. maybe you'll find it for me and if you do, i'll give you extra bread to eat. . . .*

she told me to keep my eyes peeled for a sign that something amazing was buried in the rocks waiting for her to discover it. *it's my dream,* she whispered. *the biggest find on the Frontier will be mine, i know it!*

she told me about the fires millions of years ago that killed the forests and the animals and just left gray burned bits in a little line of clay. then she shouted at me and beat me for not working. i know all about burning, smoking the skin off the back of my hand with raw Stingo so i wouldn't be a *shitzer-no-brain-waste-of-space-Galrezi-scum.*

Gim Damson said people can call you scum but they can't make you scum. he never needed to add some people are scum to the bone, whether they're called it or not. yes you, Blue Capo. someone should sew your mouth up so you can't say things that make me want to crawl inside myself and die. someone should burn out your eyes so they can't stab people anymore. maybe someone will.

*knock knock knock*

in Quarry, all those years ago, you couldn't do anything to a Capo or a Super; there were too many of them. sometimes the workers gathered in corners and whispered sssssshh what it would be like to kill all the Capos. Gim D called that crazy talk. *people get what they deserve one way or another*, he always said, meaning the bad guys would get punished somehow. *i don't think it's for us to decide. keep true to yourself, Luka, and always keep hoping.*

it's nice he could think like that. not me, though. i knew that good people should get treats and the shitzers should get shafted. that day i saved Blue Capo from drowning, i snook up to Gim's hut and tapped on the window, a special *tap-tap-tapitty-tap* that meant it was me and nobody else. the stone workers smuggled me inside, where people,

blankets, and bandages were pell-mell all around.
a few of the older men and women had already
crashed out on their bunks, but most of the
younger people had made a circle around one of
the heaters. wherever you sat you still felt cold,
so Gim D lifted up his blanket and let me creep
underneath. he had a hug big enough to make
anyone feel warm.

*look, guys, little papillon's flown in!* he said with
a smile. he knew my name then, of course, and
i'd told him all about papillons and my puss-cat
and playing at Cherry Heaven. i said he should
come and visit when we got away from Quarry.
i meant it too, only getting away from Quarry
meant going to Factory for me, and Nobody
Knows Where for him.

he said, *you're a very soggy Luka! get closer
to the fire.*

it was good to get dry, but it would've been
better if there was a pool of hot water and a
brush to scrub every last bit of Blue Capo off
my skin. most people said a friendly *hello* when
they saw it was me. the workers were always

giving me snacks or smiles. that's why i went to give them something back again. a present. *look what i've got*, i said. they all groaned when i held out my piece of rock. a grumpy bundle of blankets on a top bunk told everyone to hush before the Capos came. *no, look*, i said, giving Gim the rock.

he turned it over in his red-raw palm. *it's a funny shape. is it a fossil?*

*oh, not another fricking fossilized becano bug!* one of the stone workers said. *if i had a loaf of bread for every time we found one of those . . .*

*mind your language*, said Gim D.

*don't worry, i've heard worse*, i said.

*that's not the point*, he replied. *anyway, what is this rock thing?*

*it's not just any old fossil*, i told everyone. *it comes from the biggest dinosaur thing you've ever seen. i found it in sector 7 when i was running messages for Red-Neck Capo. the whole skeleton's huge—at least ten times longer than me.* i stretched my arms out wide in the brazier light, then brought them close together to show the size of my fossil. *this is its toe.*

*big toe,* said Gim with a low whistle.

*actually, it's a tip of its littlest toe,* i said. *i could tell when i chiseled it out.*

*jeez, it'd be something to see the whole dinosaur dug up and cleaned.*

*are you kidding?* said someone else. it was a white-haired girl who later came to Factory with me to be Packer 109—the one who crouched at Director's feet to file his nails and condition his cuticles. *who cares about dead things in the rocks? next time find some treasure, Luka, or at least something we can eat.*

*no, it's cool,* said Gim, and for a moment he reminded me of Harpo C, who was always getting excited by grisly things like blackling bones, or nests of bustling becanos. *didn't you say the Capo's been looking out for something big like this?*

*it's sick,* said the girl. *Capos should care more about us than million-year-old-rock-skeletons.*

*it's a missing link in planetary evolution,* i said carefully, so i got all the bits of the long words right. *no one's found anything like it in the whole colony—Blue Capo said so. and when you find things they're put in a museum and named after you.*

Gim laughed. *the Papillonosaur!*

the girl said, *yeah right, more like they'll name it after the Capo. like, Bitch-face Beastiesaur.*

*i couldn't resist teasing everyone.*

*i'm supposed to go tell her i've found it. you never know, she might die of happiness, if we're lucky.*

the girl's face was like a page of hate crumpled up.

*no way should you tell her! after everything she's done to you—to all of us!*

*oh, i'm going to tell her,* i said. *but not yet.*

Gim D leaned forward, enjoying the joke even though he didn't yet know what the punch line was.

*so when are you going to tell her, Luka?*

*oh, i thought about five minutes after the demolition crew explodes the whole of sector 7 tomorrow morning. . . .*

and because we didn't know then that two
men would get dead in the explosion, we all
laughed. only, as things turned out, i didn't
get a chance to tell Blue Capo about the fossil
because after the explosion i was too busy
being pulled out from under the hut and beaten,
so somehow i never showed her the only surviving bit of her big dream . . . until . . . until i followed her to town today.

*knock knock knock*

*who is it?* calls the voice i still hear in my night-
mares.

who is it? it's ME! and when i'm done with you,
Blue Capo, I'll be sniffing the air looking for the
NEXT.

# SNOWFALL II

"Next!"

Kat gave Tanka a helpful shove toward the consulting room. The medic was a chirpy woman with a too-bright orange badge on her jacket that wished her patients, "Happy Matsuri!"

"Wait for me, won't you?" Tanka begged.

"I'll be right here, drinking horrible hospital coffee, okay?"

Like the spa, Meander hospital was another example of harmonious design and beautiful building materials. Graceful papillons were chiseled into the tuff-glass dome that soared over the main reception. They didn't sparkle much that morning—the glass was too heavy with snow. The reception was full of Matsuri banners looking slightly creased, no doubt fetched out from last year's snow festival.

Kat found a seat out of the way. She was tired—that was to be expected after her long night being brainy—but her stomachache had nothing to do with breakfast. There was just too much to worry about. No matter how sternly Tanka lectured her on the evils of anxiety, she couldn't feel easy. Priming the *e.f.*, she tracked down Aunt Millijue.

"Milli, it's me, Kat . . . yeah, we're fine. We're at the hospital, no, nothing serious. Tanka's just having a checkup . . . no, my ankle's fine, just a bit sore. Where are you?"

Millijue hadn't been able to resist squeezing in a couple of hours' work before the big festivities began. She was in her office at the O-HA HQ.

"While you're there, could you just look something up for me? Well, a couple of things . . . no, I *did* try on my net link, only some of files were infected, and on others the info came up restricted. . . ."

She had to turn the volume down as Millijue's flat objections began. She quickly reassured her aunt that what she wanted to know wasn't so much top secret as hard to get hold of.

"I can't abuse my position here," Millijue said. "If things are restricted, it's because you don't need to know about them."

Kat was too used to managing everyone in the Jones family. After some persuasion, Millijue agreed to check a few files and then judge for herself whether the information was confidential or not. In the meanwhile, Kat tried to distract herself by mulling over her submission to *New Colonist*. She'd already thought up a million different variations on the "You're Mad" response she'd receive, when she remembered Tanka and went limping back to the consulting room.

She was just in time to hear her sister shouting, "No, I *don't* feel relieved to find out what's wrong, and no, I haven't ever had one before. Do I look like someone who'd get a—what did you call it—a *common* cold?" The medic's reply was lost, but the whole hospital could have heard Tanka's explosion of, "I don't care if it *can* be cured! I shouldn't've caught it in the first place. It was that freaking Galrezi porter in Santanna, that's where I got it from, I know it was! *Shitzer* Galrezi are just crawling with everything. . . ."

Kat was appalled. How could Tanka think such things, let alone say them? This was going too far! Obviously the medic thought so too. There was no "Happy Matsuri!" as she showed her patient to the door.

"Idiot!" Kat said. "You can't say that sort of thing."

"People think it; why not say it?"

"Because it's rude and thoughtless and . . ."

". . . racist and stupid and immature. Play a different tune—I've heard this one a squillion times already. What about you?"

"*I'm* rude?"

"No, silly—what about your ankle? Aren't you going to get it checked out?"

"It's fine."

"Yeah? And that's you all over—pretending everything's fine when it's not. At least I'm honest."

Kat couldn't answer. Was it true? Was Tanka honest, while she was fake? If so, why did Tanka try so hard to keep her distance from the truth of the past, from the reality of their Galrezi family? She was too keen to be carefree.

*What about me? Do I deal with it? Sure I do. Maybe. Sometimes. Can't think about that now.*

Tanka shrugged. "Gotta go get a prescription. It's something called a *cold*, which people apparently get out here in the *wilderness*. Fortunately there's a cure; otherwise I'd have to go on a random killing spree in revenge."

"How long before you stop coughing over me and start feeling better?"

"Not soon enough—this snot and sneezing's for another week, and I might lose my voice. What did you say? *Too bad?!* Don't be sarcastic!" Tanka gave her sister a playful shove, but Kat still looked stern. "All right, I'm *sorry* about the Galrezi stuff I said. I was just, you know, being a doop as usual. C'mon—we should get over to the main square for the festival! Everyone's going to be there. . . ."

The queue at the meds counter wasn't long. Most people had decided that going to the Matsuri took precedence over being ill. Kat's *e.f.* buzzed while they waited.

"Millijue? Hello? Speak up—you're really faint."

"I'm whispering," came the crackling voice. "Listen, I can't say much. I looked up the things you wanted, about the people at Cherry Heaven. . . ."

"The Papillons."

"Exactly. You were right; it was owned by Celia Papillon, the architect—she's had so many awards, you wouldn't believe it. There were three girls as well, Hikori, Mai, and Luka."

*H, M, and L.*

"Go on."

"Well, that's just it. All I can tell you. They . . . died."

"*Died?*"

"An awful incident ten years ago. A man called . . ."

*Oklear Foster.*

". . . Oklear Foster. This is terrible, Kat. Really awful." Aunt Millijue had enough memories of her own, enough trauma from the civil war.

"But you did check up on Foster, didn't you? He is still in prison, isn't he?"

"Absolutely. Brain-drained on the last day of his trial—not even time to lodge an appeal, even though he protested he was completely . . ."

The line went fuzzy. Kat had to wander around reception to get a better signal. Eventually she found a corner near double swing doors marked EMERGENCY/INCOMING.

". . . everyone was so upset by what he'd done. Hello? Can you hear me?"

Kat had a bizarre image of her aunt crouched in the corner of her office, hiding. "Are you okay?" she asked cautiously.

"Well, of course, dear. Only . . ."

In hurried whispers the whole story came out. Millijue had been following a trail on her computer when someone knocked on the door. The building should've been empty—people didn't work during the Yuki Matsuri. She'd opened the door . . . to a man from Security. "And I was right back ten years ago," she confided, "afraid they were coming to get me for something. But don't think about that now."

"Security came? What did they want?"

"Oh, we're not in trouble or anything. He was asking about that Hydro worker, you know, the Galrezi girl."

"What's it got to do with us?"

"Nothing—except this man thinks the girl might try to hide near Cherry Heaven. He asked if we'd seen anything odd in the orchard. I said there were no girls there, and it's so *cold*, how could anyone survive . . . ?"

The man had left his name and number and said any information was to be sent to him *personally*.

"He was very clear about that," Millijue said. "We're to talk to him directly, no one else."

This was bad. Kat made up her mind there and then to tell Security about the man she'd imagined and the footprints she'd seen. "Who's the guy we're to call?"

"Challis. Federic Challis. He's from Security at the factory at Santanna."

The connection broke. Tanka came bounding over with a bag of pills. Vaguely Kat thought about reminding her to take the doses properly, not down the whole lot in one go. Before she had time to tidy her brain, the unhurried hospital calm was broken by the rattle of a stretcher gurney on the other side of the double doors and a tense voice shouting, "She's stable but maxed out on pain relief! Security are on their way for questioning!"

Tanka had no compunction about pushing the doors open a little way to see what was happening. The commotion naturally attracted a small crowd. Drama didn't flare up often in the easygoing town.

They saw that snow had melted on the metal poles of the stretcher gurney, leaving it shining and wet; the pale gray cover on the patient was spotted too.

Tanka gasped. "It's K Rahbin, look!"

The geology professor's bright blue eyes were lost in a disgusting bubble of red welts and the air was harsh with the stink of some kind of antibac gel.

*How could anyone accidentally . . . ? Oh.*

Kat blinked, in sympathy. It obviously hadn't been an accident.

Following the stretcher was someone they'd met on the ferry that morning, the pushy woman with a yellow coat. Her face looked as if it had been stretched too tightly across her bones, and she had hold of one of the emergency medics with clawlike fingers.

"I keep telling you, she's highly allergic to antibac! There's no reason she'd accidentally rub her eyes with it! She wouldn't even keep it in the apartment. I should know, she's my daughter!"

K Rahbin moaned, a low rattle of agony from deep in her throat. Her knuckles went a brilliant white color as her hands bunched into fists, then just as abruptly spasmed open, letting something small and hard fall to the ground. Intent on rushing their patient to emergency care, the medics never noticed.

Kat did.

Once the stretcher was wheeled away and the fuss died down, she slipped through the double doors to pick it up.

It was a piece of rock—a fossil, in fact—hardly

the sort of thing you'd expect to get possessive about when your eyes felt like live fire. She shuddered, getting a sudden afterimage of K Rahbin's injuries.

The hospital receptionist cleared people away from the double doors and asked K Rahbin's mother to step through. He led her over to a quiet corner of the entrance hall. "She's a professor from the JC, isn't she?" he asked. "My kid goes there. Are you all right?"

"Of course I'm not all right!" Rahbin's mother said too loudly. People in the reception turned away, pretending not to hear. "I just went to pick my daughter up for the Matsuri and found her lying on her apartment floor with a big letter *F* smeared on each eye with antibac! Which part of that scenario is *all right*? What sort of monster would *blind* someone like that for no reason?"

## Forgotten

i'm blind to danger; only got eyes for the colors
all around.

lights are magic; streets are manic. the whole
town's Matsuri-mad with people, hurry here,
hurry there, where are they going? how come
they don't all crash in one big pile of bags and
broken legs? can you believe there are children
running around as if there aren't any Capos or
Supers to punish them, and guess what—there
aren't! they look like little aliens, weaving
between arcade pillars with warm bobble hats
and bright sparklers. i'm practically sneezing,
the air's so full of smells—cimarron chocolate
from one shop, honey-roast meat from another.
i scoot out of the way of a man with a tuff-cup
of coffee—not quickly enough—the hot smell
spills into the air and down his trouser leg.

ready for the fist, i turn my shoulder to cushion a blow . . . that never arrives.

*sorry, love, you're not scalded, are you?*

is he talking to me? i shake my head, moved . . . and moving away quickly. this busyness, this brightness, it's bugging me big time. how come these people get to be happy, rushing from one normal thing to another, making money, (making snowfish,) making me feel normal too? it would be nice to forget that *i'm* the alien from that other world called Factory—except when i look at kids in the crowd i only see rows of Galrezi in white Hygie suits, still slaving to the eversteady hum of the chill machine. i see Director high on his platform shouting *work, you shitzer-no-brain-Galrezi-scum: double shift!* for all i know, Packer 109's filing his fingernails at this very moment. for all i know, the new Packer 67 will be sleeping in her narrow bunk, the new Color Tech 26 will be squeezing syringes of redberry-blueberry-greenberry flavor, and the new Bottle Seal 55 will be wondering what the hell happened to the last one—me.

i stop dead in the street, and people flow around me like the river flows to Factory. F is for Forgot about Factory. SF is *Shouldn't Forget.* i want to write it in big letters, words a mile high. who'd look, though, when fun things are happening all around? what *do* they care? they drink their bottles of Blue Mountain without bothering to think where it came from. someone should tell them. i'll tell them! i'm Luka now, not a limp wimp worker! i'm going to ask the next person i see if they can help me. oh yes, we'll lead an army to stamp Factory flat into the ground, put Director in a leaky tin can and fire him into orbit, and Bossman . . . leave Bossman to me. and if that's too much to ask, could someone please give me something to eat? my stomach's had nothing but snow all day, and it's like something chews me inside when i smell the next delicious smell, from the stand on the street corner. who is that in the wool hat? is it . . . ? yes it is! i remember him—Reak the roast-nut man! same shiny nose and the sign that says, *Best Hot Snax in Meander.* hey, J Reak! remember me?

*hey, little Luka girl, i got some nuts picked
and roasted just for you.* that's what he used
to say every time, since i was old enough to walk
to town and tall enough to reach for my own
roast nuts. the last time i had nuts was my
birthday—a treat for having to go to town for
our green Galrezi stamps. Hikori and Mai had a
bag of cherries from the cryo-freeze but i
dragged them to J Reak. i was bouncing that
day! Mama wasn't working; she was doing a
party for me. *stay with your sisters,* she said.
*see you later.*

i did try to keep up with them, but they had
such long legs. and i did see her later, just for
a moment. . . .

no. hands over my eyes. i'm not looking at
that right now.

give me nuts instead.

J Reak's face is more creased and cracked
these days, but he still has betel-nuts, juli-nuts,
and pinch-end peanuts: beautiful brown and gold
and black nuts with bright white specks of salt. i
stare at them like i could eat a whole bucketful.

he obviously can't spare a whole bucketful.

he can't spare a bag.

he can't spare even one nut.

he takes one look at my face and snaps, *i'm here to sell nuts, not to give them away.*

but it's me, it's Luka! not so little anymore, and it's nearly my birthday again.

he gets a funny look in his eye, a sneaky snaky look.

*all right, girlie-girl, come over here a mo. let's see if i've got any snax for you.*

picked and roasted specially for me?

he doesn't know what in shitzerville i'm talking about. he just waits till i get close, then he grabs my arm and twists it.

*it's YOU, isn't it?*

hurray! has he remembered me at last?

no.

squashed up close i see that there's a nasty poster pasted on the side of his stand, something Director must've sent from Factory. it's me, with UNSTABLE HYDRO WORKER spelled underneath, and HAVE YOU SEEN THIS CRIMI-

NAL? J Reak figures he has. he calls for Security, and by the worst cursed luck, there's a uniform already moving through the crowds toward us, black boots squashing the snow.

*hey!* i say, squirming like a cat being wormed. *hey, you don't have to do this! you don't have to tell anyone you saw me! i'll go, i'll walk away, i've got legs, that's what they're for. please don't tell them i'm here! i won't go back there!*

*over here!* Reak waves his arm, but there's still time. Security hasn't yet seen us. . . .

*listen, listen to me! you can't give me to Security because i've got to tell people . . . about Factory . . . it's this place in Santanna and they make us work there, all the time, and people drop dead and Director's always shouting, and you've got to know about it because otherwise it won't ever stop. . . .*

*shut it, bitch!*

*i'm not a bitch, i'm a Papillon! don't you remember me?*

he can't have forgotten—he can't have! but when he looks at me he doesn't see Luka, or girl-needing-help, he just sees a shitzer-scum that makes him feel superior. he's as blind as Blue Capo always was, even before i got to her, not seeing people properly. oh, i know his type—they feel bigger by making other people smaller, squashing them down, splatting them flat.

*over here! it's the factory psycho!*

the uniform gets closer, almost on me—not going to get me! i'm hot-mad like nuts jumping in a pan. i see Reak, i see red. no, i see green— he's sicked Security on me even though he's Galrezi too! that's not right, not human, he didn't have to do that! his mouth's open and his eyes are black pellets. his Galrezi hand's pointing, my mouth's biting, the uniform's running and the street's stretching out under my feet—run, run, as fast as i can! run ran slam bam into . . .

*who?*

can't see. can't speak. can barely breathe. got a hand clamped over my mouth and a voice in my ear.

*hush, you're coming with me!*

# FIREFALL

Caught up in her own world of worry Kat ran slam bam into someone walking the opposite way. The canal bridge they were crossing was crowded with people fighting their way through the snow to the town square for the festival. For a moment she found herself apologizing to a row of coat buttons. The she realized who it was.

The very person she'd been thinking of.

Fresh falls of snow had made the sky unnaturally dark. Some landed on the ropes of Matsuri lights strung along the streets, making fine fronds that glowed orange in the lantern light. Some dusted the magnificent ice sculptures on display at every street corner, sponsored by the major stores in town. Some fell into the canal and were quickly swallowed.

She felt just as aimless as the snowflakes drifting down. Squashed up against the bridge parapet, she couldn't decide what to do next. Tanka was waving a pink glove from the far side of the canal and yelling, "Aren't you coming with us?" On the other hand, Harpo Challis was conveniently right in front of her. Just the person to interrogate.

"Hang on a mo," she called to her sister. "I've just got to . . . do something."

Harpo stared down at Kat, uncertain whether to stay or go. He'd taken unusual trouble getting ready for the Matsuri, choosing clothes that didn't clash as horribly as usual and hiding his favorite blue check shirt under a fairly respectable fleece. Not exactly owning a comb, he'd done his best to flatten his hair with his fingers. When that didn't work, he'd admitted defeat and squashed it under a hat. Now here he was, colliding with the very girl he'd spent all night and morning not thinking about.

"Kat. What's up? You look awful. I mean, you look lovely, I mean, not lovely, well, not *not* lovely, but . . . are you okay?"

"Kind of. Are you doing anything?"

"Heading off to the Matsuri like the rest of the world. Got some rockets to set off."

A snowball came zooming through the air with frightening accuracy. Kat brushed snow off her face. Tanka whooped.

"On target! Hey—meet you at the square, Kat! Don't get savaged by mad Galrezi girls—ow!" She was reduced to squealing as Aran E squashed a large handful of snow down her neck.

Harpo heard Tanka and his smile died as soon as it was born. Just when he thought it was safe to talk to Kat he got reminded of what she was— Atsumisi, and proud of it. His mum always said not to be prejudiced, and with an Atsumisi dad, how could he be? Only Kat and Tanka were foreigners, grown up in the cities where gene-clan discrimination was so much a part of life people barely noticed it anymore.

"What does she mean, mad *Galrezi* girls?" he asked gruffly.

"The worker from Linveki Hydro. We just thought—you won't have heard. . . ."

Quickly and quietly Kat told him about the attack on K Rahbin. "Not that anyone knows who did it, only you're not exactly crawling with criminals out here on the Frontier so, putting two and two together . . ."

"You figured it had to be a Galrezi, because you consider them scum, right?"

"No! It's not like that. I know what you're thinking!"

Harpo blinked. Did she? He hoped not, since at that very moment he was staring at a trickle of melted snow running down Kat's throat and thinking how pretty her hair was, with its streaks of caramel in chocolate.

"You're thinking we're racist, just because we come from the cities. Not everyone's like that."

Okay, that *was* also what he'd been thinking, and it was no use pretending otherwise. Genes just seemed to get in the way of everything.

"Your sister is pretty down on Galrezi."

Because of the crowds all heading into the town square, Kat squeezed a bit closer to Harpo. He was so tall she had a ridiculous feeling of being safe, even though he was glaring down at her. "Tanka's already threatened to kill me if I told anyone, but you might as well know, our parents are . . . *were* . . . Galrezi, both of them. You can probably guess what happened to them in the war. It was bad, and it's why Tanka gets a bit screwy on the subject. She's still upset."

*We both are. Pretending we don't really remember the day we ran from Security, knocking on every door we could find, Mum and Dad begging to be let in, to be hidden away.*

"Please don't go thinking we're horrible because we're Atsumisi. We can't help it, and you don't know what it was like with General Insidian telling everyone to forget the past and get on with the future."

She looked up. Harpo's frown had deepened, but it was more from sympathy than mistrust.

"Jeez, I'm sorry, I didn't know. I shouldn't have said anything about it."

"Yes you should! I'm getting fed up with people not saying anything when there's obviously stuff to talk about! Like why didn't anyone tell us there'd been murders at Cherry Heaven? I only just found out about the Papillon family, and everyone let us move in there as if it was a completely lovely place."

"It *is*. . . ."

"And there's all the drama about Oklear Foster. When I tried to look him up on the net most of the files were restricted or corrupted—loads of information chewed up by some kind of virus."

"That's nothing sinister. Just a glitch."

"And this girl from the factory? Is she a glitch too? Is she going to turn out to be some kind of psychopath who goes around attacking perfectly innocent people, because if she is, I don't want to live here anymore! It's not the New Frontier, it's a complete *mush-up*!"

*Breathe, girl, breathe. Hey—Tanka would be proud of me. I think that was what's known as having a rant. Must try it more often. It wasn't so bad—quite fun, in fact. I don't feel too doopish, and Harpo's not exactly looking at me like I'm from another planet.*

Harpo had to laugh. "Not afraid to speak your mind, are you?"

*Afraid?* Kat thought of her sister fearlessly throwing herself into life, while she could only watch and worry. "I guess things are just getting to me."

"I'm not surprised. And Rahbin's really been blinded?"

"Both eyes smeared with some kind of antibac."

"She's allergic to it."

"Right."

"Was she robbed or anything?"

Kat shook her head—making more snow scatter onto her shoulders. "It's very personal, going for someone's eyes. And it happened at Rahbin's apartment, which is specific, too. Maybe the attack wasn't so random after all. They say psychopaths have their own twisted logic for each attack, like O Foster going after Galrezi. Except K Rahbin's Mazzini. Oh, and there's something else. She dropped this fossil when they brought her into the hospital. It looks like it's embedded in the same sort of weak shale I saw at Cluff Wood quarry. I noticed a streak quite low down on one of the slopes. I suppose most of it would've been blasted away to get at decent stone for cladding the dam. I don't know much about fossils but it does look kind of claw shaped. Some kind of giant tarsal?"

Harpo whistled—surprisingly well. "Must've been a real monster to have a toe this size! Nothing like this has been found on the Frontier. Rahbin's always been a bit of a nut for paleontology, wanting to turn up a real-life dinosaur like the ones they had on Earth. D'you reckon she was attacked because she'd finally found one? I can't imagine her getting slathered in antibac by some jealous fossil hunter."

"I don't know! It's all mad. And you aren't supposed to have *any* crime out here on the Frontier. I read that even O Foster kept saying he was innocent, right till they plugged him into the brain drain." She shuddered at the thought of anyone messing with her mind.

"Innocent?" Harpo snorted. "They found him with a gun that matched ballistics from the murders, a list of potential suspects, and yeah, that handy *ooh I've been framed* defense at the ready. Doesn't sound too innocent to me."

Harpo did his best to keep his voice steady. He wasn't being objective, and he knew it. Kat had a bad habit of bringing up the terrible events from ten years before, when all he wanted to do was forget that day in the snow—the gunshots, the blacklings flapping up out of the treetops, running down the orchard path so fast he thought his lungs would burst. Had it been so wrong to run away? Yes. He should have stayed. Should have looked. Maybe he could have done something, saved someone. Even though he was only six years old and a shrimp when it happened.

"Don't talk like it was your fault," his dad had said, some time after the shootings. "There was nothing you could have done. You called me, I came, that was the best thing. No medic in the world was going to bring them back to life."

Even so . . .

"It was going to be such a fantastic day," he said slowly, forgetting where he was and even who he was talking to. Snow fell on his face and he didn't brush it off. "Luka's birthday. Seven years old. Jeez—only seven! We were all in town for these *shitzer* hand stamps, but after that there was going to be a party at Heaven. Aran got a call from his dad, telling him to go home straightaway—parents went mental worrying about the sniper—but after the call Aran said no way he was missing the party. In the end there wasn't one. Foster was waiting for the Papillon girls in the orchard. They were cremated, Foster arrested, end of story."

Kat meant to say something sympathetic, at least show how shocked she was to hear his quiet words. Instead she stared into space, turning the fossil over and over in her gloved hand.

*Something doesn't make sense, doesn't work, isn't logical. Something Harpo just said. Why's it bugging me?*

There was no time to chase the thought down.

A wiry little man came tumbling onto the bridge, one hand clutching a sheet of plastic paper, the other hanging limply at his side. He skidded suddenly and thudded into Kat, knocking the fossil out of her hand as she struggled to keep her balance. The fossil fell down into the canal, making ripples in the dark water. Harpo grabbed Kat to stop her going the same way.

"Where is she? Did she come over here? Did you see her?" The man was so angry his words were mixed with flecks of spit. It was J Reak, the roast-nut seller.

"What do you want?" Harpo said, pushing just a little way in front of Kat. He kept his voice polite, in the usual neighborly way of Meander people.

Reak thrust the paper at them. It was one of the posters showing the escaped Hydro worker. HAVE YOU SEEN THIS CRIMINAL?

"Bitch pushed me over and bit me—*bit* me!" They could both see a pattern of bloody tooth prints coloring Reak's silver/green Galrezi ID. "Now I've damn well twisted my ankle, too. Scum!"

Harpo C swallowed. "I'll call Security. . . ."

"She got away but she's got to be hiding here somewhere."

Kat was already scanning the street, seeing psychos behind every snowdrift. "Look, Security's here now. . . ."

A tall man in uniform followed Reak onto the bridge, crunching the snow in his black boots. Kat was amazed to see that he carried a gun. She was even more amazed when Harpo C stiffened at her side.

"Dad!"

*Dad?*

"Harpo! Nice surprise."

"I thought you were still in Santanna."

"Special project down here in Meander. I've been looking for you."

"Sweet," sneered Reak. "How about first of all we deal with the small matter of an innocent citizen being viciously assaulted?" He looked up at the Security officer with all the indignation a short man can muster.

Harpo's dad dutifully examined the printout picture of the missing Hydro worker then entered J Reak's statement on to his e-pad. "Believe me, I'm treating this whole case very seriously," he said. "I have been for some time now. Now, why don't you leave me to continue making inquiries while you get your injuries seen to? Can you make it unaided to the hospital?" For a man with a mild manner, Kat noticed that he held a surprising store of authority.

"*If* I haven't broken something I could *maybe* limp along. You find that girl, Officer. Savage, she is. Mad savage."

Still scowling, Reak walked back over the bridge, forgetting which foot he was supposed to be limping on.

Kat sighed. *One more thing to worry about.*

More than a little embarrassed, Harpo did the introductions. "Kat, this is Federic Challis. Dad, this is Kataka Jones."

"Pleasure to meet you, Kataka J" Challis slung his gun onto his shoulder and pulled off one black glove to shake her hand . . . and show her his red Atsumisi stamp. "I believe it was your parent I spoke to earlier today."

"Foster parent."

"Yes."

"You asked my Aunt Milli if she'd seen anyone in the orchard, didn't you?"

"Just routine questions. I've been working at the Linveki factory in Santanna. It's my job to track the missing girl down. It's very important I find her soon—the weather's only getting worse and she can't survive long on her own. If you do see any sign of her, call me personally. Here's my *e.f.* contact."

"Sure," said Kat. At the same time, the thought niggled: *Why's he so insistent that we call him and no one else?*

F Challis pulled his glove back on. "Harpo— sorry I haven't been in town for a while, but your mother and I need a word with you. Soon."

"I swung by the store a couple of minutes ago," Harpo said. "Clariss told me Mum's lying low with a headache or something. I'm off to the Matsuri now."

"It's important. . . ."

Harpo was very conscious of Kat standing next to him. She was important, too. As if on cue a massive spray of red sparks catapulted into the darkening sky and the sound of cheering echoed from the main square.

"They're starting already, Dad."

"Fine. I'll see you after the fireworks." F Challis turned to go . . . and turned back again.

"Kataka J, one more thing. You might want to be extra careful walking home tonight. Make sure you all go together. Keep alert. You, ah, haven't seen the Galrezi girl around the old cherry orchard, have you?"

"No. Why would I?"

"No reason."

*No reason.*

Kat didn't believe in "no reason." She knew every action had cause and effect, like ripples from a rock falling in still water.

Somewhat subdued, she and Harpo trekked along to the town square, where a massive bonfire burned, meters high, too hot to look at for long. More fireworks colored the sky, brief illuminations in the darkness. They were, of course, sponsored by the O-HA, and the great Q Essnid himself was rumored to be at the square. People surged forward to meet him, on the far side of the bonfire.

Kat held back, suddenly shy at arriving with a boy.

Harpo made a beeline for the donut stand. "Not as nice as Mum's," he said, coming away with a bagful. "Ginger and sugar. Want one?"

"One? Three, at least!"

The smell was delicious and the taste even better.

"Mmm. Isn't that your sister?" Harpo C gulped his second donut down. "Looks like Aran's introducing her to his dad."

Kat quickly brushed sugar off her coat and looked over at the far side of the bonfire. Her view was distorted by a heat-haze rising. At first, she had the confused idea that *two* men were circling the fire, one a misshapen shadow, one half lit by sparks as bright as the gold on his fingers. Then the image merged and Quinn Essnid appeared properly. His progress was slow as he said hello to everybody, shook everyone's hand.

There he was, the man himself. His smile was genuine, his eyes were kind. He looked relaxed and confident—the sort of guy people loved to be around.

Kat was mesmerized, like everyone else. *Taller than I expected, athletic, too. What should I say to him when he gets here? What if I muff it up and say something completely inane and he laughs, and everyone at the Matsuri laughs and I want to shrivel up and die?*

Suddenly wishing she'd downed a whole box of Tanka's chill pills, she glanced at Harpo C, to see if he was nervous, too. Not at all. He wasn't taking the slightest notice of Q Essnid. His face was skyward, watching the fireworks. Kat smiled to see him being happy.

He noticed her smile just as a firefall rocket filled the sky with magic. That did it. In a moment of madness he took one look at her lips and leaned forward to lick the donut sugar off. The lick became a kiss, a good, long kiss, and somehow Kat ended up kissing him back.

If Harpo wrapped his arms around her, it was purely to steady himself in the crowds of people. If Kat shivered, it was probably from the cold. If Harpo pressed even closer, it was almost certainly to keep her warm.

Q Essnid walked by unnoticed and everything was sweet.

## Found

sweet's nice. sweet's trickling down my throat
each time i gulp from the hot cup. fingers are on
fire just holding it—they've forgotten how to
hold anything but cold.

   *take it easy*, says the voice at my side, soft
and warm like a favorite towel. *don't drink too
much at once.*

   gently, gently she eases the empty cup from
my hands. everything is quiet and dreamy—
clouds of steam rising around, my breaths in
and out, the sound of bathwater running as she
helps me onto the wooden bench in the shower.
*we'll get you cleaned up before you go in the
bath—there's more dirt on you than flesh*, she
complains softly. i just sit there looking down at
the toggles on my stolen jacket. my hands seem
a long way away and i can't make them move.
*shall i help?* she whispers.

help? does she know how magic those words are? gently, gently she takes off the layers, folding them neatly and putting them on a stool beside me. she's about to take off my shoes when she realizes i don't have any. my white Hygie socks have long since worn away to scraps. *your poor feet!* i can tell she's counting the bruises and bashes all over my body, still visible through my Factory shift.

*it's all right. i put Stingo on all the cuts and i heal real quick.*

somehow this doesn't cheer her up as much as i thought. can't she see i'm not sick? i'm lean, strong, and surviving! i'm a stray cat come in from the cold. if i *could* purr i *would* purr.

holding the showerhead, she runs some water. *just lukewarm to start,* she says.

i smile. just *Luka* warm!

gently, gently the water runs over my feet, and bits of dirt run down the plug hole. my skin goes from bluey brown to pinky white and i can wiggle my toes again without them feeling like they'll crack off. she lifts the shower higher and heats the water some more, it glide-slides over my shoulders, running in rivers around the scabs and scars. i still can't seem to move, so she sets the water up high and i just sit underneath—oh warm! it's so beautiful. there's nothing so wonderful in the world as this easy waterfall. when i breathe it's like i've never breathed before, and when i close my eyes, it's like my skin's being kissed all over.

there's a snap of plastic and a sudden scent. *shampoo*, she says. *it's very mild.*

mild—smiled! the smell is so delicious i'd like to swim in it or swallow it.

gently, gently she rubs some of this heaven on to my head till i'm all soft with bubbles. *mind your eyes*, she says, just like Mama used to say. i can't speak. i'm afraid that one single sound will break the spell and magic me back to Meander's cold streets again. but . . . *don't take those!* the words break out of my cracked lips and i grab the woman's arm to stop her leaving with my things. i don't have much and i need all the not-a-lot i've got. i need the stole-stuff more than the real owners do, and there are still things tucked away in secret, oh yes, little things and big secrets!

*we'll not worry about washing these yet, then,* she says, her top lip curling at my clothes. they are gray and horrible next to her fuzzy pink sweater. *i'm going to get you some more food,* she adds. *lock the door if you want, while you're bathing. and call me if there's anything you'd like, Luka, anything at all.* my eyes go wide like two full moons. my fingers shake as i make letters on her palm—L-U-K-A. she knows my name! she hasn't forgotten who i am!

off she goes to make more cherry malloey. once done in the shower i'm ready to get naked and enjoy the big bath in a way that no one normal can ever understand. as i sink underwater it's like i've been given everything wonderful just when i expected the very worst. it's still hard to believe that Harpo's mama had me, grabbed me, and gave me a place to hide, murmuring, *i'll keep you safe till we can sort things out.* she pulled me into the back of her shop and up some stairs.

what i want to know is, how come some people are sweet and some are sour? how come J Reak ratted on me and J Challis helped? i reckon people are like fruit—the ripe ones taste best and the bitter ones need to mature some more. i need . . . oh, i need nothing more than what i have now. thank you thank you thank you thank you thank you thank you thank you!

first, warm water Bliss, then warm room snugness, sipping sweet in a mug, eating sweet off a plate. it's coffee—real coffee in a proper cup, not tuff-stuff plastic—and donuts—fresh ginger donuts! *plenty more where they came from,* Harpo's mama said. good. maybe she'll let me stay here for a bit. hopefully—full of hope—full of ginger donut! ginger donuts are both warm and nice. when you eat them you get crumbs on your lap and your fingers go sticky. i eat them alone cos the bringer of ginger's brung ginger and gone.

i like it here. it reminds me of somewhere else. there's a little table in the middle of the room, low to the ground. you sit with your legs under the thick cloth covering the table because there's a heater underneath and it keeps you toasty warm. there's a board on top of the cloth and that's got a bowl of fruit on it (three apples and a bunch of redberries), also two magazines with curled-up corners, three empty packets of snax, one mug of tea (old), and one mug of coffee (new), a photo of a boy with red hair, a pile of plastic tokens, two pens, one pencil, one e.f., and lots of brainy-looking homework notes—I can't see how many to count them. the reason this room reminds me of someplace else is because i've seen most of this stuff before, in a different house. that house was in the valley, near the river, not far from my cherries. have you guessed? do you know who the boy in the photo is? it's my friend Harpo C! he's bigger than he used to be, though small in the photo, of course. i didn't know he'd moved out of the valley into town, though i guess he had to when Bossman's dam was done and the houses were flooded. somehow it feels right that i'm

here. it's everything Factory isn't—warm, color-
ful, messy, and safe. but is it safe? is anywhere
safe while Director's still searching and
Bossman's still the badman? Harpo's mama had
to go downstairs again, into the shop. she's
nice—doesn't throw stones at me or call me
mad. she put her warm hands on both sides of
my face, and when she said, *poor Luka Papillon,
we all thought you were dead*, she was crying.
she comes back upstairs with a real eye-smile,
then she sits down on a cushion beside me and
holds my hand, the horrible hand. *who did this
to you? who ingodsname did this?*

   *oh i did this*, i say cheerfully. *i had to burn off
the green Galrezi-scum square when i sneaked
out of Factory. it was the only way to get past
the alarm scanners, you know. Security never
spotted me.*

   she's really good at swearing. she says a
whole load of words i never heard even at
Quarry, well, not that often at least. she's making her mind up what to do, i can tell. i'd like to
ask her if Security are going to come and get

me, but there isn't a chance. she says, you can't stay here in case someone sees you, but i'll make a snug hideaway in the storeroom, so you'll be safe. first we'll get you some clean clothes. Harpo won't mind lending you some. you remember Harpo, don't you?

i stare at her in amazement. remember him?! i can't wait to see him again for real, especially now i smell nice, not of Stingo.

Harpo's room is even messier now than it used to be. there are clothes all over the floor, and on the bed the blankets are jumbled up with books and bits of computer. on the desk by the skylight there's something i always wanted—a microscope. they can show you all those magical things our eyes aren't strong enough to see, like patterns on spider-silk or the million mirrors of a bug eye. there are shelves around the room, but they're not like the ones in Factory, filled with boxes and bottles and tubes of Stingo. Harpo's shelves are loaded with rocks. i learned enough from Blue Capo to know what sort they are. one fossil becano bug is in a top spot, on show—don't know why, doesn't look anything special to me. next there are lines of glass jars with leaves in and living becanos, busy doing whatever they do. another jar has a single stick of cherry tree, no blossom. dangling off the stick is a little white bag shape, like ones i've seen a million times before, hanging off the twigs in my cherry orchard. it's a papillon bag, called a pupa. in spring the papillon chews the pupa till it's out in the sunshine along with hundreds of others. they spread their wings and dry them and fly away. papillons love cherry trees. so do i—can hardly wait to have cherries. my mouth goes juicy at the thought of it. mind you, before i leave the room i plan to open the lid on the jar so the papillon can fly out when it's spring. you shouldn't keep things locked up. it's not nice.

i tell you what else isn't nice: while Harpo's mama digs in drawers for clothes, i suddenly look in a mirror and think, WHO IN SHITZERVILLE IS THIS SCABBY TABBY LOOKING BACK AT ME? no way is that me! no way do i look like that! i can't believe i really look like that—all scabs and scars and dark eyes. i touch the mirror. i'm as tall as the Hikori and Mai marks on the bedroom door frame back at home. even Factory couldn't stop me growing; only being dead can stop you doing that, which means i have a pretty unfair advantage over Hikori and Mai, because i'm not dead, even if everyone thought i was. huh. i still look like a dead girl standing. nothing pretty to see here. wait, though . . . what was it Gim Damson once said? he said, *look at the rocks, Luka girl, all rough and ragged and dull. just watch what happens when I chip a bit away* . . . then he chip chip chipped a bit away to show a sparkle inside, where you'd never think it would be. could i chip chip chip away at me and be pretty again?

# STARFALL I

The evening sky looked granite hard and cold, chipped with pinpoints of starlight. The Blue Mountains were a remote, sharp white and the reservoir was black. It was strange to be standing at Q Essnid's villa on the far side of the water, looking back at Cherry Heaven. Against all logic, Kat found herself staring across the darkness to see if any movement disturbed the snowy orchard. Nothing. By unspoken agreement both she and Aunt Millijue had made sure that all doors and windows were securely locked before leaving the house silent, and they'd both checked for fresh footprints in the yard. Again, nothing, just their own tracks and virgin snow.

It was achingly cold. Aran E had come to collect them for the party, skillfully steering his boat through sheets of ice that were hardening all around the edge of the lake. Kat hated every moment of the journey. The only thing that took her mind off the dark chill of the drowned village was the remembrance of ginger donuts. She licked her lips, still tasting sugar.

Now they were braced to enter Top Class society in the New Frontier. Aran E held open the front doors of the Essnid villa, a serene two-story building some way up from the shore. Prester and Millijue went forward as a team. Their usual dislike of parties was balanced by an immense sense of pride at getting an invitation. Already other guests were appearing, bright, jeweled, and excited. Some had come by sleigh from Meander, others had private boats to fetch them from fine houses in the Blue Mountain foothills. Kat hung back. The only reason she'd agreed to come was because she was afraid to stay alone at Cherry Heaven. Tanka, looking luminous in a wild turquoise outfit, suffered no such hesitation.

"I didn't spend three hours getting ready just to turn blue from the cold. Come on in, Kat, what's the worst that could happen?"

"Er, I have to talk to people I don't know?"

"You'll be fine."

"I'll curl up and die."

"Look, I'm on meds for this cold thing, so you might as well have these." Tanka fumbled in a pocket and pulled out a packet of peps. "One should do the trick—you'll be an instant worry-free zone."

"I don't think—"

"Good plan: *don't think*. Enjoy! And we *will* know people. There's Aran and Prester and Milli. Too bad your ginger boy won't be coming."

"He won't? I mean, *so?*"

"Want to know why not?" Tanka distracted Kat long enough to get her into the hall, where discreet staff took their coats and directed them toward the main reception rooms, which were dazzling with

Matsuri decorations of the very best quality.

"Maybe he had too much schoolwork? He's helping with this really neat project to do with audiovisuals at the rally. The INTENS thing."

Tanka rolled her eyes. "Are you the only person on the planet who doesn't know that the Challis family are totally troublemakers? Why would Essnid invite anyone who doesn't rate the O-HA? Aran won't even talk to Harpo C if he can help it. I've seen them go totally *blank* if they ever meet at school. And personally, I think Harpo did pretty well to survive your clinch at the Matsuri, considering what happened to the last boy who tried to kiss you. . . ."

Aran E chose the worst possible moment to listen in. "What boy?"

"Get this—a guy called Rudi G went to perform tonsil gym on Kat and she stabbed him in the leg with her pen and threatened to pee in his pool if he ever tried it again."

"I was only little!" Kat complained.

"Last year," Tanka smirked to Aran. "Now, how about I get an exclusive tour of your home, gorgeous?"

"Happy to oblige. Coming, Kat?"

Aran's smile was wide but Kat sensed something forced about it. Instead of being more relaxed on home turf, he was strangely tense. She wondered if there was any truth in Tanka's comments about Aran and his dad not getting on well.

She let them go off into the music. *I'm a sensible, intelligent, capable girl, so why can't I just relax and enjoy myself like Tanka says? Why am I always worrying . . . noticing things? How about I just slink into a dark corner and hide for the rest of the night? No one'll mind I'm not around.*

Too late. Uncle Prester's voice drifted in from the next room. "My other girl? She's here somewhere. Yes, yes, got all the brains in the family—oh, you're too kind, but really, Kataka J's the genius, not me. All sorts of bright ideas . . . ask her!"

Alarmed that someone could be about to pounce on her, Kat tore the silver pill foil.

*One should do, enough to take the edge off things. It's only a party, after all, just a ritual gathering of humans in pleasant surroundings, nothing anyone logical could get worried about. Maybe two peps— two for good luck.*

She backed away into a quiet garden room running the length of the villa. Subtle lighting picked out charming architectural details, like the papillon patterns worked into the sandy grain of the stonework. It was yet another building designed by Celia Papillon. It seemed ironic that everywhere she went on the Frontier there was a reminder of the family from Cherry Heaven ... and what Oklear Foster did to them.

*Just one more pep. Three's a nice round number. They're mostly sugar anyway.*

The wall facing the lake was made entirely of glass, the roof also. Because the lights were so low, the constellations still showed quite clearly and Kat could just about make out her lucky star, impossibly far away. Letting the peps dissolve on her tongue, she closed her eyes and made a wish—for everything to be all right again.

*Bit of a tall order, I know*, she murmured to the star, turning slowly around, brushing her fingers against the blooms of expensive hothouse plants and growing dizzy on the scents. When she opened her eyes again she was facing a display of photographs, most showing Aran and his father doing various vigorous sports, or posing alongside famous colony landmarks. They seemed to have met every VIP in the cities. Kat recognized the actor Zee Homarlo, and a pose with the late General Insidian himself. She stopped to look at one photo in particular, a scene from the Frontier heartland. Q Essnid and his son were part of a line of trekkers, all with hunting guns slung comfortably across their backs. Kat was vaguely aware she ought to feel worried by guns, especially after seeing Harpo's dad handle one so casually . . . only she wasn't. While part of her brain began to purr, another part seemed to detach itself and float over the worry, analyzing it with vague amusement.

*Guns kill people*, she thought. *Was that how Aran E got his scar? No. A bullet wouldn't follow the contours of a face like that. It's more like . . . more like . . . more like . . . whiplash, like the cut on my hand from those trees at Cherry Heaven.*

The photo began to move. Startled, Kat stepped back, hoping this wasn't one of the pep side effects, and if it was, that it would stop *immediately*. Q Essnid's face seemed to have expanded until it filled the whole photo frame. For a second there were two Essnids—one in the picture and one reflected in the glass. She gasped and turned around.

There he was in person. Smiling and stunning.

"Kataka Jones, I presume? I'm Quinn Essnid."

He held out a hand. In a dream, Kat watched her own hand grasp his. His rings were cold to the touch. "I was worried there'd be too much ice on the lake for Aran to get the boat over. Such a fine night, though, don't you think? Perfect for star-gazing. It almost makes me wish the colony didn't have a ban on powered flight—imagine soaring over such scenery! Still, keeping the planet clean comes at a price, as do most things."

"A price worth paying," Kat said, the words tasting fizzy on her tongue.

"Oh yes," he answered slowly. "You'd be amazed how hard it is for most people to appreciate that."

Something about his words made her uneasy, but Essnid quickly smiled and moved on.

"Now I know this is meant to be a social gathering, but there's something I need to talk to you about. Can we have a chat when you've got a moment . . . ?"

Kat could only nod.

He wasn't the sort of man you could refuse, not even when he gestured toward the party and said, "Shall we . . . ?"

"There you are!" Tanka found Kat wandering in a happy daze. "You've got to come and meet the guest of honor—his family are so-o-o big in City Five. Hey, are you okay? Oh, I get it—you've had a little *sparkle* to get the party going, right? Good for you."

The guest of honor—Ant Linveki—was already in the water, soaked in both senses of the word. He lounged at the far end of the fabulous Essnid pool with a bottle of wine in one hand and a plate of cimarron sweets close by. When he saw the sisters approach he submerged briefly then rose again. Water ran in rivulets over a gold neck chain embossed with diamonds that flashed his initials: A. L. He was very well groomed. His nails were buffed and clippered to perfection.

"And I thought the party was going to be dull," he began, sending Tanka and Kat a perfect white smile. "I'm Ant Linveki."

"I'm Tanka Jones, hello!"

"Pleasure to meet you," he replied. "And you are . . . ?"

"Kataka Jones. Don't you work at the factory where they bottle Blue Mountain?"

"I *own* the factory, yes—I'm the director. Actually, we've filled this lovely pool with Blue Mountain water tonight, just to swim in." He spread his arms out suggestively.

Tanka's eyes widened. "Has anyone claimed the Zee Homarlo prize yet?"

"Aha! Yet another fan of the movie man. I'm afraid everyone will have to wait a couple more days for the competition results—I can't be giving away any secrets now! You know, Tanka J, you remind me of someone I dated back in high school. Someone pretty, of course. A real cutie."

"You know what you remind me of?" Kat said bluntly, oblivious to manners and modesty now that the peps had taken hold of her. "There was this fair that used to come to City Five. Tanka had a huge crush on this slimy lad who took tickets for the wave-rider roller-coaster—remember, Tank?"

"*No.*"

"Sure you do! The one you were sick all over when the ride stopped." Some sort of explanation seemed necessary, since Linveki was frowning and other guests had gathered around to listen. "This guy went strutting around like he was something special, with his shirt open and his sarong all low slung, except his teeth were brown and he'd got that, you know, receding hairline thing, and he was *way* on the wrong side of young, still grinning at all the girls and thinking he was A-one supremo, not some slimy wannabe. Hey, Tank, we don't have to leave! I'm enjoying myself."

Tanka dragged her sister away to the pool

changing rooms and savagely set out their swimming things. "Are you out of your mind? How many pills did you take?"

"One. Two."

"Just two? Huh. I guess they're more powerful if you're not used to them."

"Three, four . . ." Kat started counting on her fingers.

"Kat, this isn't just a gang of kids having fun. This is a really important party. Jeez—Q Essnid's party! I thought you'd want to impress him, since he's into all that science stuff like you. Don't screw up on the big night."

"Essnid's smart," said Kat serenely. "You worry too much. Um, five, maybe six? Definitely not more than six. Or seven."

"Seven?! You're on your own from now on, kiddo. I can't bear to watch you acting like a complete doop."

"Acting like a complete *you*, more like."

"Fine," Tanka snapped. "Be like me, but don't expect me to go all stuffy like you. Remember the peps can wear off pretty quickly, sugar—crash—and—burn!"

"It's not the peps," said Kat happily. "I wished on a lucky star."

"Good. Now wish on the whole fricking universe of them that Ant Linveki will accept your apology."

"My what?"

"*Apology*. Put your swimsuit on and get groveling!"

Of course, everyone wanted to swim. The Essnid pool was magnificent, surrounded on all sides by glass and topped by the classic Papillon carved ceiling. There was an outstanding subaqua sound system and a marvelously well-stocked bar. Sleek underwater in her best swimsuit, Kat felt the Bliss like never before. She only surfaced because, amusingly, Tanka was quite serious about the whole apology thing, Aran E, too.

"Just for my father's sake," he said, acutely embarrassed for himself and Kat. "He has this big party every year and it means a lot to him. When he was younger, people didn't take him so seriously—not till the success of the O-HA."

"You're pretty loyal to Daddy," Kat said.

Aran looked horrified. "I'm not! I mean, yes, except . . ." Then he actually blushed.

"Don't you think Linveki's a complete mushhead?"

"Well, yeah, but you can't go around saying it—even on peps!"

"There's too much people don't say around here," Kat insisted stubbornly. "Keeping your secrets snug. You think I don't notice? I do. Okay, okay, don't look so panicky. I'll play nicely. Say, Tank, you haven't any more, have you? I feel fantastic."

"*No!*"

Linveki was surrounded by quite a crowd in the water. They were, inevitably, talking about the brilliant Matsuri celebrations, and about the spectacular show Q Essnid had planned for the O-HA rally, set to take place two days on. He was very excited about the fact that he would be hosting it from the top of Meander dam, saying, "It's been ten years since the O-HA started and foundations were begun for the dam. I think we can be excused a special celebration . . . something the Frontier's never seen before!"

"Wouldn't miss it for the world!" said Ant Linveki.

"Will it be safe?" asked an attractive woman at his side. "I heard about the attack on that professor yesterday."

"Shocking news," agreed Essnid. "Kristie Rahbin will be blind for life—I've never seen an allergic reaction like it."

"Nasty stuff, that antibac," said Linveki helpfully. "Expensive too. We get through vat fulls of it up at Santanna, and the multi-boxes don't come cheap. I tell you, it's a nightmare trying to educate the workers about the importance of absolute hygiene."

His companion nodded sympathetically. She was a stylish older woman with straw-blond hair and enough money of her own to impress even a member of the rich Linveki family.

"You've no idea how much stress the girls cause me." Linveki yawned, looking up at her through long, darkened lashes. "They're so greedy and ungrateful. And then this shitzer girl—excuse my language—she goes soft in the head and somehow gets past Security and out!"

"Who is she?"

"A pain in the ass! According to the file she's some leftover from the war years. Rumor among the factory girls has it she's called Lyka, Lurka,

Luka . . . something. A Galrezi, of course."

Q Essnid's eyes narrowed. "A Galrezi called Luka? You used to have a friend called Luka, didn't you, Aran? One of the Papillon family. Poor thing—they never found what Foster did with her body. What's your missing worker's family name, Linveki?"

"Couldn't tell you, never asked. None of the workers are family types, you should know. Gives me no end of trouble. Lost, they are, without me and my Supers to look out for them. Not too bright . . . know what I'm saying?" Looking over the water and seeing Kat, Linveki's bravado diminished.

"I'm surprised you managed to let her escape, and that you're far from finding her again." Essnid's criticism was gentle, but unmistakable. Then his frown vanished like a spent ripple. "The Hydro gives Galrezi a good, steady job in life. That's what the O-HA's all about, after all—*one people, one world.*"

"Yeah," said Ant Linveki abruptly. He didn't like

being blamed for anything. "Overseas in the cities they're not open-minded enough to employ the scummy little shitzers like we do! Maybe Oklear Foster had the right idea after all, putting them out of their misery—*bang, bang!*"

The pool water stilled and everyone went silent.

Even in her happy haze, Kat knew there was something seriously wrong. Linveki's friend opened her mouth to object, then took a drink instead. Q Essnid just sighed, as if he was so used to Linveki's idiotic outbursts it wasn't worth arguing, certainly not at a party. Aran E started to speak, but one look from his father stopped him. Kat calmly observed everything and thought she'd join in. Even she was surprised at the words which tumbled out.

"If your factory's such a fabulous place, how come a girl would rather run away and risk dying than work there?"

Then the words turned to bubbles as her despairing sister pulled her underwater.

## For You

my own bottle of Blue, bubbles and all.

wish Director could see me now, drinking it down
instead of watching it go past on the conveyor.
nothing as nice as real cherries, but good
enough for now. too bad Color Tech 26 can't be
here with me, she wouldn't mind being snook
away in a storeroom, not when there's warm
clothes and food. J Challis says i'll be secret
and safe here. yeah right. what does she know
about safe? there is no safe as long as
Director's around and the only secret Bossman
hasn't found out is that i'm still alive, and it's
only a matter of time before he knows I AM.

   can't say i'm happy to stay hidden, cos i haven't
done anything wrong, well, maybe one or two
things. Harpo's mama asked about someone called
Kristie Rahbin. i said, *who?* she said a woman got

blinded. *oh her,* i said. *she was blind already—couldn't see people, just green for Galrezi.*

all i can see now are boxes, walls, and shadows. it smells back here in the storeroom, of dried tea and plastic wrap, of sawdust and cherry bubbles. *want another drink?* J Challis asks. *redberry, blueberry, or greenberry flavor?*

no need to think about the answer, i just point to the picture on a bottle and wonder how Label-glue 11's getting on. wonder if other girls got punished instead of me. wonder if Director's busy at his big party. soon be time for mine.

*oh too bad, your bottle top's blank,* says Harpo's mama. *guess you didn't win that hot date with Zee Homarlo. my girl, Clariss, loves his movies, she goes all dreamy for him. not that she's got a hope in heaven of meeting him. funny what people set their hearts on, isn't it, when there isn't the slightest hope of it coming true?*

i tell her you've always got to keep hoping. she says there's hope, and there's being mush-headed.

*try another bottle,* i say, with a secret smile.

*you could get lucky. go on—try.*

she pretends not to get all excited, saying it's a load of hooey. *i'm just remembering what it was like to screw all those bottle tops on.* she closes her eyes to open the bottle, then sneeks a peek. of course, the next top's blank, too. i knew it would be, cos there's only one winner out of thousands—tens of thousands.

*what'd i tell you, honey? mush-headed. hey ho, the world keeps turning whether i want something or not. i'd best get back to the shop, help Clariss with stock-taking now we're shut for the night. not a peep from you, though—not when you've got half the Frontier looking for you.*

I ask, can't i peep if i see Harpo?

she thinks about it.

*Harpo's no idea you're still alive, honey. you know what he's like—doesn't see something unless it's on a slide under a microscope. i don't think anyone could recognize you from those posters the factory sent out.*

you did.

*ah, well, that's different. i notice things. i'll*

*check in on you in a while, love. remember, keep
ssssh, okay?*

wait! i grab her arm. i'm not done with giving
presents yet—hardly even started! i gave Packer
67 some soap, Color Tech 26 a nice lie, then Blue
Capo got some Stingo. now i've got a present for
J Challis because she's been nice, and Gim
Damson always said people get what they
deserve one way or another. Harpo's mama
deserves this. i fumble in my secret bundle of
Hygie suit to find it and press it into her hand—
it's small, round, and plastic. *this is for you.*

she starts to look. she stops to listen. someone's in the store, calling her name.

*hush!*

have they come for me? is he here? is Director
standing at the counter with that smile in his
mouth and that foul *hey cutie?* i crouch low and
spy through the door. no—not Director. first, all
i see is a pair of black boots. my stomach goes
upside down, thinking of boots crunching the
snow, squashing cherries flat. i'm feeling fear as
the gun whines ready for another shot. hearing

the cackling of blacklings up in the sky. . . .

these boots belong to a man in a gray uniform, a man i recognize—who could miss that
red hair? he grabs J Challis and squashes her in
a hug. they whisper, but i've got ears so sharp
they can hear the soft pad-pad of a Supervisor
sneaking up from several rooms away.

*you're back!* Harpo's mama says. *you look
frozen.*

*warmer for seeing you,* says Harpo's dad. *how
are you? did you look at the packet i left?*

*i haven't had chance to open it yet. come and
get near the heater, you're cold as ice.*

*no, i can't stop. i want to go back out for
another search before the next lot of snow
comes. They're predicting blizzards for the early
hours, something to spoil Essnid's party, maybe.*

*oh, come on, love, you've been out long enough
as it is!*

he blows on his hands and warms them at the
shop heater. his silver/red stamp shines.

*i've been all around the orchard,* he says. *there
are tracks, definitely, more like a man's been*

there, but no sign of the girl, and there's no way
she could survive in this, Jo, the snow's so deep.
we shouldn't have stopped looking for her before.
if i'd known she was still alive! it's just so incredible that she is . . . if you sure that's her in the
posters?

Jo says, oh, i'm sure. i had a funny feeling
about that face as soon as i saw it. it's Luka
Papillon all right. i haven't told anyone else yet,
especially not Harpo.

F Challis looks around the shop, blinking. i just
thought Foster must have buried her body, that
we'd find it in the thaw. that's the story we
heard and we all believed it! and she's been at
the factory all this time, practically under my
very nose, and i never knew!

J Challis puts her finger on her lips and looks
back at the storeroom.

you did what you could. the files are still
wrecked and Foster's equally useless in prison.
but listen, i'm trying to tell you: there's something i've got to show you. . . .

his eyes spark as she whispers in his ear.

*she's here? she's actually here? those black boots take a couple of steps toward the store-room door. so many years . . . so many years i've been wanting to sort this mess out, and she ends up hiding in your shop! well, Jo, best we get this over and done with—finish it once and for all. . . .*

# STARFALL II

*Best get this over and done with, before the humiliation kills me once and for all.*

More than ever Kat wished she could hide in the magic world of peps again, instead of making a crash landing into reality, just as Tanka had warned she would.

The middle of the night was past and most of the guests were mellow in the pool room. Bundled in a robe, she hovered at the edge of the bar, where Q Essnid was temporarily alone, staring at a white plate of cherries. When he bit into one he looked like a man tasting memories. Then he noticed Kat.

"All these years in the cryo-freeze and they taste as delicious as ever. The cherries from Heaven used to be legendary, you know."

"That's what people keep telling us. Look—I'm really sorry about . . . about how I was earlier. I'm not normally like that, and I shouldn't have been rude to your guest."

Essnid's voice was as calming as a whole packet full of peps, and it was only after he spoke that she realized he was being ironic. "Linveki's oversensitive to criticism. It comes of being so perfect, I suppose. Don't worry about it."

"You're not angry?"

"We all make mistakes. There are more important things I want to talk about." He didn't explain this straightaway. Instead he seemed preoccupied with his own train of thoughts. Eventually he set the cherry stone on the snowy white edge of the plate.

"I'm sorry you've had to find out about Oklear Foster. Your aunt told me. It must've been very upsetting. Perhaps I should have waited longer before renting out the orchard house. Somehow I thought ten years would be far enough in the past. After all, there does come a time when we have to leave old things behind when they weigh us down. Wouldn't you agree?"

Again Kat felt uneasy for some reason, but all she murmured was, "Forgive and forget, you mean?"

"Exactly. I'm glad you agree. We have to stay focused on what matters: the future. With this in mind, I've actually been waiting to speak with you ever since I read your online submission to *New Colonist*."

Kat's face glared pink. "You *read* that? It was just . . . I shouldn't have. I mean, it's a completely crazy idea."

"It's a completely brilliant idea," he said firmly. "I had to laugh when I finished it—here we are, with one of the best research centers on the planet, and we're still struggling to make communications even fifty percent reliable, then along comes a school student turning all our ideas on the head with a dazzling new theory."

"Not dazzling," Kat mumbled. "It's just perspective. My sister was bugging me about not being able to call her boyfriend, I mean, Aran, well, you probably know about that, and I thought there had to be a way to nullify the effects of the mont-halo ore."

"Exactly what we've been wishing for the past few decades."

"But then I thought, why not look at things a different way. Instead of working *against* the ore, why not try to harness the power of the very thing frustrating us? Those notes on the net are only preliminary . . . I need to do a more sophisticated analysis."

She became more confident as they discussed technicalities, then Essnid held up his hand.

"Enough for now—you've convinced me already! Look, I'm a big believer in promoting talent wherever I find it. When I first came to the Frontier I was flat broke and friendless, and *absolutely determined* to make something of myself. All this—this house, this pool, the O-HA, peace even—it's the result of my efforts. But I'm not so assured of my own brilliance I don't need to surround myself with all the best people. We're looking for bright students like you. Forget the past: you're the future. If you can overcome your sudden dislike of the Hydro director . . ."—here he smiled briefly—"I'm pleased to tell you Linveki Hydro Company would be interested in offering you a sponsorship to fund advanced tuition for the rest of your years at school. There'd be a job at the end of it. A very good job."

Kat nearly fell in the pool with surprise. "Linveki Hydro Company? You have to have a brain the size of a planet just to fill in the application forms for that setup!"

At this point Q Essnid laughed out loud. "I

don't think you quite realize the implications of your ideas about mont-halo ore. A flawless, reliable communications system is something we'd all appreciate. Don't worry, we'll get our money's worth out of you!"

"I'm not sure—"

"I am." He held her gaze with his own. "You're old enough to start getting ideas about the way the world works, to know it's a luxury to think there are no difficult choices, no hardships to face. God knows I've had a lot to fight against myself."

She saw he was stroking the silver/blue Mazzini stamp on his hand as he spoke, and wondered if he was conscious of the gesture. She was certainly aware of the fact that out of all the guests that night, there were few other Mazzini, and no Galrezi. She had a growing suspicion that Q Essnid knew perfectly well that he was richer and more respected than any Atsumisi on the Frontier ... and that this pleased him.

*Would I feel the same if I was Mazzini—wanting to prove that I was as good as the Atsumisi, and better than Galrezi?*

Q Essnid seemed to have read her mind. "Don't ever let other people tell you what you're supposed to be like, or what your limits are, Kataka J. I'm a big believer in people getting what they deserve one way or another, and you deserve to be the best you can be."

"It was just an idea I had. . . ."

"And this is just an invitation to try to make it work—with the full support of me, Linveki, and the O-HA. Think about it and call me . . . when you can get a signal!"

Essnid excused himself and went back to his other guests.

Kat took her robe off and sat on the edge of the pool, letting her mind go supernova as all the compliments sank in. Q Essnid was sensationally inspirational! In just five minutes he'd got her thinking that maybe—just maybe—wishing on a lucky star would work after all! With his support she could become whatever she wanted! Do anything! Forget ghosts and Galrezi girls: the New Frontier was a fabulous place after all!

She stayed in a dream until Aran E swam over and hauled himself onto the poolside next to her. He looked particularly sleek in his swim shorts, and she shivered, thinking of Harpo's sugary kisses by the bonfire. He also looked unusually nervous, like he had something bottled up inside.

"Dad didn't eat you alive and spit out the bones?"

"No. Not at all, he was great."

"Wow. That's a first—him being cool about criticism. Listen, there's something I need to talk to you about, actually a couple of things, while Tanka's not around. D'you want a drink?"

"Yeah, cherry Blue, please."

"Coming up."

She felt uncomfortable being so close, even

though the pool room was still full of other guests. She had a clear view of his scar.

". . . obviously I don't want Tanka to know," he was saying.

*Mush! I didn't hear a word he said. Act cool, Kat. Pretend to agree.*

Aran swallowed. "You seem pretty sound, and I reckon I can trust you to keep a secret. You see, I've been planning this for ages. . . ."

"Planning?"

"Yes."

"This?"

"Yes." He took another hasty gulp of water. "I, er, heard you and Harpo were . . . an item," he said, definitely not looking at her legs.

Kat scotched that rumor as quickly and convincingly as possible, then added, "You two aren't friends, are you?"

" 'Course we are! Not close, but friends. Always have been."

"I just wondered why he wasn't invited."

"No reason. Look, it's not just the Tanka thing I wanted to check with you. I'm supposed to be giving this speech at the rally, too, and you see, there was this other thing I've been wondering about, and maybe we could meet up. I need your opinion. . . ."

It was no good. She couldn't resist reaching out to touch his scar. "Go on, tell me where you got this. It's whiplash, isn't it? Some kind of tree branch?"

He sat like stone, not even moving when Tanka came padding around the pool. Still burning mad at Kat's irresponsible behavior, she'd been keeping her distance. Now she almost choked to see Aran and Kat so cozy together.

"Oh, I may be the thickie sister but I'm not so stupid I can't figure it out what's going on here."

Aran E jumped, then stupidly spouted the classic line, "It's not what you think. . . ."

"Oh, so you do concede I *can* think, after all?

Well, I *think* that's you and me finished, Aran Essnid! And as for you, Kat, maybe you're not brainy enough to work out he's only taking *pity* on you. Like we all do."

"No he wasn't!"

Kat suddenly felt horribly sick, another side-effect Tanka hadn't warned her about. Unfortunately, the nearest thing to grab to steady herself was Aran's bare leg. When he pulled away she slumped forward over the pool edge.

"Oh god." Tanka was there in an instant. "Don't you *dare* puke in the pool, Kat. Open your eyes—open them!" She snapped at Aran to fetch some more water then get lost, which he did, rigid with embarrassment and mute apologies. Luckily, most of the other guests were distracted by something going on outside the pool room, so Tanka could safely shake Kat without anyone noticing.

"You've been a total doop all night! Why'd you have to embarrass me like this?"

"Um, because I could?"

"*Because you could?* What sort of shitzer excuse is that?"

"The one you always use."

"Only when I'm stacked on peps . . ." Tanka started to say. "Oh, this stinks! You're already brainier and faster in the pool, and now you've started going after my boyfriend, too. Couldn't you just leave me one thing to be better at? *One thing?*"

"Ssh. My head hurts."

"Good. Drink this."

Kat took the fresh glass of Blue. As the nausea passed she became aware of a group of people clustered at the far side of the room, Ant Linveki among them. He hadn't bothered putting a robe on when he left the pool. Admiring his own reflected physique with wine in one hand and a woman in the other, he'd made a funny discovery.

"Hey, looks just like someone's been drawing on the windows," he burbled. "Might have a go myself—could be fun. Knew this would be a good party!"

Each and every pane of glass had been smeared in red paint.

Kat squinted.

*The letter* F, *backward. Some kind of Frontier joke?*

"*F* for what?" Linveki wondered.

"Filthy windows!" The woman laughed.

"Funny!" barked another guest.

*Smash!!* Linveki only just had time to duck as something came cracking clean through the glass. Kat didn't think twice. Like catching the weight in waterball, she was in the pool instantly, diving after the object. When she surfaced and gulped in lung-air, the other guests were shivering as snowflakes came blowing in. Shards of glass on the poolside showed that the writing wasn't done with red paint, but blood.

Linveki was stunned. "I nearly got hit! That

would've killed me! Call Essnid! I don't like parties where people get hit!"

Q Essnid pushed his way through the onlookers. Kat swam over to him. "This was thrown," she said shakily. "Actually, I think it must be for him. . . ."

Essnid examined the missile then passed it to Linveki.

It was a stone—possibly a quarry stone—and wrapped around it with tuff-tape was a simple, innocent object. A metal nail file. Just a nail file with the very same golden A. L. logo as the one patterning Linveki's neck chain.

"Well, happy birthday to me!" said Linveki with heavy sarcasm.

*So much for wishing on a star.*

## Frozen

only stars watch me throw that stone. to
everyone else i'm as see-through as the sky.
nobody invited *me* to the party, not even Aran
E. he's twice as tall as he used to be but not
twice as much my friend, not now he's got that
house, that pool, and fancy new people to play
with. whose side's he on anyway? friend or
phoney? that's what i've come to find out, to
see what he does when i show what i know. he
looks like his daddy. will he be like him too?

   time freezes. there's me, the ghost in the
glass, and there's everyone else on the warm
side of the windows. can you see who that is in
there? CAN YOU SEE WHO THAT IS? the bad
man. the worst man. the Bossman. the one i'm
come for. the man with a smile so wide people
trip up and fall right into it. forget putting out
stars—i want to PULL THE WHOLE SKY DOWN,

rip it to shreds, stamp the lights out one by one. you can't have me and *that man* alive in the world together! don't they know who he is? don't they know what he's done, those shiny party people who land on him like flies on bad meat? they can't know, or they wouldn't drink his water and swim in his pool. wouldn't, couldn't!

but why have one monster when you can have two? next thing i see is DIRECTOR rising out of the water, not on a platform shouting, not on Factory floor beating, here, in Aran's house, breathing, smiling. soon put an end to that—fill his smile with a stone—smash, bash, break the bone! arm back to throw, lips back to snarl, then *speed*—the stone cracks through the glass and . . .

i miss! how could i miss? he ducks, doesn't die. time to run, *run!* before Bossman bursts through the blizzard to grab me with his gold fingers. run hard, run fast. can't breathe, can't breathe, can't breathe, can't get my breath. nowhere i can run to fast enough away from Factory men. can't go back to Harpo's—he's not at home, but the man with the gun is. can't stay with Aran, not within a million miles of the other nastiness in that house, the house my mama made. i was there when she sent for workers, when they dug the first big hole for the pool, when gangers carried giant sheets of glass all the way along the path from Meander. yes, i was there when the pool was finished— me, Aran E, and Harpo C all lined up, hand in hand, one two three JUMP!

not jumping now. legs slowing, freezing from the toes up. what's the point of running? i had enough hate to throw harder than a million musclemen and i still missed. why did every punch of Director's hand smack in someone's face but i can't even send a stone straight? and if hate isn't enough to hurt him, how can i hope to bash Bossman—the man at the end of the Plan? so much for the Plan. the Plan's over, the Plan's dead, and i might as well be, buried in cold, closing my eyes, letting the snow kiss me good night, good riddance.

softly, softly, a whisper nestles in my ear.

*get up*, it says. *get up, get moving. head high,
have hope.*

is that Gim? Gim Damson?

*where are you?* i shout. he's nowhere, that's
where. it's just words on the wind. i remember
the day they took him from Quarry. it was
sunny. one single blue flower had made it
through the mud, showing spring was on its way.
i saw Blue Capo and shrank behind Gim, but it
wasn't me she was after, but him.

*you'll do,* she said. *the call's come in for help in
the heartland, special work you'll love so much
you won't ever want to leave. don't worry, pet,*
she sneered, seeing my face. *maybe he'll send
you a postcard, if he can be bothered.*

*head high, have hope,* he said as they pulled
him away, but i'd already seen that blue flower
squashed under Capo's boots and i knew there
wouldn't be any postcards or any more Gim D.

one set of whispers fades, then new voices fall
through the air.

*get up,* says Packer 67.

*get up,* says Color Tech 26. *you're not finished*

*yet. we can't do it, you have to do it for us.*

*i can't! i missed. couldn't kill him.*

the voices won't take no for an answer.

*who wants Director dead anyway? killing's too quick, too easy. he deserves worse than that, and he'll get it, if you get moving.* i start stumbling about again, blind until three red lights from the big dam show me which way to go in the whiteness. one last murmur blows in with the snow. it's Packer 67.

*think what he's like,* she says, *think what he loves, then tear it all away from him, make him hurt in the worst ways.*

what does Director love? fine wine, women, and working out with weights so he's a lean, mean shouting machine. no, more than that, what he loves is seeing his glory shining back at him from a mirror or other people's eyes. that's what you'd have to rip off him to get the right revenge. can i do that? can try! head high.

wait, too late? are those dogs barking? people shouting with their nasty lights shining? they won't stop till they find me, not now i've spoiled the party. what'll they shine their lights on? my cold body with dead eyes open and snow on my lashes? no! i wasn't killed before and i won't get dead now. hate makes me hot again. run, run as fast as i can, can't catch me cos I got a Plan! it's a new Plan and it ain't pretty. i know what to do to Director, and then Bossman will be next. i know where i'm going now—just hope i get there before my legs turn to ice and snap. i'm going HOME, yes, to my house. back past those trees and that path and my last, bad birthday. back to somewhere safe and snug where i can get warm again before i get even.

i can't just run across the valley, though, the village is gone, lost like all the old days. got to go around, a long way into shadows and snow, climbing over the freezing feet of the Blue Mountains. not giving up, not slowing down. the closer i get to home, the more the memories leap out of the dark.

*let's go swim in the river!* yelled Aran E.

*let's go make soda volcanoes,* said Harpo C.

*let's go skating, sliding, stuffing our faces,*

racing, writing, fighting, swinging, anything! let's
do it! and at the end of the day i'd say, *let's go
back to my house and eat cherries.*

oh, the old, gold days of Cherry Heaven, giddy
with fun, lolling lazy in the sun. everything fun,
everything yum, everything yum in the sun.

yum fun in the sun.

yum sun fun.

*gun.*

wish i had one.

# FREEFALL

The sun was still several hours away when someone started knocking on the door of Cherry Heaven. Kat was alone downstairs, with a gun and a cup of coffee.

The gun was Q Essnid's idea. As soon as he saw what had been thrown through the window he'd rushed outside, barefoot and furious, but heavy snow hid any trace of the culprit. He checked and checked again that no one had been hurt, even taking time to congratulate Kat on catching the rock that had been thrown. He'd stared for a long time at the nail file taped to it, and examined the bloody letter *F*s smeared on the window panes. Eventually, he'd mouthed one word: *Factory*.

Everyone looked at Linveki, who was strangely pale under his orange tan. The whisperings started, the wonderings. His friends pulled away and women stopped flirting once his sparkle dimmed.

The party was over then. Guests were politely and persistently encouraged to leave. Security were called in from Meander to escort everyone home who could get home. Some, unwilling to face the cold or the escaped criminal, bedded down at the villa. The Jones family were determined to go back to Cherry Heaven. They were all astonished when Q Essnid sought them out and presented Aunt Millijue with his own sleek power rifle. She was shocked to see the gun, taken back ten years to the tension of the war. Uncle Prester looked just as shaken.

"Idiot proof," Essnid reassured them. He gave clear instructions how to use it. "It's just to be on the safe side. I'd come with you on the launch myself, only I'm setting up a couple of teams to track this girl down. If we don't find her soon she'll freeze to death, and mad though she is, nobody wants that. If she turns up at Cherry Heaven . . ."

"Is there any reason why she should?" Aunt Millijue stammered.

"Why would she?" he countered. "This is just a precaution. If she turns up let her in, of course, but keep her under observation and *don't* let her talk or overexcite herself. It could be fatal in her condition. I'll deal with the matter personally as soon as I can get to you—send me an *e.f.* message. If you can't get a signal, try the net or sit tight till you can."

"Is everything going to be all right?"

He smiled grimly. "Oh yes. Everything's going to be just fine. One screwed-up Galrezi girl is *not* going to sabotage peace in this continent. That's not how it's meant to happen."

The knocking obviously wasn't loud enough to wake everyone else in the house. Kat took a tighter grip on the gun. At that moment she preferred to face whatever was outside than her own family.

Coming off peps had been like hurtling down from orbit—a breath-defying freefall of emotions. She began to understand why Tanka was rarely without the pills. Even though they weren't technically addictive, who'd want to stop popping them if the aftermath was so bleak? In fact, no one had enjoyed the journey home across the ice-crisp reservoir. Aunt Millijue was all for packing their bags to get on the first ship out of Santanna, but Tanka said there was no way she'd go near the ocean again, then Uncle Prester wanted to know why Kat was looking peaky, which was when she admitted to the peps. Cue a long and surprisingly coherent rant about the stupidity of taking anything chemical as a mood enhancer. He tore Kat's bag from her and threw it over the side of the boat, so the last of the pills were gone.

Which was a shame, Aunt Millijue murmured,

because she could've done with a couple herself.

All in all, it had been an evening worthy of one of Zee Homarlo's more histrionic movie plots, and the fun obviously wasn't over yet. Kat was too tense to sleep, so she'd bundled her duvet on the sofa downstairs and turned to cherries for consolation. When the knocking began she was up in an instant, thinking, *This is it. The watcher in the wood's finally come to get us! Fine. I'm tired of being afraid of everything!*

She took a deep breath, hiked the gun higher, and pulled the front door open.

"Don't shoot! It's me!"

The snowman on the doorstep fell forward mid-knock.

"Harpo? What are *you* doing out here?"

"What are *you* doing with that? Is it primed?"

"The orange light's on. . . ."

"Looks dangerous."

"Get inside before you freeze."

"Too late," he shivered. "Lost sensation in my hands and feet. You might have to amputate."

Kat locked the front door again and propped the gun nearby. Harpo's fingers were too stiff to undo his coat so she helped him strip off a couple of layers. He poked the limp pile of snow and clothes dampening the floor. "I did dress for the weather, only I *didn't* plan on getting completely lost in the snowstorm. It's blowing a real blizzard out there."

"What exactly were you doing out in the first place? It's so late it's early!"

"Is that coffee I smell?"

"Come on through; I'll brew a fresh pot. *Then* tell me what's going on."

Harpo blinked in the harsh kitchen light. "You look awful."

"Thanks. That's a fairly accurate description of how I feel, too."

"Sorry, I just meant, are you all right? Stupid question. Anything I can do?"

"Sugar?"

"Huh? Oh, no thanks, just cream." He couldn't help remembering that the best sugar he'd ever tasted had been from Kat's own lips, not so long ago. "Were you, ah, expecting someone else, or was the gun thing for me?"

"You're the *last* person I expected to see out here."

She spooned five sugars into his mug before she realized what she was doing. Then she was suddenly overwhelmed by how normal everything seemed in the kitchen—just cupboards, electrics, food, and dishes—compared to the craziness of every other part of her life.

*Oh no, not now, don't start the waterworks while Harpo's watching!*

Too late. "I never cry," she said, between sniffs.

"Me either, except when I do." He passed her a piece of kitchen towel.

"I should be completely happy—the most

amazing thing happened at Aran's party."

She told him about Q Essnid's praise for her *New Colonist* submission, and his offer of a job one day. Although Harpo's eyes brightened at the science talk, he was surprisingly lukewarm about the scholarship with Linveki Hydro Co. She was a little hurt. After all her agonies of indecision over what to do with her life, couldn't he at least be happy that she'd been offered the chance to work toward one of her dream careers?

He was oblivious to her disappointment. "I tried to call you," he said. "When I couldn't get through I thought I'd swing by the house, only it kept disguising itself as a particularly deep snowdrift and it was dark, and the blizzard started . . . and I somehow survived and made it here eventually."

"I can't get any calls." She sighed. It should have been the perfect opportunity to discuss the finer geeky details about her ideas on *e.f.* communications. Instead Harpo looked unusually serious.

"Come on through to the sitting room; it's warmer in there."

He already knew his way around, having visited Cherry Heaven many times in the past. It certainly seemed smaller now he'd sprouted so tall. Kat darted ahead to pull her duvet and pillow off the sofa.

"Sorry—were you asleep?"

"Er, no, just not ready for bed. It's been quite a night."

"You're telling me! Look, I'm not a complete nutter—I wasn't out in a blizzard for the fun of it, and I'm not stalking you just because we . . ." *Kissed. Repeatedly. All the way through the Matsuri celebrations.* "I, er, came here to talk to you. Actually, to warn you."

"Warn me?"

Once again she felt herself falling off the edge of *safe* and *normal.*

"It's a bit of a mess really."

Harpo stalled for time, looking around the sitting room with a sick sense of remembrance. This was where the birthday party would have been—the balloons, the cakes, the presents. How many times had he come bounding through the door asking if Luka wanted to come out and play?

"It's about the Hydro worker—the missing girl."

"Have they found her?" she asked. "I heard Q Essnid ordering dogs out and calling Security."

"Not exactly . . ." He looked away. Was it safe to tell her? To trust her? Why else had he risked the snowstorm? She had to know; it was too dangerous to keep the secret. He had to tell her his suspicions—how he'd come home to find his mum behaving strangely, his room disturbed, and a lingering stink of antibac in the air; how he'd noticed the lid had been removed from the jar with the papillon pupa.

Kat was amazed. "You think that girl was at your house? Did you call Security?"

"What, my dad? Funnily enough, he spent the day searching your orchard, checking it was safe. No sign of anyone, you'll be glad to know, at least not in the last day or so. Maybe if there was someone camping in the trees they cleared off with all the search parties around. No, Dad wasn't home when I set off."

He pushed his hand through his hair, making it stand alarmingly upright. He should have looked doopish like that, but Kat was comparing him to Aran E's near-perfect good looks and thinking Harpo's strength of mind made him much more handsome.

"Why would your mum hide an escaped criminal?" she asked. "She'd get into trouble."

"That's just it. Mum's not exactly afraid of trouble. People have probably told you loads of mush about how she fought the O-HA over building the dam and other things?"

Kat went pink, remembering Tanka's gossip at

the party. "A bit. I didn't take much notice."

"It doesn't matter. I'm used to it. As me and Clariss got older Mum toned it down so we didn't get hassled at school about it, but I wouldn't put it past her to help the girl just to spite the powers that be. Plus . . . plus there's another reason Mum might be involved." He stared at the bowl of cherries, suddenly feeling sick. How could he be sitting snug in this house, talking about these things? It was too strange, too horrible.

"We know the girl," he said slowly. "We thought she was dead—everyone did. Apparently she's quite hard to kill. Oklear Foster tried the first time around, not far from here. On the path. In the snow."

He put his hands over his face.

Kat said, "You mean . . . one of the Papillons?"

He nodded. "I think it's Luka. I think she's alive."

"How can she be?"

"Good question! It's what kept me slogging through the snow tonight, trying to figure it out! She was shot—I was *so sure* she was shot! Jeez, if I'd known! I called my dad when it happened and he was first on the scene. Said Foster had taken one body—Luka's. It was never found. They asked him over and over what he'd done with it and all he could bleat was, *I'm innocent!* Yeah, well *so were they*! It was her *birthday*, too!"

He looked around the room again and shuddered.

"Celia Papillon didn't see her kids much, you know how it is—single parent, always busy working—but she was going to make a really big thing of Luka's birthday. She stayed home, fixing balloons and musical holograms and mountains of food. We were going to have games and a treasure hunt—the usual stuff."

"Why were the girls in the orchard if Luka was having a party?"

"That's the sick thing: they went into town for their stupid gene-stamps that morning—the actual morning they were killed for being Galrezi, can you believe it? I'd already had mine done and it didn't bother me one way or another. I was Mazzini, like Mum. Dad was Atsumisi—no big deal, we all thought. We'd only got tested because . . . because that's what everyone was doing. It was a new law, not supposed to mean anything. But I didn't walk back with the girls cos I had to go fetch Luka's present from my house. That was before the valley was dammed, when I lived in Cluff village. Aran called to say he'd join me at Heaven, only he was pretty nervy cos his dad had actually banned him from leaving the house—not even to go to the party—because of the danger from the gunman. Aran's dad wasn't someone you wanted to disobey. Not that we were scared of the sniper. Being total doops we thought it was kind of exciting, like a movie or computer game. Not real. Not something that would happen in Cherry Heaven."

Kat found herself touching his hand. It was warm to hold, and Harpo didn't seem to mind. "Sorry, I'm being dim, but were you actually *there* when the girls were shot?"

Another nod. "That's what I'm trying to say— that I should've known Luka wasn't dead after all. If my sock hadn't been rucked up in my boot I wouldn't have slowed down to sort it out. Maybe I would've walked in on the whole thing as it happened." His voice softened. "I guess Hikori and Mai went first. They were always walking ahead, making Luka run to catch up, cos she was only little. I heard three shots all together, then a fourth, then . . . just silence. You can't imagine it. I was . . . I just bolted, like a complete spineless wimp. I ran all the way home to get my dad. He wasn't even there."

Kat thought of F Challis and his gun. Shocked by everything she'd heard she murmured, "Harpo, you don't think . . . ?"

"No!" He pulled his hand away. "My dad wasn't the sniper! I told you, I got hold of him in the end—he was first on the scene. I heard him tell Mum he'd never seen so much . . . blood."

"I'm sorry, it's just a crazy idea I had, your dad being Atsumisi and all, maybe having a racist thing for Galrezi, and he has been in Santanna working. He could have tracked Luka there somehow hoping to . . ."

"What? Finish her off? Stop her from accusing him? No, it's not like that. Oklear Foster was found with the gun, the Galrezi names, everything."

"I know, and they said he was guilty and he's brain-drained. Only, it doesn't seem right somehow, Foster waiting in the orchard with a list of people to kill that morning."

*That's it! The thing that's been bugging me about the Foster shootings. He was already in the orchard. . . .*

"Why?" he snapped. "We heard a lot of shitzer

propaganda against Galrezi from your General Insidian. Why shouldn't someone decide to take matters into their own hands and kill the sub-humans? It's what happened in the cities, isn't it?"

Kat went cold, thinking of her own parents. She was so very tempted to give up and dive under the duvet to hide. Everything was awful, whichever way she looked at it; there were no silver linings, just clouds. However, logic was still logic, and her brain was still working even if her heart was heavy.

"Tell me how Oklear Foster could have been in the orchard waiting to kill the Papillon girls, when he *didn't even know they were Galrezi*."

Harpo blinked. Stared at her. Blinked again. His face went very white, making his freckles look even browner. "He must've known. . . ."

"How? The only way he could've known was if he followed them from town and saw their hand stamps . . ."

"He didn't follow them. *I* followed them; *he* was there waiting."

". . . or if he had access to the test results before anyone else."

"No, he couldn't have. He was just a ferry worker from Anabarra; no way would he have access to stuff like that. Only someone in Admin could find it out."

"So who had access to Admin?"

"Some clerks. Town governors. Security."

"See what I mean? It's most likely to be someone official." She shook her head, as if hoping to dislodge the horrible implications. "It was so cold-blooded—to wait there for freshly greened Galrezi, just to shoot them. Shoot children."

"No way was it my dad, Kat. No way."

"I don't *want* it to be him, only he did find the bodies, and he did have access to all the crime files on computer. He could have planted that virus to chew them up so people wouldn't be able to get clear information about the crimes and start suspecting things. I'm amazed they could even bring Foster to trial with such patchy evidence."

"Everyone knew he'd done it! You don't understand—people were afraid, panicking, wondering if it'd all blow up into a race war, like the one in the cities. That trial saved a lot of lives and hundreds of people signed up for O-HA peacekeeping to put an end to all the racist fighting. Good came of it."

"Oh brilliant. So now the end justifies the means?"

"No, but facts are facts: there were no more Galrezi killed once the O-HA got massive."

"Thank god. That doesn't necessarily mean your dad isn't connected to the case."

"My dad doesn't hate Galrezi. He fought in the war with the peacekeepers. He went to the cities to save them!"

The clouds never thinned to let dawn through. Harpo and Kat sat side by side. Somehow they were holding hands again. It seemed to help. Kat heard how Federic Challis had spent two years in the cities on a peacekeeping mission with the O-HA. He'd been one of the first to find the ash-coated canal banks where many Galrezi had been killed. Afterward he'd taken the job in Santanna in an attempt to discover more about the fate of Galrezi in the New Frontier.

"At first he couldn't find out a thing," Harpo said. "Linveki Hydro, where lots of Galrezi are said to work, it's a closed shop. They have inspections a couple of times a year, but it's always reported as a model facility with excellent hygiene standards and care for the workers. I guess they spruce things up big-time when the boss calls—that's Quinn Essnid. You've probably seen the official shots of the Hydro factory on the Linveki net-site. Now look at these. They're pictures Dad arranged to have smuggled out of the factory. He left a packet of them for my mum at the store, only she's so scatterbrained she didn't even open the envelope, just put it on the coffee table. My guess is that they're planning on sending them to the newschat channels—if they haven't done it already. Chances are they won't be published. It's peace at any price on this planet," he ended bitterly.

The photographs had been copied and they were creased from where he'd crammed them in his trouser pocket. They were mostly badly focused and poor quality. They were definitely *not* pictures of a worker's paradise. They showed gaunt staff, cramped conditions, and the occasional white body bag on the factory floor.

Her head aching, Kat said, "I'm really sorry; I had no idea. I should never have thought that about your dad, especially with him being a war veteran."

Harpo surprised himself by reaching over to give her a big hug. Her hair smelled lovely, so he shyly kept his face close and she let him. He left a small kiss on her brow and she kissed his cheek. They were silent until eventually he said, "You see why I came now? If I'm right, and that girl is Luka, then she's spent nearly ten years in this factory hell and she's not going to be happy about it."

"This is her house," said Kat, looking at the room with a whole new perspective. "She's going to want it back again."

"That's why I came to warn you."

She smiled at him, and he returned the smile—a very welcome bit of comfort. Then she heard a soft scratching at the window and twisted around to see what it was. "Probably just the stray kitty."

Harpo's grip on her hand tightened. "Not a little white one, with a black-tipped tail?"

"Yeah—it prowls in the yard all the time but never comes in."

"Luka had a white cat, well, a kitten. Called it Puss, or something mushy."

"You're joking? I suppose it could be the same one, gone wild. I made a shelter for it in one of the sheds. I'll just nip out and give it some more nosh, poor thing."

Harpo grabbed her arm and pulled her back. "Actually, I don't think that's a cat. . . ."

He pointed to the white face at the window. Blue fingers scratched at the frosted glass and a thin voice was singing:

*Happy Birthday to me . . . Happy Birthday to me . . .*

## Finally

Home.

right here where i left it, not changed much.
  door opens. no Mama, only a girl with a gun.
stagger in. look around. Mama made pancakes
there, and crunchies and cherry pies with cream.
snuggled on the sofa there, with Puss-cat, read
stories when the wind howled. Puss-cat's back,
a wiggle of white, all grown up too, like me.
  there's the window where we watched for
Mama walking down the orchard path. there's
the shelf where we hung old papillon wings when
we found them on the ground; they twirled and
swirled in the breeze. and this. this is the floor.
  *is she dead?* asks a voice. a girl.
  *she ought to be,* says someone else. a boy.
warm fingers pull ice off my clothes, rub my
hands.

*is this what they call hypothermia?* says the
girl.

*it's what they call a bloody miracle,* says the boy.

i smile inside my mind. good old Harpo, here
for my birthday—better late than never. he
seems to think i'm not well. i seem to agree,
because i can't actually move. i want to know
where my mama is, why this strange girl's in my
house, when i saw her last at Bossman's bash.

*we have to keep her torso warm before every-
thing else,* Harpo says. *pass me the duvet and
the pillows.*

it's later when i open my eyes. i'm buried under
mountains of soft stuff and there's a girl with
chocolate hair rubbing my feet.

*she's coming around.*

actually, i want to say i'm *going* around.
around and around and around and around . . .
then Harpo's with me and the room stands still.

*hey, Luka.*

*hey, Harpo.*

*long time no see.* his eyes are wet.

*no kidding. will you come to my birthday?*

for some reason his eyes get even wetter.

*'course i will. i'll bring you lots of presents, too. but just take it easy now and get warm. this is Kat J, by the way. she's a friend.*

she swims with slime, i growl. *nasty people.* throat hurts. can't get words out. can't yet tell Harpo about Factory and Quarry and the gunman in the snow. *where's my mama?*

Harpo looks at Kat. *tell you what,* he says, *drink this up then we'll get you some warm food. and cherries. . . .*

yes! there really is a big, blue bowl of cherries right next to me! just smelling them makes me crazy-happy.

*give them here!*

Harpo and the girl look at me like i'm some sort of zoo animal. i suck on those fat, red cherries and line up the stones and hum that rhyme we used to chant at school:

Atsumisi, Mazzini, Galrezi, *dead.*
Atsumisi, Mazzini, Galrezi, *dead.*
Atsumisi, Mazzini, Galrezi . . .

*steady on*, says Harpo. *you'll make yourself sick, eating so quickly when you've been starving.*

fading in, fading out. Puss-cat's curled on top, whiskers tickling, purring. can't believe i forgot this place, can't believe i'm here now. different things, pictures, people. where's Hikori and Mai? out in the snow. fallen on the ground with blood all around. where's my mama? what's that noise?

Harpo lets go of my hand, leaps up. there's a shock of knocks and bark of dogs. Puss-cat runs and i would too only i can't move. Cherry Heaven goes crazy. Kat J leaps up to close curtains, old people come downstairs in dressing gowns, and a new voice yells, *who the hell let that thing in?*

*keep the noise down, Tanka*, says Kat. *Milli, tell Prester not to open the door!*

*what's she doing here?* asks the man.

WHAT ARE YOU DOING HERE? i want to shout.

*what's HE doing here?* Tanka hisses, looking at Harpo. *and is that the escaped mad girl? don't*

touch her! she's probably infected! she threw
that stone, she tried to kill us!

i wouldn't mind killing her, but she'll have to
wait, ugly bitch. i've got another name at the
top of the list first.

the knocking's getting louder.

i'm opening the door, says Prester. Security
can deal with this.

the woman, Milli, pulls his arm.

wait a moment. everyone just stand still and
keep calm. i need to think. Kat, tell me what
that girl's doing here.

she's escaped from the factory. you've got to
see these pictures, what things are like there.
tell them, Harpo.

Harpo speaks quickly and quietly. he tells them
a story about three girls walking in the woods.
two of them get shot, the other one is me.

look, says Prester, i'm sorry for this girl, but
whatever's going on at that factory isn't our
problem, so we'll let the proper authorities deal
with it.

not our problem? Kat's hissing with frustration.

*how can you say that when we're living in her*
*house and swimming in her pools and, for*
*godssake, we've all eaten the cherries!*

ice-white silence.

Milli says, *we can't let them in. remember*
*what happened last time we let Security do*
*their job? we could've hidden those people—your*
*mother and father—maybe saved them, but we*
*didn't. we were scared.*

*we saved the girls,* says Prester.

i don't know what they're talking about—don't
care. save me! save me! hide me now before they
break the door down. stop fighting, DO SOME-
THING!

then the nasty girl's face twists up.

*open the door,* she says.

scum. if i had any energy left i'd smash her
face in for being such a stick of shitzer. she
says something next and i remember what Gim
Damson told me: that there are nice people in
the world if you know how to look for them.

the girl says, *but give me a moment first.*
*Prester and Millijue have to pretend they've only*

just got up. Kat, you hide the girl's clothes under your duvet and . . . and look like you were too scared or too busy snogging to answer the door. this Galrezi . . . i'll hide her. well, don't just stand there looking at me—i do occasionally use my brain, you know!

yep, she has a brain. she's also got a tough grip, she drags me upstairs even though my legs are stabbed with knives, two steps at a time. and how many times have i gone up these stairs before? usually running up cos i'd forgotten something and was late for school, or crawling up cos it was bedtime and Mama was close behind me, coming to tuck me in. where is my mama now? the girl yanks me past my old bedroom and into the small pool room, the one with all the wooden papillons. she starts turning high power taps. we crouch, we listen. downstairs the door opens to let the badness in.

finally! comes a voice like bleach down a blocked-up toilet.

hearing Director in my house is like eating sick. he's only being nice because half the people

who've stolen my house are lucky, lovely
Atsumisi. he's also being something else, too. i
can hear the shake in his voice. he's scared. it's
started—just by being alive i make his mirror
crack and his stars fall. Packer 67 and Color
Tech 26 would dance if they were watching.

*we saw the light on and figured you were up.
can we come in?*

sorry, says Millijue. *we were fast asleep—
tired after the party, you know.*

*some party!* says Director. *thank god for the
snow to sober us all up, right?*

*have you . . . have you found the girl you're
looking for?*

*not yet, but we will.* Director pushes past
Millijue into the house. i can't see him but i can
almost hear his gold chains clinking—see the
twink of his bright white teeth. there's someone
else with him.

*Aran E! you look like a snowman,* says Kat J,
all fake brightness.

*hi, Kat,* says Aran. he doesn't sound right
either. *awful weather, isn't it? i don't see how*

anyone could last long in this, without shelter, but we're still looking. hey, Harpo! what are you doing here?

Harpo's voice has got a grin in it. oh, i was just in the neighborhood.

to see me, says Kat.

how sweet, says Director. sorry to interrupt the smooch. mind if we take a look around? the dogs are really keen.

Prester jumps in. they can probably smell the cat.

i didn't know you had a cat, says Aran.

and i'm allergic to dogs, says Milli.

guess we'll just have a nosey round ourselves, says Director. he's used to getting what he wants. tie the dogs to those trees in the yard.

after that i'm hiding and don't hear much until the knock on the pool room door.

come in! calls the girl, sitting up in the water and pushing me down. i'm gagging. who the hell gets their gills gunged with bubbles, for godssake?? Aran E's voice comes through the froth. since the girl's practically sitting on me i couldn't get up to say hello, even if i wanted to. which i don't.

god, sorry, i didn't realize, Tanka. we were just looking for the lost girl.

i can see what you're looking at!

look, he says in a funny voice. about earlier, at the pool with Kat, there was nothing going on. . . .

she stiffens. oh really. why exactly were you huddled up with her?

i can't tell you. it's a secret. i don't want to spoil the surprise.

well, you're just too damn full of secrets, Aran E, and you know what really surprises me? it's why i'm even listening to you right now. and it may have escaped your notice that i am butt naked in here! (that's a lie. she's still got her 'jama bottoms on. they're pink with silver stripes. wish i had some 'jamas. i'd have pink ones too.) now if you'd be kind enough to piss off, and close the door behind you. . . .

fine, says Aran E bitterly. be like that. there's a long pause. i can't imagine what's going through his mind. last time i knew him, he wasn't old enough to have girl trouble . . . or secrets. then he finds his voice. *if you must know, Zee Homarlo's coming to the O-HA rally and i wanted Kat to help fix up a meeting with him, since you seemed quite keen on the guy and you hadn't won the Blue Mountain competition yet, but, hey, like you say, i'll just piss off. . . .*

the girl wants to leap out and run after him, but if she does he'll see the jimjams and know something's wrong and i'll get found, so she slumps on the poolside instead. when the door closes she goes to get up. too late. quick as gunshot i've grabbed her.

*now tell me where my mama is!*

*ow! how should i . . . ? oh. you mean Celia Papillon? i guess . . . i think . . . she's dead.*

# DOWNFALL I

"It's like she's dead!"

Tanka waved her fingers in front of Luka's face. No response.

She kept her voice low, they all did, creeping around Cherry Heaven like mourners at a funeral. In every room they were imagining the ghosts of the Papillon family and Tanka hated being so crowded by the past.

"We can't keep her here forever. What are we going to do next?"

*Good question*, thought Kat.

Since Luka had come scratching at the window, one strange hour had followed another. Dawn became day—a long day with bursts of conversation between anxious stretches of silence. Night followed, then brightened to a new morning.

Waking from an uncomfortable doze, Kat was cheered to see that the blizzard had passed. Frost, ice, and snow bound the landscape in brilliant beauty. Soon deep-heat machines would cruise along clearing the pathways around town and through the orchard. It was good to believe that outside was innocent again. For once she had no sense of someone secret in the orchard. There had been no visits from Linveki's hunting party, and no sign of Security either. They must all have headed off to the great event of the day, the long-waited O-HA rally.

*What are we going to do next?*

She looked over at Luka. Dazed by news of her mama's death the Galrezi girl had stumbled down from the pool room submerged in towels. She'd eaten more cherries and drunk Blue Mountain, bottle after bottle, even though Tanka was all for tipping it in the reservoir and never touching a drop from the factory again. Then Luka talked—

yes, she'd certainly talked. She told them about the quarry, the factory, "Director," and "Bossman." If anything, her calm descriptions of everyday brutality were more upsetting than the actual details. She was surprised they were so disgusted by treatments she'd long since taken for granted.

"It's okay," she reassured them. "That was normal."

"That's *not* normal," everyone said in unison.

Harpo asked the most searching questions. At first Kat thought he was being insensitive, grilling Luka over the tiniest things. When he asked for pencil and paper she understood. Drawing was his way of understanding something—like sketching rocks at the quarry. Drawing also gave Luka's memories more impact, almost as much as the photographs he'd filched from his parents.

Occasionally Luka drifted into something like sleep, but nobody else was comfortable closing their eyes for long, not when the house felt haunted. Every so often the frown between Luka's eyes would deepen and she'd use her fingers to count, like a child, "One, two, three, and . . . four." Even in her sleep she carried on murmuring.

"What does it mean?" Tanka wanted to know.

Only Harpo, remembering the sounds of gunshot in the trees, had an idea of the memory Luka was searching for: one shot, two shots, three shots . . . and a fourth. Three sisters and a mother dead. This last memory, the one she'd blanked the longest, was becoming clearer.

Gradually Luka lost her voice, only counting in a dim whisper. Then she curled up in a corner of the sitting room, and that was that.

"Like she's dead," Tanka said. "Just given up."

Kat didn't think so. She watched how careful Luka was with every word, every movement. It was control, pure and simple. Luka was holding herself as still as possible so she wouldn't crack completely.

"That's quite enough playing dead!" said Uncle Prester as sternly as he was able.

"Come on now, wake up and have a cup of tea," were Aunt Millijue's tentative instructions.

Harpo held Luka's cold hands, saying over and over, "It's okay, you're with friends now—friends."

For seventeen hours straight Luka was lost to them. Then it was the morning of the big day— the rally day. The O-HA's glorious birthday.

What were they going to do next?

Prester and Millijue spent the morning in the kitchen, wading through an argument about the war years—what they could have done, what they should have done, what they did; who was still alive, who was dead. The others kept watch over Luka, pulling blankets around her and checking her pulse. She was oblivious to the cat in her lap.

Kat commandeered one end of the sofa. Harpo was cross-legged on the floor beside her, still sketching page after page. Every now and then he looked up at Kat and held her gaze . . . then drew some more. Her hand occasionally brushed his shoulder and her eyes often wandered to the smile that sometimes showed in the corner of his mouth.

"She's seriously screwed up," Tanka whispered, jerking her head toward Luka. "Should be in hospital."

"What, so we can have her house back?" said Kat.

"I didn't mean that! But can't the authorities sort her out?"

"Yeah right," said Harpo. "Cos the authorities have such a good track record with her."

"Things were just *fine* until she turned up. I wish I hadn't hidden her."

"Why did you, then?" he asked, a little scornfully.

Tanka buried her face in a cushion. Kat could just make out the muffled reply: "Because no one hid my mum and dad."

"You did the right thing," Kat said gently. "While we were all standing there like complete idiots." She was proud of her sister—an unusual feeling.

*But what are we going to do next?*

She pulled the problem apart a hundred different ways in her mind. It was like the puzzle of mont-halo ore: she felt she could solve it if she could just get the right perspective. The clues were all there, even if the information was muddled. One thing was clear: terrible crimes had been committed even while the sun shone on the New Frontier. Beautiful Meander dam would never look the same now she knew who'd built it and how they'd suffered. Blue Mountain water would always taste flat, despite the bubbles. As for Luka, who'd spoken so serenely about slave labor and lies, what other, darker secrets were still tormenting her?

*I can't fix things if I don't know things. There's too much going on!*

Luka's disappearance had obviously shaken things up out in the real world, too. Kat now had her *e.f.* tuned to hear the latest broadcast about an "anonymous informer" who'd submitted photographs allegedly showing abuses at the world-famous Hydro factory in Santanna. Kat guessed that Harpo's parents had sent the photos, so that the truth would be told and justice would be done.

So why wasn't the story even making headlines? Some newschat channels barely mentioned it at all, acting as if no one wanted to hear about corporate corruption and Galrezi girls, when the New Frontier was gearing up to celebrate ten years of peace and prosperity. People were waiting to see pictures of the fabulous rally arena, not suspect shots of something like a prison camp.

The *e.f.* signal was too fuzzy to get full details.

"Anything new?" asked Harpo.

Kat shook her head. "Same old stuff. Hang on . . . Quinn Essnid's made a statement, apparently—says he'll investigate the allegations personally . . . that the photos may not even be authentic."

"Of course they are! My dad wouldn't fake stuff like that! He waited *years* to get evidence!"

"Keep your hair on—I'm just saying what he's saying. There's more: Essnid's reported to be shocked and saddened to think that there could be any truth in the . . . wait a mo . . . something, something . . . awful crimes against Galrezi but nothing certain yet . . . Very sad . . . Escaped worker probably dead in the blizzard . . . body's not found . . . Ant Linveki *not* available for comment . . ."

"I bet. He's slunk off to some rat hole to hide till the heat's off him."

"Here we go—main news coming through loud and clear: the gates to the rally arena are due to open in three hours, plus they're announcing the winner of the amazing Zee Homarlo competition after the next commercial break."

Harpo flung his pencil down in disgust. "Supreme! Basically, nobody cares, and Essnid's going to make sure that Linveki takes the rap for any *allegations* about the factory while he comes out smiling and rosy."

"Who says Q Essnid had anything to do with the factory!" Tanka protested.

"Who do you think Luka's *Bossman* is?"

"She never actually said his name."

"Er, actually, she did," Harpo objected. "She said, 'Bossman, the badman, the Essnid daddy.'"

"Oh, like that makes perfect sense and will stand up in a court of law!"

Kat was, as ever, the voice of reason. "To be fair, Q Essnid could be the 'Bossman' Luka knew, but maybe he really didn't see anything of these working conditions." She nodded to Harpo's drawings. "If he just made routine inspections, Linveki could've tarted the place up, making it look like a worker's paradise, and Essnid wouldn't know any better."

Harpo muttered something fluently rude.

"I'm just saying!"

She resorted to chewing the ends of her hair while she figured things out. Cherry Heaven was so peaceful that day it was hard to believe that crimes could happen out in the real world. There was the smell of fresh cherry tea from the kitchen. Harpo's pencil made soft sounds on the paper. General Insidian's portrait stared down on them all.

*It's okay*, she thought. *Maybe everything's still muddled, but there is something we can do to wake this world up, and something's better than nothing.*

"Here's an idea. . . ." she said out loud, suddenly sitting up straight.

"Are we going to the rally?" Tanka panicked instantly. "Cos I'll need plenty of prep time if we are. Zee Homarlo and Aran'll be there, and I haven't even *started* wondering what to wear!"

Kat smiled. At least some things were still normal. "Go play in the wardrobe, then, and ask Milli to get ready too, but Uncle Prester should stay here to look after Luka. I think, I *think* I've figured out what to do next!"

Not long after they'd gone Luka lifted her head. Soft words slipped out from between her teeth.

"One dead, two dead, three—that was me—but I could still see—saw you, gunman. Saw *four*—saw my mama shot to the floor."

There it was. The darkest memory.

She opened her eyes, breathed deeply, and smiled.

She knew exactly what she was going to do next.

# DOWNFALL II

It was going to be the most magnificent party the Frontier had ever seen—the best birthday ever. Ten years of peace was a lot to celebrate for a world still reeling from memories of war.

Lines for the entrance to the rally arena began to form overnight, covered by deep-heat canopies. Coffee and conversation kept people awake as the hours ticked by.

"Did you hear on *e.f.* . . . ? Did you see on TV . . . ?"

"Some pictures, that's all. No big deal. Probably fake."

"Who sent them?"

"Who cares?"

"What have they done to the dam?"

"It's awesome—everyone says . . ."

No newschats had been allowed to see what the workers had been busy rigging up for weeks. When the entry gates opened mid-afternoon, people surged forward with excitement . . . only to stop dead in awe.

It was like a cathedral from the old world, they said, but bigger, grander, more inspiring. The dam rose up as high as a mountain, topped by three dazzling towers of light. The wide pool of runoff water had been boarded over and covered with massive tiers of seats facing toward the dam— enough for the many thousands of Frontier citizens. Tuff-lite screens and awnings protected everyone from the worst of the winds and there were vast hydro-powered heaters to keep the temperature pleasantly mild. Giant flags in red, blue, and green hung down from transparent poles; sparks of light led the way to stalls with free food and drinks. Beyond the dam, millions of liters of ice-cold water were kept at bay in the reservoir. At the foot of the dam, thousands of revelers poured in to find a place.

Jo Challis did her best to distract them as they jostled in. Her voice was hoarse after only half a day protesting, "It's peace built on people's suffering; it's power made from lies!" She carried a heavy homemade banner that shouted: WAKE UP MEANDER! TRUTH AND JUSTICE!

Would Meander take any notice?

Kat watched from the edge of the crowd. Some people were laughing and joking so much, caught up in the celebratory mood of the event, they genuinely didn't spot the one-woman demonstration. Maybe they wouldn't be so hard to convince, once their eyes were properly open. Others spared a glance for J Challis, but there was pity for her efforts mixed with their sympathy and they soon looked away. Worse still, there were people who looked on the demonstrator as if she was mad. Would they be the ones who would only shrug when the truth was revealed, no matter how appalling it was?

"Security's watching her," Tanka murmured in Kat's ear. "Will she be all right? Will we be all right?"

"Are you sure you're still up for this?"

" 'Course! As long as I don't get arrested or any-thing."

"Can't promise . . ."

"But think how much you'll be in demand by the newschat channels if that happens," Harpo consoled Tanka. He was rewarded with a haughty look.

Kat gave him a quick hug, then he squeezed through the press of coats and bodies and was lost to sight. Would he make it? He said he had a free pass to the control room of the amazing INTENS system, thanks to all the work he'd done with the techs for his school project. They were expecting him to turn up for a behind-the-scenes seat at entertainment central. What he had in mind was far less passive and a lot more educational. . . .

It was just as well he wasn't around to see Security sidling ever closer to his mum, who kept right on hollering, "Nothing but the truth, Meander! Nothing but the truth!" even though *nothing but the party* was the implicit reply.

"D'you think they'll let him near it?" Tanka whispered to Kat.

They'd arrived at an elevator with Aunt Millijue, ready to be whooshed up to the top of the dam with other privileged guests. Aran E had sent tickets for all of them, although when Tanka spoke with him she said he'd sounded strange. She took this to mean he was devastated at their breakup, and wondered how long she should leave it before engineering a passionate reconciliation. Kat was more uneasy. Something wasn't quite right about Aran's behavior. One minute he was the confident wonder boy, the next he had a guilty look about him. What had he been trying to tell her that night at the pool?

Tanka prodded her. "I said, d'you reckon Harpo'll get into the INTENS room?"

"He seems to think the techs'll be friendly. They've been helping him with his school project."

"I guess it's one of those rare occasions when being a geek counts for something." Tanka's attention switched to more exciting matters—the O-HA tenth birthday party. "I reckon the whole continent's here today! Thank god we're not with the crowds. Tell me when you see Aran E—I owe him the world's biggest apology for thinking he'd even glance twice at you when all he wanted was to fix me up with VIP seats. Do I look nice, Kat; do I look completely gorgeous?"

"Completely. Hey, your outfit even matches the carpet."

The elevator doors opened on to the dam parapet, ridiculously high above the main arena. The entire walkway was covered in thick crimson and shaded by a deep-heat system. Beautiful holograms of the O-HA silver mountain graced every cushioned chair and there was a goodie bag for each visitor.

"At least we get something for our trouble," said Aunt Millijue. "I feel badly leaving Prester home alone with Luka. He'd've loved all this—material for his next book."

"Give him a call," said Kat.

"I tried. No signal."

"Don't worry about it. He's probably gorging on pancakes with extra syrup as we speak. Or asleep in front of the TV."

Tanka pushed through them both to lean over the parapet. She laughed at the crowd below. "They're so small! What an a-ma-zing view!"

"Supreme," Kat echoed weakly. She was staring over the opposite side, where the ice-crusted reservoir pressed up close, only a few meters down. This whole rally felt like a big mistake in so many ways. Now that she was surrounded by normal people, noise, and fun, Luka's stories seemed ludicrous— lunatic. Was it too late to track down Harpo and tell him the plan was a no-go? That she was probably wrong about Linveki and Essnid—Director and Bossman—all of it?

She was just heading back to the elevator when Tanka grabbed her arm.

"Stop right there, Jones! *Have you seen who's sitting in the front row?*"

A tall man with granite eyes, designer stubble, and a mathematically square jaw turned in his seat to smile in their direction. Tanka expressed a desire to melt into a pile of goo on the floor. Kat just stared at the movie man of the millennium, Zee Homarlo himself. So Aran E hadn't been kidding when he said he wanted to wangle a meeting!

Tanka tried to spot her ex, to give a belated thanks. Fat chance. Although Aran seemed equally anxious to speak to her, he was surrounded by a thick cloud of photographers. Kat thought he looked nervous, but he was still enough like his father to keep up appearances, especially for the media. Whenever the cameras flashed, he made sure it was the scar-free side of his face that was turned toward them.

She prodded Tanka. "Shall we sit down, then?"

"No way can I sit next to Zee Homarlo!"

"You're joking, right?"

"Kat, I've had no peps for *eons* now—do I look like I've grown a normal sense of humor in the meanwhile? *You* sit next to him."

"I can't believe you've got your dream come true and you're too afraid to—"

"Tanka Jones?" Zee Homarlo rose and came toward them, looking so heavily muscled he probably needed two seats all to himself. "Aran said you'd be joining us. And you must be Kataka and Millijue Jones? Can I get you ladies some bottles of Blue?"

• • •

A single rocket shooting up into twilight signaled the start of the tenth O-HA rally. Down in the arena every face was turned skyward to watch the rocket shrink until it was no bigger than a star-dot in the sky . . . then it exploded and pushed the evening away with silver/blue fire. Sparks began to fall all around. People cringed, afraid they were going to get burned, but then fear turned into smiles and laughs because the sparks began to float dreamily down, transformed into light illusions of snow that seemed so real thousands of hands reached up to stroke the flakes, only to find their fingers grazing thin air. The imaginary snow thickened as the state-of-the-art INTENS system went on to full power, working its magic from a myriad of tiny projectors hidden around the arena. Bass-heavy music started to pound out from connected speakers. Even on the parapet the very stone seemed to vibrate. People whooped exuberantly as a shock of lasers began to scatter more wild patterns of light in time to the beat.

"This INTENS is off-world!" Homarlo shouted to Tanka, pointing over the parapet. "Have you seen what they're using as a projection screen?"

"Holy shitzer," she gasped. "I mean, excuse my language. We're *sitting on it*!"

The bright quarry stone of the dam's great curve was brilliant with silver light which was shattering into a million O-HA symbols. The INTENS system was so sophisticated there was barely any distortion on this unusual screen, even though it was a good two-hundred-meter spread.

"How can we see the screen if we're on top of it?"

"Relax," said Homarlo. "Quinn's thought of everything."

And so he had.

A few people in the arena actually screamed when they heard giant spumes of water spurting up behind them, created by dense rows of jets. It was a simple enough idea and all the more impressive for that: as well as creating a sparkling backdrop for the crowd, the sheen of water became a screen for a new wave of INTENS cameras projecting a second, identical pattern of silver O-HA signs.

Homarlo was right—the INTENS system *was* the most amazing thing. Kat was so impressed she started wondering if it wouldn't be worthwhile switching her research from mont-halo ore. Then she remembered Luka's descriptions of factory life and she knew she'd never be able to do anything for Linveki Hydro Co. now. That bright dream was over.

*But there's no point in worrying about the future when there's plenty in the here and now to keep me stressed. Like going two nights without sleep.* In theory, Kat still knew that all clouds had silver linings; in practice, she didn't have the energy to lift her head to look for them.

Zee Homarlo read from the souvenir rally guide. "INTENS has full spherical projection capabilities for live-action or prerecorded images. It's a whole new way of looking at things. INTENS stands for Illumination Network Trans— *Hey!* That's me they're showing now! Can you hear everyone cheering?"

"The Blue Mountain competition," Tanka exclaimed. She leaned forward in her seat even though she knew she hadn't won. "Clariss Challis?! What a rip-off! Why should *she* have all the fun? I bet they rigged it at the store. I bet L—"

Kat tugged at Tanka's arm before she could say anything about Luka.

Roving cameras picked Clariss C out of the audience, homing in on her unusually glowing face. "I just drank lots of water," she told newschats shyly. Her parents had already warned her not to mention the fact that Luka had handed the lucky bottle top to Jo Challis before running away from the store that night. The cameras didn't dwell on her for long—they didn't want to give too much exposure time to the sticker on Clariss C's coat front: NOTHING BUT THE TRUTH.

The shot pulled away—so quickly the crowd felt as if they'd been yanked away with it. Abruptly, all INTENS sound died.

A gentle cherry-scented mist wafted down on the crowd, followed by equally gauzy odors of red-berry, blueberry, and greenberry flavors. Music grew slowly, gently. The lights grew too, and there was the man himself, Quinn Essnid, magnified onto the far-off sheet of water, with a double image on the dam wall. When Kat dragged her eyes away from the INTENS she saw that Essnid was actually standing close by, just beyond Zee Homarlo. He was in front of a row of cameras on the parapet, microscopic to the crowd below but at the same time as huge as the dam itself, and as marvelous as the wall of water. One image smiled back at the other. One man showed many faces.

Behind Essnid the INTENS pictures morphed into a smoothing ripple of blues—water so enticing it looked as if you could slide right into it and feel the Bliss. When Q Essnid spoke, he sounded just as gentle and wonderful. He was their friend, their savior, their adored peacekeeper.

"People of the New Frontier! Friends. *Welcome* to the tenth anniversary of our O-HA and another wonderful year of Frontier achievements. Thank you, all of you, for joining me to make this our happiest birthday ever!"

He waited several minutes for the crowds to revel in their cheering, then he spread his hands for silence and they were ready to listen again.

"I'm sure you'll agree we couldn't have picked a more fitting spot for our celebration—here at our wonderful Meander dam. It's a miracle of engineering that guarantees everyone on the Frontier clean power for life."

*At what cost?* Kat wondered rebelliously.

"So please put your hands together and let's hear it for everyone who's worked so hard to make this party possible!"

Again, there was a long wait while the crowd hollered. Again, Essnid's timing was perfect.

"Of course, things don't always go according to plan. There's been some bad news the last couple of days, hasn't there? We've all been shocked at allegations about Ant Linveki's conduct at the Hydro factory in Santanna—behavior so contrary to everything humanitarian we, as decent people, believe in. Contrary to everything I've dedicated my last ten years to. Contrary to the spirit of the O-HA!"

"*O-HA! O-HA! O-HA!*"

"We've been troubled to hear about war crimes being investigated over in the cities. I don't know about you, but I've about had enough of dwelling on past mistakes."

"Hear, hear," muttered Aunt Millijue.

"Let's not get dragged down by bad deeds done by other people in other times. Let's bury our mistakes and forget old wars. Let's have a fresh new way of looking at things, feeling stronger and better than ever before. For the next ten years of the O-HA I offer you the gift of a bright and amazing future!"

As one the crowd was on their feet. They punched the air and chanted again: "O-HA, *one people*! O-HA, *one world*!"

Kat stood up too, though she couldn't cheer. Not so long ago she would have thrilled to hear Quinn Essnid's promises. Now she could barely believe them, not when she knew how Luka had been broken by the *mistakes* and *old wars* Essnid was so willing to wash away. She sent a silent message to a certain redheaded boy: *Come on, Harpo— now's the time.*

Essnid stepped away from the static cameras to

let the INTENS system fill both screens with his stunning vision for the New Frontier. Then he frowned as the cheers died away. The crowd went as quiet as snow. Over on the sheen of water pictures of Essnid's paradise were still being paraded. What he couldn't see were the strange images now projected monster-size under his very feet.

First came the photographs, the shadowy shots of the Hydro factory. They weren't so easy to shrug off and forget when two hundred meters wide. Then came the pictures, all drawn with Harpo's scientific precision. The crowd began to murmur. What did it mean? Who were these skeleton people lugging stone in a quarry? Who were those beasts with twisted faces beating workers emerging from the silt of the dam foundations? Was this the way their dam had been built? These ghosts in white, were they the ones filling bottles of bubbly Blue Mountain? Those bodies on the factory floor, were they actually *dead*? Dead so they'd never get up again? And this photograph filling the screen, was it a girl—a real, live human girl?

It was the last image. Luka's face.

Her scabs and scars were magnified many times over. Her skin looked so pale it was almost see-through. One second later, and her face was showing on the water spray too.

Kat eventually remembered to breathe. He'd done it! Somehow Harpo had fed the INTENS on both screens! There was nowhere the crowd could look without staring straight into Luka's hard, bright eyes.

Suddenly, a few thousand people flinched as the photo *moved* and the face cracked into a tooth-chipped smile.

There were murmurs of concern. What did this have to do with the future of the Frontier? Who was this girl?

Kat went cold all over as she realized she wasn't looking at an image of Luka, but the real, live girl.

Luka was there on the parapet in front of the cameras, an uninvited guest, with a gun. The very same gun given to protect Cherry Heaven. She left no one guessing what would happen next. Pointing the weapon at Q Essnid she said, "I've come to kill you."

# DOWNFALL III

"Kill the sound! Kill the cameras!" Quinn Essnid cried. "Switch to prerecorded." His voice was strong and pitched for obedience. "Let's all relax. We don't want any trouble."

"I do," said Luka. "You're Bossman. You've been bad."

Kat shivered. *Bossman.* The ultimate bully. The people's hero . . . The man facing a gun. This wasn't part of the plan! Where was Uncle Prester? And why couldn't someone magic that gun away?

Only Luka and Essnid stayed standing. Everyone else was either crouching behind their chair or facedown flat on the parapet floor. There were only two Security officers present on the dam top. One was Federic Challis, who'd let Luka sneak inside, thinking she just wanted her chance in front of the cameras. The other was downright terrified—he didn't dare shoot in case anyone innocent got injured.

Q Essnid let out a quiet sigh and spoke in his most reasonable voice. "You've been through a lot, Luka. It is Luka, isn't it? You're confused; it's understandable. Why don't you put that gun down? You won't need it now, you're safe."

"You're not."

"I see you're upset. Why don't we go somewhere warm and talk, find out what you think is the matter."

"*You're* the matter. *You*. One, two, three, four— *bang*. We all fell down and only I got up again. Came back again. Saw you again."

Down in a quiet corner of the INTENS control room Harpo was faking innocence badly as the techs tried to wrestle for control of the system. Unable to get at the glitch directly, the head tech reached for the master switch.

"Wait," said one of the staff. "I want to know what she's on about."

He wasn't the only one.

*What's she talking about?* Kat had to grip her hands into fists to stop herself leaping up to shake some sense into the girl, or maybe just to shake her to stop her saying such terrible things. *You know. In your heart you know what she's saying.* Everyone was frightened—not nearly as much as they would be when they'd worked out what Luka meant.

*Got up again*—she'd survived the shots in the snow.

*Came back again*—she wanted revenge.

*Saw you again*—she'd seen him before. In the snow.

The sniper.

*No way. Too incredible. Too terrible. Can't believe it. Who could? There's Essnid, so smart in his suit, so patient, so reasonable ... there's Luka, half-mad, half-mangy, fired by revenge for so long she doesn't know when to quit.*

It was so tempting to hide her face in her hands, like Tanka. To hope there wouldn't be sudden moves, sprays of gunshot, more blood, more deaths. But Kat couldn't tear her gaze away.

Quinn Essnid never stopped smiling. That was what scared her the most. If only he'd looked shocked, or offended, or at the very least angry. His calm words were chilling, not soothing.

"This is a little ridiculous. You're talking about Oklear Foster, yes? We all know what terrible crimes he committed. It's why we're here today, one Frontier family, side by side, to make sure we have peace, lasting peace, and nothing but peace."

*He's quick to understand. Too quick?*

"Oklear Foster?" The murmurs grew, all around the arena. Down in the control room, the techs stared at their multiple screens as if willing the action to fast forward, the tension was so unbearable.

Kat found herself holding her breath.

Was Luka telling the truth? Was this the deep secret she'd carried with her, from the orchard, to the stone works and, finally, from the factory, face-to-face with the culprit? Did she really know for sure who'd killed her family? Unlike the rest of the Frontier, she wasn't pointing the finger at Oklear Foster. No. She was pointing a gun. At Quinn Essnid. With every indication she was going to give him the ultimate birthday present. To shoot.

"Put that thing down," Essnid said.

"You didn't."

"We don't want anyone to get hurt."

"I do."

His breathing quickened and his eyes narrowed.

So he was human after all. What on earth was going through his head as he looked into the end of his own gun? Was he scared? Ashamed? Guilty? Perhaps all of these emotions . . . or none of them. The only thing that showed on his face was a convincing flush of confidence. Standing on the dam he'd built, overlooking the people he ruled, he quite simply believed he was invincible.

"It's over, Luka. It stops now. You can say whatever silly things you like; it doesn't bother me. Who's going to believe you anyway?"

Silence.

Luka blinked.

She hadn't expected this, the ultimate punishment. To fight, to survive, to speak . . . to have her pain so casually denied.

Then, two words.

"I do."

The words were so faint the microphones didn't pick up on them the first time, so Kat cleared her throat and spoke out again.

"I do. I believe her."

Slowly, shakily, she got to her feet, mesmerized by the gun in Luka's hand. It was the most frightening thing she'd ever done in her life.

Harpo saw her on screen. He was at once

fiercely proud of her and horrified: he could see only too well how the human body provided a large target for gunfire. He found himself willing Luka to stay steady—or at the very least to put the safety catch on.

"I do," said another voice, a bit less wobbly than the first. Tanka stood *behind* her sister, but she did stand up, stubbornly keeping her nose in the air as if city girls faced dangerous situations all the time, without so much as a smudge of mascara.

"I believe you," came a rich, deep voice. Federic Challis stepped forward. "Only would you put the gun down?"

"I believe you," mouthed Jo Challis, far below in the arena.

"I believe you," said Aunt Millijue, to her own great surprise.

"You believe *lies*."

The words smothered their solidarity in an instant. Q Essnid spoke as soberly as if he was correcting a class of schoolchildren. "It's sad to see how a bright young girl could stoop to this. Even sadder that she has you caught up in it too." His voice was so full of regret they began to feel ashamed for causing him so much trouble. "Lies," he repeated mournfully. "All lies."

"*It's not lies!*" Luka screamed in a sudden fury. "How can you stand there and say that? You know what you did! It's—not—lies!" She turned around to shout it again and again to the terrified people on the parapet, and the gun swung around with her, ready to fire with just one twitch of her finger. Even down in the arena people screamed and ducked, the images on the INTENS were so overwhelming.

Kat pulled Tanka to the ground again. The two of them cowered behind Zee Homarlo's solid bulk.

That was it, then. They'd tried. Failed. Essnid would die to the shrill sound of *not lies lies lies!* and the world would only remember the murderer whirling with her gun. Nothing and no one could stop the girl now.

Then: "Luka!"

A new voice broke into the mayhem.

Still shaking, Luka steadied the gun, not at Essnid this time, but at Aran E, who rose up from the mass of frightened guests on the floor to stand between her and his father.

"I'll kill him!" she said. "You too!"

He shrugged unconvincingly.

"Get away from here!" Q Essnid snapped, slowing unrolling from a defensive hunch. "Keep away from that gun!"

Aran took a step closer to Luka, even though his father was dragging him back. His face was a strange mix of fear and determination. "Please don't shoot anyone, Luka."

"*It's not lies!*"

"I've been looking for you. It's funny to see you again. I guess we've both grown up a bit. Ten years is a long time."

"It's not lies!"

"I always thought it was so cool you were my friend, when you were a whole year above me. I was six and you were seven." He held out a hand a little way in front, as if resting on a young boy's head. Luka's eyes flickered down.

*Don't go so close, you idiot!* Kat scrunched her eyes shut briefly, almost too terrified to see what would happen next. Tanka was squashed up beside her, not moving, not hiding, just crying.

"Keep back, Aran!" Q Essnid commanded.

"I got you a microscope for your birthday, went halves on it with Harpo. We knew you'd always wanted one. Dad said not to give it you, though, not to go through the orchard that day. Said it wasn't safe with the sniper. We all knew about the gunman, of course, but I was only little, I went anyway, on my own: you were having a party!"

"My birthday."

"Leave it, Aran!"

"Your birthday." Aran's voice was hoarse, but he

didn't falter. His hand flew up to touch the side of his face. "You know, people often ask me how I got this scar, and I joke around, telling them any old story, but nobody ever guessed. Not even my dad. It was a tree, actually. A tree in your orchard."

"A cherry tree?"

"Yeah. We used to eat cherries by the bucketful, didn't we?"

Quinn Essnid could only watch with a sick kind of fascination as his son showed just how thoroughly he'd inherited the famous Essnid charm. *Like father like son.* He had the sense not to interfere now, believing Aran was doing all he could to distract the girl, to disarm her.

"I like cherries," said Luka.

"Hikori had a bag of them," said Aran, his voice going dark. "She got shot first, didn't she? Then Mai."

"Hikori, Mai, then me. He shot me!" Her voice rose to the verge of hysteria again and her grip tightened on the gun.

Aran quickly calmed her, even though his face was pale with fear. "But he missed, didn't he?"

She grinned and relaxed a little. "Yeah."

"He was walking over the snow to see how well he'd done, only then someone came running out of the house. . . ."

*Are you mad?* Kat thought. *Making her remember this when she's already spitting for blood?*

But Luka was crying now, the first tears she'd tasted for a long, long time. "That was my mama. He shot her last."

Aran's eyes were bright too. Kat didn't know how he could hold himself together as well as he did. Down in the tech room, they worked to get the microphones sensitive enough to pick up his trembling confession.

"I should've done something, Luka. Said something. Stopped him! But the gun was so loud! I'd never heard one before, not so close! I ran and ran like a complete coward, never ran so fast in my life, right across the valley all the way home. Swiped my cheek on a cherry tree as I ran and bled for ages."

He wasn't even looking at Luka now. His eyes had wandered northward over the reservoir.

"Dad came home later, and he was great, really great. He sat with me and told me he had bad news for me, that a wicked man had killed my friend, but they'd caught him. Put him in prison, where he'd never hurt anyone again. He said the . . . deaths . . . were a terrible tragedy, but not to worry. Daddy would take care of me. Daddy would take care of everything. Daddy would make sure there was peace and no war."

"That's enough now, Aran," said his father. "Let me deal with this."

"You've done enough! Don't you all under-stand?" Aran shouted out now, across the stunned arena. "He's done it all—all of this. Look at it! Celebrate if you still feel like cheering! He gave us what we wanted—our peace, our prosperity, this giant monument to all things great and glorious! All it cost was a few Galrezi lives. He said it was all for the best, that good would come of it. Yeah, like the ends justified the means, *Daddy*."

He turned the bitterness on himself.

"I was so *stupid*. I made myself forget. Told myself it couldn't be true. That it couldn't have been my father standing there with a gun, shooting one round after another. But I was close, so close. I could count the creases around his eyes as he focused to fire. He killed them, the Papillons. He killed them, all of them, dead in the snow."

He turned and stumbled away, trailing a broken "I'm sorry" behind him. Q Essnid automatically reached out to help, oblivious now to the gun.

Luka's eyes glittered as she fired one shot— straight up to the stars. "You see?" she called out. "*It's not lies!*"

She threw the gun on the ground and herself over the side of the dam.

# FEARLESS

With an action yell worthy of Zee Homarlo, Kat scrambled to her feet and leaped after Luka. The ice on the reservoir cracked but held, as did her ankle, which was still shooting fire after her fall at the quarry.

She took a moment to check she wasn't dead, then set off shuffling after the girl, still visible in the glare of the red tower lights.

*This is such a bad idea, Kataka Jones. Mere centimeters of frozen water between me and nasty blackness. How deep is it? And if I go through the ice, will I get sucked into turbines and come out all frothed up in the pool?*

Luka seemed oblivious to Kat's approach. She was kneeling on the ice with her head tipped back and one hand—the scarred hand—raised up to the night sky. One by one she was putting the stars out and letting them shine again.

Kat squashed her panic. At least she didn't have to deal with a gun now, just a mad girl and a dark-water phobia . . . plus the biting cold.

She knew she ought to do something.

*What's the right thing to say? Maybe not, "WHAT THE HELL WERE YOU THINKING?" Maybe something more like, "Hey, are you okay?" Huh, yeah, as in—are you okay with the fact you've been abused for ten years and nobody helped you and you just faced up to the man who stole your life and he denied doing anything, and it turns out your best friend actually watched it happen and wimped out on telling anyone?*

Luka looked around. "Are you okay?" she asked gravely.

"Mostly. How about you?"

"Mostly. It's better out here, away from everyone. We never had a lake before. It's like standing on old air."

"Yeah? Well, I'm glad it's more solid than air, though not as solid as I'd like. So . . . what do you want to do next?"

*Please don't say "stay out here all night stargazing. . . ."*

Beyond them, on the dam top, people were shouting and lights were flashing.

"Actually, nothing," Luka said eventually. "There's no moons to make a tide, nothing new pulling me now. I did it. I gave Bossman exactly what he deserved."

"But you didn't shoot him—I thought you were going to."

"Shoot him? Oh, the gun thing. Didn't you see what I gave him instead? Look!" Luka showed Kat one closed fist then opened it slowly, revealing an empty palm. "Nothing, that's what I gave him, and it's exactly what he's got left: nothing."

"Nice logic." *How about we get off the ice now?* "I guess death would've been a pretty final judgement."

"I was afraid at first," Luka whispered. "Ten years I buried what he did, while he buried bodies and said someone else fired the gun. He's been so big in my head! I was going there thinking one look from his smiley eyes would make me drop down dead, even if his bullet missed me. Then I saw him for real, and he's not so tall, not so tall at all! He's not the whole wide world, just a stick of shitzer I wouldn't dirty my hands on, not even if I could scrub 'em with Stingo after. It's all about perspective, see? Put the stars out, let them shine again! He'll get what he deserves, one way or another."

"You reckon?"

Kat knew only too well how convincing Essnid could be. The law courts would probably love him and let him go. . . .

"I don't reckon—I know. Gim Damson said so."

*Fair enough. Whoever this Gim Damson is.*

Luka suddenly shivered. "It's cold. What's the plan?"

"The plan? Whatever we do we're stuffed! Sooner or later Security will come up with a way of following us onto the ice without cracking it— that's if we don't fall in ourselves or freeze to death first. If we head for shore it's only a matter of time before you're arrested for assaulting the top bod on the Frontier, as well as my geology prof, while I'm locked up for . . . for some crime or other they'll concoct on the way to prison to be brain-drained."

"Cheerful, aren't you? How about *I* make the plan? What d'you say we head back to my house for hot malloey tea and a big bowl of cherries?"

Before Kat could agree this was a very good plan, she was interrupted by a strange noise. A sort of a groan.

"Was that you, Luka?"

"No. Was it you?"

"No."

Luka suddenly hunched down and balanced herself with her fingertips.

"I don't think the ice is as thick as it looks. . . ."

The groan turned into a *crick-crack* splitting sound.

"That kind of helps with the plan," Kat muttered. "Okay, fine. We crawl to spread our body weight, and we get to land quickly. We head north-westish till we see the wind turbines and the lights at Heaven." A horrible thought occurred to her. "You didn't do anything to Uncle Prester, did you?"

"The snoring man? No, I just borrowed his gun. He wasn't using it."

"Fine. Jeez! I don't want to sound dumb, but ice is *really* cold! Let's crawl *quickly*."

So they crawled, two dark specks on the ice, each blowing clouds of cold breath. As long as they didn't look back at the bright dam towers, their eyes got used to night vision. Kat could just about see Luka, off to her right, and she was once again struck by how tough the girl was, to keep going when she'd already been on the run for several weeks, when there was little hope of everything turning into a happy ending. Most people would just have given up. Then Kat remembered Luka's stories and knew that the people who *had* given up were the ones who'd been hauled out of the quarry and the factory in white body bags. No wonder Luka just wanted to get home again, to feel something like safe.

Thinking all this, she was amazed when Luka broke the silence to say, "Maybe we shouldn't go back to my house after all. . . ."

"You're joking, right?"

"Joking? No. That would be something to make you laugh and this isn't funny. I don't want to go home now everyone's dead. I don't want to be on my own there."

"Don't be a doop," Kat said in a gruff voice. "You're not on your own. I'm coming with you,

and that usually means Tanka won't be so far off—
*sisters stick together* and all that. *If* we can drag her
away from Zee Homarlo, of course."

She wondered whether Tanka would get a
chance to talk to Aran in the next few crazy hours.
She wished she could get that final image of Aran's
face out of her mind—how haggard he'd looked.
Haunted.

"He should have said something before!" she
blurted out.

"Who?"

"Aran!"

"Maybe."

"Then Bossman, I mean, Essnid, couldn't have
gone around lording it over everyone, and that
man Foster wouldn't have been stuffed in prison
when he was innocent. There wouldn't have been a
factory or the slave labor in the quarry."

"Is that Aran's fault?"

"No-o, only . . ."

"Only you wish everything had just been happy and okay?"

"*Yes!*"

Luka shook her head. "It was never going to be okay. Not from the moment Bossman picked up that gun. He pulled the trigger, he spread the lies, he got all the reward. You want to blame someone, blame him. I do!"

"I guess you're right. Jeez, six years old and seeing your dad do that! No wonder Aran blanked it." She couldn't help thinking of another couple of children in the war years, watching as their parents were ripped away. There were just too many ways to be damaged by a fight. Too many children learning to live with the aftermath. "People do whatever they can to squash the bad stuff out of sight, even when they're kids. I suppose Aran did the right thing in the end."

"He bought me a microscope for my birthday. Wonder if he's still got it? Did you ever want to look at leaves under a lens, and papillon wings, and snow and . . . ? Oh. You've already got one, haven't you? I saw it in your room."

"You can borrow it any time you like. Jeez, you can *have* it, but only if we get off this ice pretty damn soon!"

Patchy snow clouds still covered parts of the sky. Kat's lucky star, previously quite bright over the Blue Mountains, was abruptly snuffed out.

A cold whisper came over the ice. "Kat?"

"What?"

"Nothing."

"What?"

"Thank you . . ."

"What for?"

"Not being a *shitzer-badbrain-wasting-lives-Atsumisi-scum*."

"Oh. Okay. You're welcome—anytime."

"I mean it."

Kat reached for Luka's bare hand. "So do I."

After hourless ages of crawling they finally spotted the row of wind turbines, and they knew they were almost at the shore. Much as she hated being on the ice, Kat still dreaded what they'd find at Cherry Heaven. Maybe the little white cat, padding about in the snow with fastidious steps. Maybe Security with stun guns and handcuffs.

Luka was oddly chirpy, quizzing Kat about revenge.

"Would you do it?" she was saying. "Would you shoot? No, really, would you? Could you kill someone, make them dead, then stamp on the memory of them so they were nothing but mush? Is there someone you'd like to punch, beat, shoot, stab, strangle, burn, and beat? Someone you hate as much as I hate Bossman?"

Kat didn't like all the talk of beating and shooting, not when the motion-sensor lights at Cherry Heaven suddenly switched on. Who was there? Uncle Prester? No. Someone else. A tall figure standing in silhouette. Someone big and bad, with brilliant white teeth.

His voice uncurled to meet them.

"Hey, girlie-girls!"

Kat got to her feet unsteadily; Luka stayed low, struggling with the fact that she'd just got away from Bossman only to come face-to-face with another bag of bastardness.

"Nice night for a walking on water," Linveki mocked. He began bashing the butt end of his gun on the ice. Little pieces skittered about, making strangely musical sounds. "Say, the ice is frozen pretty thick."

*Like your head*, thought Kat.

"Whoa—it's not *solid*, though! Hey, look—it's cracking! Watch out you don't fall in! It could still be pretty deep and it's definitely going to be cold. . . . You'd better get over here, Kataka J, get warm. And her—she could do with a dunking, don't you think?"

The ice rocked unpleasantly and cracks shivered toward them.

"Go get safe," Luka called to Kat as she lurched for a handhold. It was no use. The ice really had broken and her weight was making it slope down into the water. "He won't shoot Atsumisi."

"Oh, come on now. It can't feel that cold after working in a fridge for ten years," Linveki taunted.

Struggling to keep steady herself, Kat could only watch as Luka began to slip-slide into the darkness. It all happened so quickly. The last part to go under was her red-scarred hand.

"Oops," said Linveki. "Now how about you come on over and let me warm you up, Kataka J? Hey! Where are *you* going?"

Against all self-preservation instincts, Kat skidded over to the hole in the ice and fell in, feet first.

Her whole skin swore. How could anything be so cold!

Worse, she was suddenly cramped by the horrible awareness that she was now trapped under a roof of ice. Even more dangerous than the cold and the claustrophobia was the fact that she couldn't breathe because her throat was wrapped in layers of winter clothing!

*How long have I got before I die? Maybe three minutes before the cold kills me. Less than that if I can't get my gills free . . .*

She thrashed about, struggling with all the scarves and woollies that had been such a comfort just a few moments before. The weight of her sodden clothes was dragging her deeper underwater, where there was no light. She couldn't help it—she had to get air—she opened her mouth instinctively but only ice cold rushed in. It was the most horrible sensation. She kept tearing at her throat, even though her fingers were as stiff as claws. Finally she had her neck free. The freezing water was agony on her gills, but, mercifully, a sharp kind of Bliss filled her blood and she knew it would be cold that killed her, not drowning.

She had to clamp one hand over her nose and mouth to force herself not to cough anymore. With her other hand she felt about in the darkness. She knew she wasn't so far from shore, that she couldn't be anywhere near the eerie ruins of old Cluff village. That didn't stop her imagining ghostly shapes of walls and windows just out of reach of her fingertips. Somewhere beyond her feet was the great looming wall of Meander dam. Somewhere close by was Luka Papillon, maybe swimming, maybe already a cold corpse.

It was too much! She'd go mad, imagining Luka's last breath gliding over her own gills! She had to find the girl . . . she *would* find the girl. . . .

She *did* find the girl.

Her hand suddenly felt something smooth and hard—a faintly warm wind turbine. Wrapped around the turbine were two arms, two legs, a body—a Luka.

Still alive?

Yes?

Kat was at the last edge of panic as she pushed Luka's heavy body back onto the ice.

"Get out!" She gasped as soon as her lungs were choking on air again. "Get moving."

But Luka turned back to help Kat. Somehow they both found the strength to get flat on the ice. This time they simply threw themselves toward shore, regardless of the fact that Linveki was still standing in the line of lights, this time with his gun unslung ready to fire.

"Tough little bitches, aren't you?" he said in a poisonously pleasant voice. "I knew it was you who threw that stone into Essnid's pool, that you weren't dead in the snow. I knew I'd be the one to find you, Bottle Seal Fifty-five."

Kat managed to prise some words from between her chattering teeth. "S-S-Security are coming."

"Like I care," spat Linveki. He rumbled out an

alcoholic burp. "At least there'll be a nice pool at prison—I'm sick of washing in snow."

Luka got a few words out too: "You—look—like—walking—shitzer!"

It took her last bit of stamina. Her eyes closed and she sagged in Kat's arms.

"God, you could really get to hate a place!" Kat half-laughed, half-cried. "Nothing's worked out the way it's supposed to, and those damn Blue Mountains aren't even blue!"

Miraculously Luka's eyes snapped open. "Who told you they weren't blue? 'Course they are, idiot."

That was when the ghost appeared, a tall ghost with snow-speckled hair and a shaggy coat. Kat just couldn't get any more astounded. There really *was* a watcher in the woods and he'd finally mooched into view as if he didn't have a care in the world!

Linveki almost dropped his gun in surprise, but he quickly squared his shoulders so the ghost couldn't see how scared he was. "You're trespass-ing," he snarled.

"And you're forgetting an old friend," replied the ghost.

Luka's voice was a faint echo. "Old friend . . . ?" She tried to stagger to her feet.

*Who's this guy and where's he come from? And if he's Linveki's friend, how come Luka seems pleased to see him?*

Linveki frowned. "Do I know you?"

"Class of one-fifty-three Saint-Antel's High, Linveki. Not that long ago—I reckon about ten years, give or take a war or two."

The old friend stepped closer. Did he notice Kat and Luka frozen together in the snow? Did his eyes twinkle, or was that just a trick of the light?

"Clear off and forget you ever came here!" Linveki shouted. "This is a private Security matter. I'm arresting a known criminal, wanted for savage assaults on Frontier citizens."

The old friend whistled. "Way to go, Luka. Was one of those decent citizens *you* by any chance, Linveki? No? Then maybe I should do something about that."

The first punch had the factory director reeling backward, blood flying from his nose onto the snow. "What the hell d'you do that for?"

"That's for my sister."

"Your *sister*?"

"Yeah. She said you were a real creep and I can see you haven't changed. What, you don't remember her from school? You should do; you dated her once. Her name was Pelly D."

Linveki wiped his nose on his glove. "Jeez! You're Gim D? From high school? No way!"

"All the way. Gim Damson—one and the same."

"But you—"

"Grew up? Grew a beard?"

"No, well, yes, but I thought you were—"

"Dead? I get that a lot. Sorry to disappoint. No, nothing more dramatic than your basic life of slave labor and *finally* a successful escape attempt from a work camp in the heartland. But that's another story. I'm here for Luka. I guess she got free before me. Tough little tyke, isn't she?"

"Not so little," Luka murmured.

"Hey, Papillon! Do you know how long I've been scoping this place, waiting for you to show? And what do you do? Turn up just when I was skulking around town for a change, seeing your face on posters everywhere! I thought I'd come try some of those cherries you kept boasting about."

Luka looked at him as if she'd swallowed the whole skyful of stars.

Kat was just plain confused. "You're the creepy guy who's been hanging out in the orchard spying on us!"

Linveki tried to impose his authority on the situation. "Look, Gim, you can't just turn up and—"

The second punch had him flat on the ground, making a very still snow angel. Silence fell around him. Gim Damson rubbed his knuckles and went to give Luka the biggest hug of her life.

"Sorry you had to see that. I've always said that violence isn't the answer. Only sometimes, I've got to admit, it just feels so *good*."

## Blue Mountains

I'm out of the bad place and here in a good place, in my opinion no place better. It's the most beautiful spring in the history of springs since time began. Cherry blossom blizzards make the air soft and sweet. I like soft and sweet. I like my Cherry Heaven.

Here I swing, lazy in a hammock under the trees. I like trees. Trees grow. Trees reach roots deep in the ground. Trees remember things. All around my head are papillon pupae, ready to burst like hundreds before. The papillons climb out trembling at every breeze. When their wings are dry they're free to fly wherever they want. Like me.

I'm not going anywhere fast, though—mostly cos no one's quite ready. We're meant to be off on a picnic, only Tanka J's late—as usual. At least Kat made it here on time, and wherever

Kat goes, Harpo C's not far behind. They're sitting in the shade looking at papillon wings through my new microscope, the one that Harpo and Aran bought me for my birthday.

"It's kind of a late present," Harpo said. "Hardly worth the wait."

Much he knows.

Anyway, I'm not shifting till I finish my bowl of cherries. It's the last of the ten-year-ago harvest. Every single one of them came from the trees when my mama was still alive, Hikori and Mai, too. That should make them taste bitter but they're still sweet to me. Do you know something about cherries? Kat's Uncle Prester told me (and he knows his history) back on Earth in the old days, trees used to mean different things, and fruit, too. Cherries meant innocence. Innocence is when you're not guilty of anything, and who can honestly say that? Maybe that's why it's mostly cherries that are innocent, not people. Certainly not the people in Meander.

Softly, softly they creep to the orchard and lay their innocence or guilt at my feet.

"We're sorry, we didn't know," most of them say.

The more truthful ones admit, "We're sorry, we didn't want to know."

They're not sorry they still have their dam, or their good lives on the Frontier; they're sorry they've been made to feel guilty about how they got these wonderful things. Maybe that's not fair. Maybe some of them really do feel bad. Oh well, as far as I'm concerned they can be sorry as much as they like. I tell 'em, "Next time you eat cherries, remember who picked 'em. Next time you swig water, stop and wonder where it came from." Plus, "Do you think you could help with this-that-and-the-other while you're busy being sorry?"

Some clear the weeds, some prune the trees, some just come to stare and wonder about Quarry and Factory and all the secret Galrezi-scum stuff. At least the orchard's looking beautiful now I've got people to help. It's going to be an A1 supremo harvest.

It's a funny thing about innocence—seems to

me all the wrong people think they are, while the nice people get twisted up being guilty. Take Harpo's mum and dad. Federic Challis always knew there was something wrong about the Oklear Foster story, what with my dead body being missing. For ten years he tried to find out what had been going on, and that was even after sailing overseas to fight in the war to stop more Galrezi being killed. He's what I call innocent, but he still worries about it all so much he's got snow white bits in his fire red hair. Mostly he stays at Challis, now he's quit Security, selling cherry-malloey tea and giving interviews to hungry newschat channels.

As for Jo Challis, she's just a magic lady. She can't be my mama, nobody can now, but I love it when she comes to visit. She's very good at baking ginger donuts. Isn't it nice that she planted the Hikori-Mai trees? Back during the horrible Quarry months Bossman wanted to live in Cherry Heaven but a plague of papillons came and ate all the cherries, so he didn't; he just took all my mama's money instead. And her life.

Some reckon he must hate Galrezi, to do a thing like that. I'm not sure. Seems to me he killed them and climbed on their corpses to say, *Hey everybody, let's all be nice to one another and not kill cos that's bad. Don't we just hate it when nasty people kill those cute Galrezi? Instead, why doesn't everyone make mountains of money and vote me in for Big Man Bossman jobs?*

And they did.

When Heaven farm died, that's when Harpo C's mum snook through the orchard and planted three cherry stones near the shed. Three stones for three dead girls. She hoped I was still alive cos Harpo's dad told her he hadn't found my body, but no one knew what had happened to me, not even Bossman. I suppose he thought I was frozen solid in the snow somewhere, or maybe he was so used to telling people I was dead he came to believe it too. If he hadn't made the hell that was Quarry to get lost in, he might have met me again sooner.

"You planted them too close," I told J Challis

when I found out it was her who put the cherry stones in the ground to grow, coming back later to carve the letters onto the saplings. "They're both tangled up now."

She ruffled my new tufts of hair. "Give over complaining! I just sell cherries; I don't know how to grow them. I did the best I could."

"Your best was brilliant," I said. "Even if the Luka stone didn't grow."

"Guess you didn't need a tree, honey—you were still alive all along, just how I hoped." That's when she hugged me, and I let her.

Kat and her family still feel guilty too, and I wish they wouldn't, even though when I first saw them in my house I wanted to squash them dead for being there. They wouldn't stay at Heaven. I told them there was lots of room and that I'd make sure Puss-cat didn't leave too much white hair all over Prester's best suits, but they said don't be daft. I had to ask, "You aren't going back to the cities?" because I didn't want to lose any more nice people.

"We're getting a house in town," said Millijue.

"Near the spa!" said Tanka.

"I've got my book to write," Prester beamed. "It's a history of the O-HA with a completely up-to-date section on the events of the tenth anniversary . . . even though someone tied me to my chair while I slept so I couldn't actually be there."

See—I'm not innocent either. No hard feelings. Prester says he's going to write a bit in his book about me!

Apart from being in a book, I thought I'd be in a movie, too, cos Harpo's sister Clariss had a really nice time when she spent a day with Zee Homarlo, and my plan now is to have plenty of nice times, too. According to the newschat channels, Zee Homarlo says he's *not* going to be in the film about my life. Just as well, really, cos he's too tall for Bossman and too handsome for Director. Hiding under a fake name, I went along for a thing called a screen test at a movie studio in Santanna. Harpo rehearsed me for the part of "Luka Papillon." I had to practice talking without twitching my fingers or scratching the ghosts of old Stingo sores. It's too bad the film people told me I "didn't have credibility as the character" and that I "didn't look the part." Harpo and I nearly bust ourselves laughing afterward. Of course I don't look the part anymore! I've been eating mountains of food for starters, plus I've actually got hair, and warm clothes, and no one's making me look small or offering to beat me to pulp.

I don't know who they'll pick to play me instead.

To be honest, I don't think I've got time to be an international superstar anyway. I've got my guests to look after. All sorts of people mean-der along the path through the cherry orchard now—friends from Factory and Quarry who've come for a long swim and a soft bed. I wish I'd been there to see everyone's faces when the chill-machine stopped, the conveyor belts ground to a halt, and someone from Outside came in to tell the workers to quit working. At first they thought it was one of Director's cruel tricks, then some nice people from the O-HA (*proper* nice people) came to take more photos and to give out chocolate and snug clothes.

Label-glue 11 had to sit down and rest after the walk from the ferry, she's grown so fat. Good for her. She complains about the blossoms making her sneeze. We don't like to tell her it's not the blossoms but symptoms of a non-curable respiratory disease caused by solvent poisoning at Factory. She wouldn't understand all those long words anyway. Besides, she's happy—slowing dying in sunshine rather than in pain. We'll all give her a hand to get to the picnic, cos when you've missed out on life like she has, you should say "yes!" to doing as much good stuff as you can.

It's too bad Packer 67 and Color Tech 26 couldn't be here for the picnic too. I've started a new garden in Packer 67's honor. She'd've liked the sight of strong green shoots bursting out of the soil. As for Color Tech 26, oh boy! If she was here I'd've given her as many juicy cherries as she could possibly eat, and then some!

My old friend Packer 109 came by in deep

winter, bringing a few more leftover laborers with her. Now she spends her time trimming her own nails and cuticles, not Director's, or lolling around in the big pool room watching her white hair float in the water. She's sleeping in one of my spare rooms till she can figure out where her home's going to be next. Like most of the Galrezi who came from the cities, there's nothing for her to go back to, but I reckon there's room on this Frontier for us all to show people how good we are at being alive and working for ourselves instead. 109 goes along with the "being alive" bit; she's just not so sure about ever working again. Who cares? We'll get the harvest in anyway.

She did laugh when she heard what I did with Director's old nail file.

"I've already offered him a free manicure ready for the trial," she said with a smug look.

Oh yes. The trial, well, *trials*, because there are many, which is only fair when you know what the old Earth meaning for cherry trees is:

DO ME JUSTICE.

I did what justice I could. One by one I found my enemies and got my own back. Took from them their favorite things. Director lost his good looks and everyone else's good opinion. Bossman lost his shine—and his son. Blue Capo's mother says I ought to be brain-drained for what I did to her daughter. I tried to explain that Blue Capo was blind way before I slathered her in Stingo, the sort of blindness where you can't see how cruel you are to other people. Luckily, Blue Capo's so busy being bullied in court she hasn't time to accuse me of anything.

The trials are in Santanna, not far from Factory. Whoever's found guilty will go off to prison to have their brains drained. I'm not sure what I think about that. It's hard to hate a walking vegetable, and it means they'd lose so much mind they'd never ever be able to remember what they did and *squirm* with guilt. Plus I can't help thinking of Oklear Foster, cos they now reckon he never murdered *any* of the Galrezi who were killed. He was innocent, like he said all along. Like me. No amount of "oops, sorry, mistake" is going to get his life back again. Or mine.

Which doesn't mean people shouldn't keep trying to get things right, to DO JUSTICE. The War Crimes Commission never thought they'd have to send investigators to this part of the world, where no one would admit there *had* been a war, a secret war. Now people in the cities are greedy for newschat on Director, cos he used to live in City Five. Security were glad to get their gloved hands on him all right. We tied him to a chair in Cherry Heaven (once we'd kindly set Prester free). Director's oily, but not so slippery he'll ooze out of *all* the charges of racial inhumanity, gross negligence, violence, and manslaughter (Kat's words, not mine). Brain-draining *him* will only be an improvement in his intelligence levels.

Bossman's the tricky man. They want to get him, oh yes they want to convict, but no court on the continent can make a case against him.

I think he's built a dam around his heart, with a reservoir of guilt backed up out of sight behind it, so his eyes seem to shine with innocence.

"Where's the proof?" his friends whine. "Proof that an honest man like him would know what Linveki did in secret? Proof that he was anywhere near Cherry Heaven when the Papillons were killed?"

"What about people who saw him?" I screamed at Kat when she told me this. "How many hundred Factory workers watched him arrive?"

"They didn't get a clear view of his face."

"I saw him in the orchard! I saw him shoot my mama and walk away!"

"I know you did, but you were only six at the time."

"Seven. Just."

"Seven, then. It won't make any difference in court. They might be sympathetic or they might resent all the trouble you've stirred up by speaking out. They might try something called a credibility attack—say you buried the memories so long you *wanted* to believe it was Boss—I mean, Essnid—because you needed to see someone punished."

"That's mush! What about Aran? He saw his

dad—he knows what he did."

Kat agreed that Aran was a strong witness. "Poor doop. Tanka says he's staying with family in the heartland until this blows over and he doesn't get stopped in the street . . . more than once or twice a day. He'll have a horrible time testifying. At least no one can say he was being vindictive when he stood up and spoke on the dam."

She had to explain what "credibility" and "vindictive" meant. In fact, she had to explain a lot of things. I don't understand! Why can't Justice be as simple as saying, "You were bad so I'm going to be bad back at you"? Apparently that's called Vengeance, and it's not the same thing, even if Justice sometimes means that bad people walk away free.

They still get what they deserve, though. This is what I had to explain to Kat.

"Maybe Bossman won't go to prison or get his brain drained, but he'll always have to live with the fact that he's one of the scummiest people on the planet. Nothing will work for him, no one will love him even though he says he did every-thing to make the Frontier a wonderful place, and he'll probably never see his son again except in court."

"But he'll be officially innocent," she said.

Yeah, that innocence thing again. So what if *officially* he'll be a free man? Unofficially he'll get what I call Justice: he'll never be able to enjoy the real beauty of a spring morning like this one, or go on a picnic with people who actually *like* him. That's still a kind of punishment, even if it's not as satisfying as some others I could think of, like blasting his brains out, feeding him to a giant mincing machine, locking him in a cryo-freeze, throwing him off the *wrong* side of the dam so his gold fingers scrabble for a handhold before he lands *splat smash* on the ground below, or gets mashed up in that pool of frothy water or . . .

I could go on.

Kat says I have to stop thinking up horrible ways to kill Bossman. She's probably right, as usual. Apart from it being not-so-healthy for me,

I have to behave nicely whenever people are looking so I don't end up on trial myself for being a
mad-psycho-bitch-who-blinds-people-on-purpose.

I don't follow the trials—I can't stand to see
pictures of Factory or Quarry—so Kat watches
every program and keeps her new e.f. on alert for
updates. She's been downloading a lot of legal
textbooks from the net, all paid for by money
she got thinking up a brilliant new idea for communications (I don't really understand the technical stuff, something to do with mont-halo
ore). A lot of naughty people are going to start
being extra-twice nice to her now she's decided
what she's going to do when she eventually
leaves school: join the War Crimes Commission,
that's what.

*We'll nail the scumbags,* she says cheerfully.

She's made a start already, and not just her,
Tanka, too. They're tracking down what happened
to their mama and papa in the war. Once, I
caught Tanka chewing the end of her e-pad pencil, actually looking *thoughtful.* Kat said it
wouldn't last, that Tanka's conscience was just

a new fad brought on by, well, by me I guess. I'm not so sure. Tanka's been reading a book that got her thinking, a diary. How the diary ended up in Cherry Heaven is a story all by itself, and it's all to do with Gim Damson.

Did you think I'd forgotten him? I *never* forgot him! If I'd known he was waiting in the orchard I might've skipped all that vengeance stuff to go find him first. He was alive!

I won't say he was the same. He'd been in the heartland, working first, then put in some kind of prison—ten hard years he won't even tell me about. "Not yet," he says. "Not yet." But he's as big and brilliant as ever! He's right at home here in Heaven. We make our own family, now both of us know we don't have anyone else left alive.

Gim sleeps a lot, eats a lot, and works even more, though I told him not to bother. He says he can't help it. He has to keep busy. He pulls up miles of tangled weeds and digs new flower beds in the yard. He was out in the orchard with me when a stranger arrived, bringing a diary with him.

It was one of the workers from the cities who'd come in a gang to set up for the rally. Apparently he'd been all over the Frontier asking, "Do you know Gim Damson?"

Most people said, "Gim Damson? A Galrezi? Never heard of him."

But the boy kept asking, and some of his friends did too, the other workers. It was like a kind of mission with them, a quest. A Plan. Even though lots of them were Atsumisi, they were the first lot to volunteer to be at Factory to help Galrezi who'd been set free. I don't know who told them about Cherry Heaven, but I'm glad someone did. Here's what happened. This stranger, a young builder called Toni V, came walking along the orchard path on a wet winter morning, so big and bulky he looked like a sort of beastie in brown. Me and Gim were out on the edge of the trees, just clearing deadwood and stuff. This Toni V had a real shy way of talking, and he couldn't keep his eyes off Gim's silver/green square.

"Are you Gim Damson?"

Gim was like a cat waiting to bolt, and I don't blame him. "And if I am, what of it?"

Toni V didn't look as if he was going to drag anyone off for a lifetime of misery and exploitation. He stared at Gim like he was seeing a film star in the flesh. He fumbled in his jacket and took out a small packet wrapped in clear plastic. "I read about you in this. We all have. That's why we've been looking for you in the Frontier." He paused, not wanting to part with the diary. Some presents are hard to give.

Gim's face was whiter than snow when he opened the packet and saw the notebook inside.

He's read the diary lots of times since then— the diary of his sister Pelly D. He's flicking through it even now while we wait for the picnic, with my white Puss-cat curled on his lap. You aren't normally supposed to nosey in other people's diaries, but Toni V's given it to hundreds of people on the net, plus now they have a copy in the vaults of the War Crimes Commission, so I guess thousands of people know what the diary's about. Amazing how something can start so small and get so big.

Sometimes the diary makes Gim laugh and sometimes he cries trickly tears when he thinks no one's looking. It's strange, having a piece of someone's life when you can never have the person again. Strange and heartbreaking. Gim can't believe this Toni V came all the way over the ocean to track him down, and Toni looks just as surprised.

Before Toni V left Cherry Heaven I took him into a shed to show him some boxes of my mama's things—files and books she used when she was studying to be an architect—because Toni says he's going places. "Onward and upward!" He grins. He doesn't want to be doing grunt work all his life. If he can save some money he wants to build things as beautiful as this house, and the big Meander dam. I gave him all the help he wanted—I like giving presents!—and I didn't even need to make him promise not to use slave labor. He's already learned that lesson.

Gim gave Tanka a copy of the diary to take to school so they could understand more about the war against the Galrezi and why it was wrong.

Kat's not sure even the trials or the diary will be enough to make people change.

"Colonists came to this planet because they said Earth was so bad. They said too many wars and appalling things had happened. The ships were called *Never Again* and *Never Forget* but we couldn't even get it right after a fresh start! It's all happened again and we *did* forget. I can't help thinking, what's the point of telling people over and over if they won't listen?"

Harpo hates it when she gets upset. "You've just got to keep trying, Kat. If you make only one person change for the better, isn't that worth it? It beats not trying at all."

Kat still worries too much. She can't understand why people won't make the effort to be decent and nice, at least most of the time. "Things would be so much simpler." She frowns.

We can't have frowns on a picnic day, so I

shout over to Harpo, "Tell her to stop worrying!"

"Can't be done," he yells back. "Not unless we take her brain out and replace it with something easygoing, like ice cream." Harpo's in the shade still, now sketching the papillon wing while Kat goes to check the picnic bag. "I keep telling her to take more of Tanka's happy pills."

Kat throws a cherry at him. He throws it back and she grabs it midair without even trying. They're funny like that—catching cherries and kisses.

But no, Kat J won't be happy until she's got the picnic properly packed.

"Did I put the bug cream in?" she asks Harpo. "Luka says they bite any bit that shows."

"You put the cream in."

I suggest getting hold of some Stingo, to kill off the mutant monster bugs.

"There aren't any mutant monster bugs in the Blue Mountains, Luka P, and you know it . . . unless we meet one of your mile-wide dinosaurs living rough in the wilderness!"

Kat scratches the cut on her hand, the one

she got from the Hikori-Mai trees. I keep telling her not to itch it but she does and that's why she's got a scar. It's not as bad as my Stingo-burn scar. No way am I having *that* wiped off my hand. I need to be like Aran E—keeping a scar to make me remember. Not remembering's bad. Not remembering's like planting trees in poison soil: they won't grow properly; they'll wither up sooner or later. Besides, I get to remember the good stuff as well as the bad, and all the time I lie out here in the lovely spring, I'm making new memories to mull on another day.

I'm very excited about the picnic in the Blue Mountains, and yes they *are* blue—I thought everyone knew that! They're blue each spring when the most brilliant bright flowers burst out of the ground. All through winter you have to keep remembering that they'll bud, that there'll be so many flowers they cover the mountains almost to the tops and you can see them being blue from miles around. I'm going to make Kat J *roll* in those blue flowers. That'll teach her to get mopey and miserable and think this is a bad

place. You should always have hope—always
remember that the Blue Mountains are blue
even when they look gray.

And this isn't a bad place; it's a beautiful
place. If only you could get rid of the bad people,
like pulling up weeds in a garden, but you can't.
There'll always be Bossmen and Directors and
Capos. The best we can do is keep telling new
people what we've learned to stop them going
wrong. We've also got to keep digging the past
up to make sure that no matter how long it
takes, good people don't let bad people get
away with doing bad things.

*"Time to go!"* Kat calls out when Tanka finally
appears, complete with yet another rather
yummy lad from the waterball team. Nothing like
as nice as Aran E, in my opinion. Tanka can't
help but agree. She's filling in time until he's
stopped being seriously screwed up by everything . . . or until Zee Homarlo makes her an
offer she can't refuse. Whichever comes first.

Suddenly I'm not sure I want to move. I like it

here, lazy in the sun, feeling feather-soft snow-blossom on my skin. It's been a long, hard story and it's about time for a happy ending, Tanka says, and she would, wouldn't she? Cos she's seen too many Homarlo films.

I'm not so sure about happy endings.

For starters, I don't know about *happy*. Things can't ever be properly happy again, can they? Not while the Hikori-Mai trees are blowing blossom down, not while we've all got our scars.

The good thing is, there is no *ending* either. That's the glorious bit—that's the bit as fantastic as sky, sun, moons, mountains, rain, river, reservoir, cherries, everything rolled into one. I DIDN'T END! I kept going and *keep going*, one foot in front of the other, sometimes upstairs to bed, sometimes down steps to the pool, and sometimes in the Blue Mountain flower meadows for a picnic with my friends!

We're having cimarron cake, as well as ginger donuts, roast nuts of every variety, some disgustingly delicious chocolate buns, and cherries, too, of course.

I'm in a good place now.

Maybe I know too much about bad things and bad people, but I do know something else—

god it's good to be alive!